Tasha Alexander attended the University of Notre Dame, where she majored in English and Medieval Studies. She and her husband, the novelist Andrew Grant, divide their time between Chicago and the UK. Visit her online at www.tashaalexander.com.

The Lady Emily Mysteries

And Only to Deceive
A Poisoned Season
A Fatal Waltz
Tears of Pearl
Dangerous to Know
A Crimson Warning
Death in the Floating City
Behind the Shattered Glass
The Counterfeit Heiress
The Adventuress
A Terrible Beauty

Death in St Petersburg

TASHA ALEXANDER

CONSTABLE • LONDON

CONSTABLE

First published in the USA in 2017 by Minotaur Books,
an imprint of St Martin's Press

This edition published in Great Britain in 2017 by Constable

1 3 5 7 9 10 8 6 4 2

Copyright © Tasha Alexander, 2017

The moral right of the author has been asserted.

A CIP catalogue record for this book
is available from the British Library.

ISBN: 978-1-4721-2217-9

Printed and bound in Great Britain by Clays Ltd, St Ives plc

Papers used by Constable are from well-managed forests
and other responsible sources

Constable
An imprint of
Little, Brown Book Group
Carmelite House
50 Victoria Embankment
London EC4Y 0DZ

An Hachette UK Company
www.hachette.co.uk

www.littlebrown.co.uk

In memory of my ballet teacher, Marie Buczkowski, who filled my soul with a love for Russian dance

I love thee, work of Peter's hand!
I love thy stern, symmetric form;
The Neva's calm and queenly flow
Betwixt her quays of granite-stone,
With iron tracings richly wrought;
Thy nights so soft with pensive thought,
Their moonless glow, in bright obscure,
When I alone, in cosy room,
Or write or read, night's lamp unlit;
The sleeping piles that clear stand out
In lonely streets, and needle bright,
That crowns the Admiralty's spire;
When, chasing far the shades of night,
In cloudless sky of golden pure,
Dawn quick usurps the pale twilight,
And brings to end her half-hour reign.
I love thy winters bleak and harsh;
Thy stirless air fast bound by frosts;
The flight of sledge o'er Neva wide,
That glows the cheeks of maidens gay.
I love the noise and chat of balls;
A banquet free from wife's control,
Where goblets foam, and bright blue flame
Darts round the brimming punch-bowl's edge.
I love to watch the martial troops
The spacious Field of Mars fast scour;
The squadrons spruce of foot and horse;
The nicely chosen race of steeds,
As gaily housed they stand in line,
Whilst o'er them float the tattered flags;
The gleaming helmets of the men
That bear the marks of battle-shot.

I love thee, when with pomp of war
The cannons roar from fortress-tower;
When Empress-Queen of all the North
Hath given birth to royal heir;
Or when the people celebrate
Some conquest fresh on battle-field;
Or when her bonds of ice once more
The Neva, rushing free, upheaves,
The herald sure of spring's rebirth.
Fair city of the hero, hail!

—from *The Bronze Horseman: A Petersburg Story*,
by Alexander Sergeyevich Pushkin; translated by C. E. Turner

DEATH
IN
ST. PETERSBURG

St. Petersburg
January 1900

1

From a distance, the crimson spray coloring the snow looked more like scattered rose petals than evidence of a grisly murder. Upon closer approach, however, the broken body, delicate and graceful, revealed the truth of the scene in its full horror. The victim's pale skin, almost translucent, had been slashed and desecrated in an act of inhumane violence. But even so, her beauty could not be denied. Perhaps St. Petersburg required elegance even in death.

Peter the Great's city, on the banks of the Neva River, was purpose built to impress, not with the heavy, fortified architecture one might expect from an all-powerful tsar, but instead with its refined civility. After traveling through Western Europe, he rejected Moscow and the Kremlin, with its citadel-like walls, and sent an army of serfs to dig canals that would remind him of Amsterdam. Alexander Pushkin, Russia's favorite poet, wrote "his will was fate." For a hundred thousand of those serfs, fate meant death, a price Peter did not hesitate to pay for his new imperial capital.

Historian Nikolai Karamzin said the city was founded on tears and corpses, but one would never guess that from its wide boulevards, gilded steeples, and sprawling palaces. The feathery snow that blanketed the city in the winter served as a scrim curtain through which peeked the bright walls of neoclassical buildings, painted in shades of pale blue, pink, coral, and pistachio. Sleek sledges, their runners gleaming, pulled occupants wrapped in sumptuous furs along icy white streets. To an outsider, it seemed more fairy tale than imperial seat.

And a fairy tale was precisely what had enchanted me that evening in the Mariinsky Theatre, home of the Imperial Ballet. Seated in its gilded perfection in a box adjacent to that of Tsar Nicholas II's, I felt the world around me fade into nothing as I watched the story of a princess turned into a swan and of the prince whose love might have saved her. The impossibly graceful dancers, standing en pointe, mesmerized. At least they mesmerized me. As for my husband, Colin Hargreaves, I could not be sure.

He had come to Russia for his work, having been summoned there with increasing frequency over the past few years. As one of the Crown's most trusted agents, his familiarity with the intrigues of the Romanov court proved invaluable to Queen Victoria, whose granddaughter, Alix of Hesse and by Rhine—now called Alexandra Feodorovna—had married the tsar. Not only could Her Majesty count on Colin to handle any political situations that might impact Britain, she could also trust him to take note of anything potentially threatening to Alexandra's happiness. St. Petersburg might be considered a beacon of culture and society by some, but to the queen it was little more than a thuggish backwater.

I do not mean to suggest Her Majesty was prepared to intervene on behalf of her granddaughter. She felt herself above petty court controversies, but this did not dissuade her from wanting to hear all about them. Although my husband would never comment on her motives, I remain skeptical that they went beyond a desire for base gossip.

Regardless, Colin spent a great deal of time in Petersburg. Our century had proved difficult for the Romanovs. Alexander I may have emerged victorious over Napoleon in 1812, but this was not the beginning of a glorious period for his family. His grandson Alexander II survived five assassination attempts before being murdered in 1881. The martyred tsar's son Alexander III responded by refusing to continue his father's liberal policies, and in 1887 police arrested a group of conspirators plotting to bomb the emperor's carriage. Nicholas II, his successor, bore a long scar on his forehead, the memento of an unsuccessful attack by a sword-wielding man who had been part of Nicholas's protection detail during a trip to Japan.

Safety was not something a Romanov could take for granted.

I knew little of Colin's precise responsibilities in the city. Covert activity, alas, must remain covert, even from one's spouse. I had long ago abandoned any attempt to persuade him to confide in me, although I am quite certain he enjoyed my efforts in that direction. He admitted to me, on more than one occasion, that they provided some of his most treasured memories from the early days of our marriage.

Accompanying him while he worked was ordinarily—and necessarily—out of the question, and I had begrudgingly grown accustomed to waiting—and worrying—at home in England. This time, however, an irresistible opportunity presented itself. My dear friend, Cécile du Lac, had invited me to join her on a visit to Princess Mariya Alekseyevna Bolkonskaya. Masha, Cécile promised, would show us that the season in St. Petersburg made London's attempts at high society seem the work of rank amateurs. Who could refuse such an offer?

Colin might have insisted I do just that, but he was already away, having left for Russia on Boxing Day. Our twin boys, Henry and Richard, and our ward, Tom, as dear to us as any son could be, lamented his absence even before his departure. He loved to indulge them and had constructed an elaborate zoo out of blocks on the floor of the library at Anglemore Park three days before Christmas. The boys had populated the enclosures with the small animal figurines their father brought them from Hamleys every time he went to

London. Tom would turn four in another month, and the twins would follow suit in the spring. No sooner had they learned Colin would be away from home immediately after the holiday than they started to keen and wail like small Vikings mourning the loss of a beloved leader.

Colin informs me that Vikings neither keened nor wailed. I assume the astute reader understands my choice of the Viking analogy for its romantic yet masculine qualities and will not insist on a pedantic adherence to nothing but facts.

When Cécile's telegram arrived (mere hours after Colin had left), inviting me to join her for the New Year celebrations in St. Petersburg—the highlight of the Russian year—my excitement faded as I realized it would be impossible to make the trip in time to usher out 1899. Then I remembered that the Russians still used the old Gregorian calendar. Their January 1 was our January 14. I booked a sleeping compartment on the *Nord Express* via Berlin and Warsaw, delighted to find the entire trip would take only two days. Thus, I was able to welcome 1900 twice: once in England, and once in Russia. Furthermore, as the Orthodox Church celebrates Christmas on the Feast of Epiphany, January 6, I would be present for those festivities as well.

Often when he was working, Colin stayed in neighborhoods that could be described, at best, as dubious. I had visions of him taking rooms in a building much like that of Dostoyevsky's Raskolnikov, skulking up filthy, narrow staircases and arguing with a conniving landlady. On this trip, there was to be no such adventure. He had booked an extremely comfortable suite at the Hôtel de l'Europe on the corner of Nevsky Prospekt and Mikhaylovskaya ulitsa. Fearing he might try to convince me to stay home if I gave him the chance, I delayed to the last minute the sending of a telegram of my own, informing him of my impending arrival and suggesting that I could stay with Cécile in the princess's palace if my presence proved inconvenient. The affectionate manner of his greeting when I arrived in his rooms told me there was no need to consider alternate accommodations.

And so he worked, disappearing for hours, and sometimes days, while Cécile and I went to the opera, balls, soirees, and other elegant gatherings. St. Petersburg charmed me thoroughly, and I was convinced no other city was so perfectly beautiful.

Until I stepped out of the lobby of the Mariinsky Theatre to see blood splattered like rose petals on the snow and the broken body of a slim dancer, still wearing the costume of the Swan Queen.

Ekaterina Petrovna
November 1889

Ekaterina Petrovna Sokolova had been at the Imperial Theatre School for more than a year now, but she still cried every Sunday when her brother, Lev, left her at the building on Theatre Street after they'd attended service at St. Nicholas Naval Cathedral. All the other students went to the small chapel on the school's second floor, but her grandfather, whom no one dared deny anything, had got permission for Katenka to worship with her family.

What little of them was left. Along with her, it was only Grandpapa, Mama, and Lev. Grandpapa, a great hero in the Battle of Borodino, had never quite recovered from losing his son, Katenka's father, to the icy waters of the Gulf of Finland during a naval training exercise. That was why they went to St. Nicholas even though Grandpapa was an army man. Her other brothers and sisters—six of them—had all died in a cholera epidemic, and the old man had pinned his hopes on Lev, who was meant to continue the family's glorious military tradition.

Katenka didn't care why they went or what Lev was supposed to do. She liked nothing better than walking to and from the cathedral with her brother—well, almost nothing. Dancing, that was as good, but not good enough to keep her from being consumed with sadness when Lev held the heavy doors of the school open and waved as they slammed shut, separating her from him for another week.

Lev, seven years older than his sister, had showered her with affection from the day she was born, calling her his little angel. Katenka had started to dance almost as soon as she could walk and, when she was ten, had cried tears of joy at the news that she had won a spot in Petersburg's Imperial Theatre School. She had not anticipated how different living as a *pépinière*—a boarder—would be from the warm, loving home to which she was accustomed. She imagined tulle skirts and tiaras and the golden boxes and twinkling lights of the Mariinsky Theatre, not a hard bed in a cold dormitory and exhausting days spent practicing tendus. The dancers she had admired on stage worked hard to create the illusion of effortless grace, and now she, too, would have to learn how to ignore pain in the service of art.

Katenka dedicated herself to her training, hiding her homesickness as best she could. She loved ballet and adored the ritual of daily class, studying the perfect technique required by Marius Petipa, ballet master of the Imperial Theatre. Katenka would never become a prima ballerina if she could not satisfy his exacting demands. She had no trouble focusing on dance; there was nothing else to distract her. Making friends had never come easily to her, and her natural talent and the praise her efforts earned from her teachers made the other girls in her class envious. During that first year, only one reached out to her: Irina Semenova Nemetseva.

Irusya had no need for jealousy. She moved as if weightless. Her long legs, slim and muscular, carried her across rehearsal rooms as if she were flying rather than jumping. Unlike Katenka, whose shyness was often mistaken for aloofness, Irusya, gregarious by nature, drew others to her. When her parents sent a package of sweets, she shared them, telling the other girls fantastical tales of the enchanted woods that surrounded her family's dacha. Katenka would sit away from the group, never feeling welcome despite Irusya's invitations to join.

7

In the evening, after the lights were out, Irusya would flout the rules, slipping out of her narrow bed and into Katenka's, where they would snuggle close. They would discuss the day's activities: who had done well in class, who had shown fatal signs of laziness, who had failed to complete the dreaded work they were given in ordinary school subjects. Irusya excelled in all but mathematics. Katenka, to whom it came naturally, offered to help her but was denied.

"I shall never need mathematics," Irusya said. "A prima ballerina assoluta has no use for such things."

They heard the sharp sound of footsteps in the corridor: matron was coming. Stifling their giggles, they made themselves as small and still as possible. The door opened, letting in a sliver of golden light. A moment passed, and the door closed. In the morning, Katenka would scratch a small mark on the wooden trunk at the foot of her bed, marking another night they had successfully avoided being caught breaking the rules.

January 1900

2

After the curtain fell on the final scene, the crowd exited the Mariinsky Theatre bursting with energy and brimming with emotion, profoundly affected by the story of Prince Siegfried and the cursed Odette, who could be united only in death. Never before had I seen dancing like that, and from the animated chattering around me, I knew the rest of the audience had been as delighted as I.

We had all expected an exceptional performance. Irina Semenova Nemetseva, the young dancer only a few years out of school, whose meteoric rise through the ranks of the Imperial Theatre was already the stuff of legends, would make history tonight as the first person other than Pierina Legnani to dance the dual roles of Odette and Odile in Tchaikovsky's *Swan Lake*. Marius Petipa, the great choreographer and ballet master of the Mariinsky, had named Legnani the first prima ballerina assoluta, the highest rank a dancer could achieve. He adored her and all but gave the ballet to her. He had developed the choreography especially for her, and she had caused a sensation by adding thirty-two fouettées, in which the dancer whipped her leg around while turning en pointe with impossible speed, to her solo in the third act, a feat she had first performed in Petipa's *Cinderella*, years earlier. Now close to her fortieth birthday, and no doubt knowing retirement was not far away, Legnani had agreed to let someone else dance the role and chose Nemetseva as her successor.

The audience had not seen the girl's fouettées.

An extra element of excitement was added to the performance when, before the third act, a man—Petipa himself, I learned from the more experienced ballet goers around me—had stepped out from behind the heavy red velvet curtain and called for silence. We all obeyed at once, as if God Himself had made the request. Then, in a loud, steady voice, he announced that the dual role of Odette/Odile would be danced for the remainder of the performance by Ekaterina Petrovna Sokolova. He gave no explanation, but irritation was evident on his face and in his tone. I wondered what had prompted the change, as did everyone around me. Chattering filled the theatre, and the conductor, when he appeared at his podium, had to turn around three times and glower before it became quiet enough for him to raise his baton and command the orchestra to play.

Whatever the cause of the last-minute substitution, Ekaterina Petrovna had risen to the occasion with aplomb. She looked the opposite of Nemetseva, her pale, golden hair a perfect contrast to her colleague's smooth, dark locks. This made it a tad hard to believe that she could have deceived Prince Siegfried into believing she was the same girl he had fallen in love with before the interval, but from the moment she started to move, she captivated the entire theatre. By the final act, no one remembered that earlier that night someone else had danced the role.

And now, as we poured out into the frigid night, everyone bundled in furs, Theatre Square was full of smart carriages waiting to collect their fashionable owners. I almost didn't hear the first scream, but the second was impossible to ignore. It pierced the taut air like a blade.

Nothing should have been capable of silencing the bustle in front of the Mariinsky, but by the time I heard a third scream, this one joined by a voice crying, "Nemetseva!" over and over, it was as if a sorcerer had cast a spell over the entire crowd. Everyone fell quiet and started to move almost in slow motion, following the sound of the cries. Colin, who had taken me firmly by the arm to keep us from getting separated, was the only person moving at full speed. Faster than that, in fact. He knew, as did I, that something was dreadfully wrong. We skirted the side of the building until we came to the source of the screams.

Two elderly women, their programs from the performance still clutched in their hands, were standing next to a delicate spray of crimson blood that colored the snow around the body of a ballerina. Beneath her, the oozing liquid was neither delicate nor crimson; it had pooled thick and dark. She was still dressed in a white tutu, its bodice and its full, stiff skirts decorated with feathers and glittering crystal beads. The ribbon on one of her satin slippers had come undone, but her tiara, pinned to her dark hair, remained perfectly in place.

"Stay back," Colin said, stepping forward and raising a hand to keep the crowd, now arriving in droves, at bay. He knelt on the ground and bent over her. There was no need to check for a pulse. No one could have survived the loss of so much blood. Someone shouted for the police; someone else began to sob loudly. The ballerina was on her stomach, but her face was turned to the side, visible enough to be recognized by her fans.

"Irina Semenova!" a woman cried, and dropped to her knees, making the sign of the cross. "It is not possible!"

Colin spoke a few words of perfect Russian to the policemen who had now arrived and turned to me, a grim look on his face. "Go home with Cécile and Masha. You may as well stay with them tonight. I shall be late."

I knew better—rather, I had learned after years of unsuccessful attempts—than to argue with Colin at the scene of a crime. He excelled in his role as agent for the Crown, but I, too, had work of my own, and had proved my mettle as an investigator time and time again. Seeing this beautiful girl drenched in her own blood, I desired nothing more than to apply myself to the task of finding her murderer, but I knew I could not insert myself into the investigation, at least not yet. Patience was a virtue I was doing my best to acquire; the results I achieved might generously be described as varied.

I watched my husband stride purposefully back to the theatre and disappear inside. Cécile appeared seemingly out of nowhere and took me by the arm.

"Come, *chérie*, Masha's carriage is here. I cannot bear to look at this for a moment longer."

I did not do as she bade but pulled away and approached to the dainty figure on the ground. The dancer's arms were outstretched, and her legs crossed in a hauntingly graceful manner. Even in death she looked a ballerina. I caught a glimpse of something golden beneath her. A burly policeman glared at me, but I ignored him and reached for the object. Now he intervened and stopped me, handling me more roughly than I felt strictly necessary. I gave him a stiff rebuke in his native tongue. Having always had an affinity for languages, I had, over several years, made a casual study of Russian in anticipation of someday visiting St. Petersburg. My command of the language fell far short of fluency, but I was not completely hopeless. Nonetheless, he pretended not to understand when I spoke to him. I switched to French, which was spoken by everyone at the Romanov court, but not by many ordinary Russian people. It was clear his command of that language was far more lacking than my Russian. Giving up, I crouched down, close to the body, and pointed to the bit of gold. He barked something to the other police, one of whom moved it slightly, revealing what lay beneath: a small, oval object, no more than six inches long. He picked it up, pulled out a handkerchief from his coat, and wiped a spatter of blood from its surface.

It was an egg, covered in pink enamel and perfect pearl lilies of the valley, topped with a small, diamond-encrusted imperial crown. I recognized it as the work of Carl Fabergé, but before I could take a closer look, another policeman rudely moved me away. Masha, who had stayed back with Cécile, berated him in loud Russian. He did not appear affected by this in the least and shoved me in the general direction of my friends. Cécile kept me from losing my balance on the icy pavement and bundled me into the waiting carriage.

"He need not have used such force," I said, only now starting to realize how cold I had grown standing outside in the fierce winter weather.

"It is almost as if he knows you, *chérie*," Cécile said. "A stranger would not have expected a lady to force her way closer to a butchered body."

Masha's palace on the Moika Embankment was only a short drive from the theatre, and soon we were settled into one of the smaller drawing rooms. By smaller, I mean slightly less enormous than the rest. No fewer than four large crystal chandeliers lit the space, which was decorated in pale blue, white, and gold. The furniture, in empire style, reminded one that although the Russians had vanquished Napoleon, they did not object to adopting his aesthetic sensibilities. An imposing fireplace housed a roaring fire, in front of which Masha had commanded a liveried footman to place three elegant chairs, and we all welcomed its penetrating heat. Physically, that is. Its warmth could not alter our somber mood as we lamented the horrific death of the beautiful young dancer.

"Who would do such a thing?" Masha asked. Every bit as elegant as Cécile—and her contemporary in age, whatever that might be—Masha's beauty stemmed from an extraordinary pair of chocolate-brown eyes and dimples whose charm refused to succumb to the ravages of time. Her alabaster skin, impossibly smooth, glowed when she smiled. Now, though, it looked hard and gray.

"I saw something that might provide a clue," I said, and began to describe the egg I had seen. No sooner had I started than Masha interrupted.

"It is one of the empress's eggs," she said. "I have seen it in the Winter Palace. The emperor gives her a jeweled egg for Easter every year. Fabergé outdid himself with that one. I believe it is from two years ago, perhaps, and is an absolute favorite of hers. Alix adores lilies of the valley, and the surprise in this one—Fabergé always includes a little something extra hidden in his eggs—miniature portraits of her husband and daughters that pop up from the top, are perfect for a devoted wife and mother."

"Are there no others like it?" I asked.

"Absolutely not," she said. "Fabergé would not make a copy for anyone. You may order your own egg, but you may not have one identical to the imperial family's."

Cécile laughed. "As you see, Masha is sentimental about her royals. Protective, too. I cannot explain the phenomenon. It is insensible to me."

The princess raised her eyebrows. "You would feel differently had the French Revolution ended in something other than bloody terror."

"You know perfectly well I do not discuss the revolution."

And that was the end of it. I had never been able to discover Cécile's views regarding her country's revolution, nor the role (if any) her family had played in it. Everyone close to her knew the subject was verboten.

"*Bien*, is that my champagne?" she asked a servant who was approaching her somewhat cautiously while holding a tray containing a heavy silver cooler. Almost as soon as we had arrived, this same servant had brought tea for Masha and me and a bottle of champagne for Cécile, having been informed it was the only beverage she considered fit to drink. But Cécile had sent him away without allowing him to open it, objecting to it the moment she saw the label and ordering him to bring one of the bottles she had brought with her from France. "Don't look so frightened," she said. "I am never fierce with someone who brings champagne."

"You were only just fierce with him moments ago, when you rejected his first bottle," I said.

"He did not bring champagne but rather that *vin horrible* the Russians love," she said. "It is too sweet to drink."

"Are you insulting my people?" A tall gentleman wearing the dark green jacket of an army officer entered the room, his warm, deep baritone filling the space. "I shall not stand for it, Cécile. I shall challenge you to a duel."

"And it shall end as badly for you as it did for Pushkin," Cécile said.

"You wound my country and my pride," he said in French nearly as good as hers. "Masha, you are as ravishing as ever." He kissed her hand and glanced at me. "I did not realize you are entertaining. Forgive me for interrupting. I promise I will not overstay my welcome and keep you ladies from whatever you had planned for the remainder of the evening."

"An interruption from you is always welcome," the princess said. "This is my new friend, Lady Emily Hargreaves, wife of the extremely charming Mr. Colin Hargreaves, who is even more handsome than you, Vasik. Emily, I present to you Prince Vasilii Ruslanovich Guryanov."

"The pleasure is entirely mine," he said, and lifted my hand to his lips. His face, broad and Slavic, was pleasing indeed, and his hazel eyes glowed like that of a contented cat. "I came to see how the ballet finished. Did Nemetseva manage the fouettées as well as everyone hoped she would? Given your long faces I imagine it was quite miserable."

"Weren't you there?" Masha asked. "I could swear I saw you in your box."

He poured himself a glass of champagne. "I was called away after the second act. As an adjutant to the major-general in charge of the gendarmes attached to court security, I must come when summoned, even if it means missing the ballet."

"Oh, dear," Masha said. "Then you don't know?"

"What? That it was a disaster?"

"Quite a disaster, but not due to fouettées," Cécile said. "Nemetseva's body was found outside the theatre after the performance."

"Her body?" He blanched. "Body? You cannot mean—Is she—"

"Dead?" Masha's directness shocked me. "Yes, I am afraid so. It was horrible. Blood everywhere. She was still in her costume."

The prince dropped his champagne, the glass shattering on the parquet floor. "Forgive me. This is a shock." He seemed so unsteady on his feet I worried he might fall over, but he managed to right himself. "Blood? I do not understand. Was she injured dancing?"

"I'm afraid not," I said. "She was murdered."

"Murdered?" He swayed again, swallowed hard, and clutched the back of a chair, looking as if he might collapse.

I crossed to him and laid a gentle hand on his arm. "I am more sorry than I can say. Were you acquainted with her?"

"Only a bit," he said. "She was a favorite of one of the grand dukes."

I found it difficult to believe he would react so strongly to the death of someone he hardly knew. "I am very sorry. My husband spoke to the police and stayed at the theatre after we left. He's bound to know more if you should like to speak with him tomorrow."

"Thank you, Lady Emily," he said. "I appreciate the offer, but it is not necessary. I cannot claim a close connection with her, but we Russians do take our ballet rather seriously. Nemetseva charmed us all with her talent. Forgive me if my reaction startled you."

"There is nothing to forgive, Vasik," Masha said. "Sit. We are all melancholy tonight. Losing such a bright star so young is a dreadful blow."

I left Masha's soon thereafter, not wanting to stay the night as Colin had suggested. I had every intention of being at the hotel when he returned, no matter how late it might be, in order to hear what he had learned about Nemetseva's murder. Try though I did to remain awake, I did not succeed. One moment I was sitting on a couch reading *War and Peace* (and coming to the conclusion that Prince Vasilii seemed very like a real life Prince Andrei), and the next I felt myself in my husband's arms as he carried me to our bedroom.

"Do not think, even for a moment, that I shall go back to sleep before you've told me everything," I said.

"I anticipated as much," he said and kissed me before lowering me onto the bed. Suspecting his motives were not entirely pure, I pried myself away from him and returned to our sitting room.

"Vodka?" I called out, crossing to a table on which stood an assortment of liquor.

"Whisky," he said, brushing his dark curls back from his forehead and following me. The man was diabolically handsome; it took a strong woman to resist him. Fortunately, I had strength in spades, at least some of the time.

"You ought to try to adapt to Russian culture. It's the least—"

"I have spent far more time here than you, my dear, and assure you I can handle my vodka when and as necessary. That I prefer, when in my own quarters, to return to the comforts of home, is something you ought not criticize."

"If you insist," I said and poured two fingers of the golden liquid for him. "I shall have vodka."

"At four o'clock in the morning?"

"As you see."

"You have no *zakuski*. No Russian would drink vodka without *zakuski*, the little snacks that go so well with it. You ought to try to adapt to the culture, my dear. I'm told very reliable sources insist it is the only way to travel abroad."

"You're a beast," I said. "Now stop trying to distract me and tell me what you learned."

"Not much, I'm afraid." He sat down and tugged at his white tie, unknotting it. "She was stabbed in the neck. Either her assailant knew what he was doing or his blows fell in a lucky spot."

I grimaced. "The poor girl."

"No one saw her leave the theatre," he said. "She mentioned to some of the girls from the corps de ballet that she needed to fix one of the ribbons on her slippers and walked in the direction of her dressing room."

"When did they notice she was missing?"

"She did not appear in time for the next act to begin, so the stage manager went in search of her, and when he couldn't find her, went to her dressing room. She didn't answer when he knocked, and eventually he opened the door. She was not there. By this point, the performance was already late in starting—this, my dear, is why Cécile had time for that extra champagne at the second interval—and he told the understudy to report to the stage."

"Did the understudy seem surprised?" I asked.

"You think she murdered a rival dancer for the chance to take the role herself?"

"Don't be daft. She couldn't possibly have cleaned herself up in time," I said. "But she could have arranged for Nemetseva's untimely demise."

"Had you met Miss Sokolova, I am certain you would never have suggested the theory," Colin said. "She is as quiet and meek a girl as I have ever seen. I found it nearly impossible to believe that she

18

was the same person who danced the rest of the ballet with such passion."

"I didn't think you were paying attention."

"My dear girl, one always pays attention during *Swan Lake*. How else is one to count the fouettées?"

"I had no idea you were such an admirer of the ballet."

"I never was before I came to Russia," he said, "but the dancers of the Imperial Theatre cast quite a spell, don't you agree?"

"I do," I said and cocked my head to the side, studying his handsome face. "What else have you learned in all your time in Russia?"

"Nothing more that concerns you." He moved closer to me on the couch and put his arm around my waist.

I removed it, firmly. "You haven't told me the rest."

"There's not much else to say. The judicial investigators assigned to handle the matter will have it in hand."

"And the imperial Easter egg?"

"You know about the egg?" His dark eyes danced. "Of course you know about the egg. The police mentioned a very pushy foreigner who all but grabbed it from under the body. I should have known it was you. I cannot say how or why Nemetseva came to have it, but I am confident that those charged with investigating the case will be able to answer all your questions when they have completed their work."

"You are leaving this to the judicial investigators?"

"Of course I am leaving it to them, Emily. It is their job, and I am not here to interfere with ordinary city business."

"What are you here to interfere with, then?" I asked, holding his gaze.

"You'll get further hounding the police than you will hounding me, my dear," he said. "Come now, let's to bed. I've a fiendishly early morning."

Ekaterina Petrovna
May 1890

By the time winter turned to spring and the sharp cracking of the thick ice on the Neva breaking as it began to thaw punctuated the constant murmur of St. Petersburg's steady bustle, Katenka had started to feel a bit more comfortable at school. Irusya remained her only friend, but now the older girls—those elegant sylphs who already danced en pointe and were practically real ballerinas—had begun to treat her with unexpected kindness. They complimented her on her turnout. They shared sweets with her. One even gave her a beautifully illustrated volume of Pushkin's *Fairy Tales,* not that Katenka had much time to read for pleasure. She did not understand their sudden interest in her until she saw them watching from their windows as she and Lev returned from St. Nicholas's one Sunday.

She looked up at them and then looked over at Lev, never before having noticed that her brother might be considered handsome. She'd always thought his icy-blue eyes were well enough formed but too piercing; it was as if he could look right through her. And his hair, curly and rumpled, was something of a mess. The giggling girls who were now waving at them made her rethink these long-held opinions.

She told Irusya about it that night, and while her friend agreed Lev was not handsome enough to be a prince, she did admit that she had seen many uglier a boy. This sent them both into a fit of laughter they could barely contain, but, by some stroke of luck, the matron did not single them out when she came to the room to see who had caused the disturbance. She only stood in the doorway, her arms crossed and her lips drawn in a firm, solid line.

"This will not happen again," she said.

Katenka bit down hard on her lip to keep silent. The next morning, they made another mark on the chest at the foot of her bed.

January 1900

3

I breakfasted alone the next morning. Colin had departed early, and after no more than three hours of sleep, leaving me to peruse the newspapers brought to our rooms every day. Under a bold headline on the front page of the Petersburg paper was a large photograph of Nemetseva posed prettily in costume, a thick, black border around the image. The accompanying article contained nothing I did not already know, so I turned my attention to the international edition of one of the New York papers. It was outdated, and large blocks of black ink covered everything the Russian censors had deemed inappropriate, but at least I could read what remained.

I was halfway through an inane story about some controversy over rowdy ice skaters in Central Park when a knock sounded on my door. Having left my maid in England, I opened it myself and saw Prince Vasilii on the other side. He bowed low, very handsomely, his military cap in his hand, and apologized for coming to me unannounced.

"You were so kind last night to invite me to speak with your husband," he said in his deep, warm voice after I'd settled him onto a wing-backed chair in the sitting room. "I am afraid I refused without giving the matter enough thought."

"And I am afraid that you've missed my husband," I said.

"Yes, I am aware of that. I pray you do not find this too forward of me, Lady Emily, but I came here hoping to see you, not him. Forgive me for abandoning ceremony altogether, but I feel the unusual circumstances allow me to do so. I understand you have a reputation as an investigator. I heard rumbles about it as soon as you arrived in Petersburg—gossip always follows one, doesn't it? Cécile confirmed your skills, and I find them to be most impressive after hearing her descriptions of your past successes. It is what prompted me to call on you with this bold request. Would you consider looking into Nemetseva's death for me?"

"I appreciate the compliment," I said, "but I'm afraid I can't be of much help to you in the matter. I have learned very little about the murder and am not involved in the investigation."

"I figured as much," he said. "I spoke with the officer in charge this morning. Unfortunately, he is a rather uninspired man."

"I find that is often the case with official investigators."

"I imagine so, given your line of work. May I smoke?" I nodded and he leaned forward to light the cigarette he had removed from a blue enameled case with the letter V formed from small diamonds on the top. He smoked, sitting quite still and looking at the ceiling for some time before, at last, he sighed. "It would be naive of me to think you have not deduced that I have a special interest in seeing Nemetseva's murderer brought to justice."

"Your reaction to the news of her death struck me as sincere, but I also suspected it betrayed a closer relationship to the deceased than you were willing to admit."

"Your intuitive skills are all that I hoped." He finished his cigarette and stubbed it out in the ashtray on the table next to him. "I—forgive me, I realize the inappropriateness of what I am about to say but trust that you are sophisticated enough not to be put off." He met my eyes, and I saw a profound sadness in his.

"You were in love with her."

"I was."

"And . . ." I paused, searching for the right words. "Your love was returned?"

"Just so," he said. "We've been lovers for more than a year."

This did not shock me. As the prince suggested, I am nothing if not sophisticated, and I was well aware that many young gentlemen are prone to indulging their baser instincts outside the bonds of matrimony.

"Does your wife—"

He interrupted. "I have no wife. Had I a wife, I would never—" He closed his eyes. "I should have liked nothing better than to marry Irochka, but there were many impediments to my doing so."

"Irochka?" I asked.

"Forgive me. I mean Irusya, of course. Irochka is the more intimate diminutive. She asked me to call her by it soon after . . . but that is not relevant. As I said, I wanted to marry her, but there were many impediments to my doing so."

"I understand," I said. "Pressure from one's family and society can be overwhelming."

"Indeed. I hope you do not judge me too harshly. I love her—loved her—so very dearly, and I cannot bear thinking that whoever struck her down is walking free this morning. I know enough from my position at court to have little faith in the judicial investigators. Even with the best intentions, they are unlikely to be able to penetrate Nemetseva's world so well as you could."

His countenance was very serious, and his words persuasive. Sincerity all but streamed from his pores. I wanted to help him, but how much could I do? "I know nothing about the theatre and have no connections there."

"Yes, but your rank gives you ready access to any social circles you wish to enter. Will you help me? I have no one else to turn to."

"I should like nothing better," I said, "but I am afraid I may be hindered by not being able to speak Russian fluently. My husband—"

"Your Russian is more than serviceable, and I would prefer if Hargreaves did not know of the favor I am asking you."

"That, Prince, is impossible. I keep no secrets from my husband."

"He is a fortunate man." He pulled another cigarette from his case and tapped it against the enameled top. "He will allow you to do as I ask?"

"*Allow* is a word I do not much like," I said. "Colin respects my abilities and would never stand in my way."

"Then you are a fortunate woman."

"Quite." I could not deny his request appealed to me. I had wanted to insert myself into the investigation as soon as I saw the fallen dancer's body, and he was presenting me with the opportunity to do just that. Furthermore, when had I ever refused to do what I could in the name of justice? "I shall happily do whatever is possible. To start, you must tell me everything you know that might prove useful. Are there any individuals who Nemetseva might have considered enemies?"

"None. There was always competition and jealousy in the company, but the dancers loved her. She was generous and kind. There is a man, not from the theatre . . . but I do not think he could be involved."

"Who?"

He fidgeted in his seat. "One of the grand dukes. I do not like to name him and impugn his reputation. He had made numerous overtures to her, but she rejected them all. She was devoted to me."

"A name would be helpful."

"Masha will tell you. I realize I seem foolish not to do so myself, but in principle I do not like to betray the innermost feelings of my friends. If I believed you could not get the information elsewhere, I would give it to you, but beg you to allow me to retain what little honor I can in this situation."

I raised an eyebrow. Prince Vasilii was a fascinating case of contradictions. His perfect manners and erect carriage should have made him appear suave, but instead they made him stiff. "I shall speak with Masha. Is there anything else?"

"Would that I knew more." He put the cigarette, still unlit, back in his case, slipped it into his pocket, and clasped his hands together. "I should like us to meet regularly so that you might give me updates on your progress. How soon will you have something to tell me?"

"That depends on what I learn and how quickly. I shall send you a message when I've something to report."

"I think, Lady Emily, it would be best if we planned our meetings in advance. Were you to start sending messages to me, people might draw the wrong sort of conclusions. If, instead, we were to be seen, on occasion, in a café, no one would give it a second thought."

To me, this sounded like madness, but I went along with it, deciding the poor man had suffered enough. If he believed this scheme would protect his reputation, it would harm no one to go along with it. "Very well. Do you have a place in mind?" I asked.

"Literaturnoye Café on the corner of Nevsky Prospekt and the Moika River Embankment. It is the place where Pushkin stopped for refreshment on the way to his fatal duel."

"Not a promising provenance."

"It will not end so badly for us," he said. "We've already had our fair share of death. And I've no stomach for duels."

Ekaterina Petrovna
August 1896

Now that she was about to enter her final year at the Imperial Theatre School, Katenka could hardly recall a time when she did not consider it home. She loved the small room she shared with Irusya ever since they had grown out of the dormitory that housed the younger students, loved the spacious rehearsal rooms with their enormous windows, even loved the classrooms in which they studied all subjects not ballet, though they represented her least favorite part of the day.

Lev, who had long since graduated from the Nikolayev Naval Academy, still walked her to the cathedral every Sunday, but they no longer met their mother and grandfather there. Both had died the previous year. Katenka had mourned more than Lev, who had loathed being sent to the academy. The navy held no fascination for him. He would have preferred to study literature and philosophy, and had often skived off class to sit in cafés with like-minded individuals discussing the works of Dostoyevsky and Gogol.

Their grandfather had spoken to him sternly on more than one occasion, making it clear that successfully completing his studies at the academy was essential to the family. Lev acquiesced, not wanting to upset the elderly man, but in private, later, he told Katenka that he would never have a career in the navy. He refused to serve the tsar.

Katenka was glad he had never said such things to their mother, who viewed the imperial family as sacrosanct. Now that she and Lev were alone in the world, her brother had more freedom to express his views, but he was careful always to be discreet, at least in front of her. Once, she asked him if he felt he couldn't confide in her, to which he smiled and shook his head, telling her that some opinions could endanger everyone around the person who held them. Seeing her face cloud with concern, he smiled and embraced her and told her never to worry.

Their summer had been perfection. They spent languid afternoons on boats on the Neva, roamed the halls of the Hermitage, and strolled along Nevsky Prospekt, inventing fictional backgrounds for the people they passed. Lev made most of them revolutionaries. Katenka saw them as quiet individuals secretly yearning for love.

The final fortnight before she was due to return to school, Irusya invited them both to join her family at their dacha. Perched on a hill in the countryside overlooking Lake Ladoga, the house provided an idyllic respite. They swam in the cool waters of the lake, read books to each other, and laughed from a distance when Lev got into boring political discussions with Irusya's father. Katenka could not imagine a happier time.

One night, when sleep eluded her, she crept out of her room and across the corridor to Irusya's, but her friend was not there. Walking softly, she made her way downstairs and out the front door. There, on the lawn in front of the house, she saw Irusya and Lev, sitting on the wide wooden swing that hung from a tree. They were leaning close to each other, the moon illuminating their faces, and appeared to be captivated by their conversation. Katenka started to walk toward them but stopped when she saw her brother place his palm on Irusya's cheek. Irusya smiled and reached for his hand, pulling it down and kissing the tips of his fingers.

Katenka froze.

Lev lowered his hand and kissed Irusya on the lips.

Katenka turned around, knowing she should not watch. Careful not to alert them to her presence, she made her way back to the house and up to her room, where she could hardly contain a whoop of joy. Now she and Irusya could be sisters!

January 1900

4

Colin's work kept him unexpectedly late that evening and left him rumpled and rather dusty. Myriad questions sprang to mind when I saw him, but I vocalized none of them. He bathed and changed into his evening kit at a pace that would have shamed the fastest sprinter. When we stepped outside the hotel, the dark curls visible below his fur hat were still damp and started to freeze in the frigid air. We climbed into a carriage and set off for Masha's, where we would be attending what she had billed as *an evening of entertainment*. En route, I shared with him my decision to investigate Nemetseva's death on behalf of Prince Vasilii.

"If you say he is grieving and in search of justice, I shall trust your judgment on the matter," he said, as we came to a stop in front of the house. "But let us not forget he is an adjutant to the major-general in charge of court security. Surely he knows someone who would be better suited to his purpose. Only because of connections in Petersburg, my dear; I do not suggest anyone is in possession of better deductive— let alone intuitive—skills than you."

Masha worked hard to earn—and maintain—her reputation as one of the best hostesses in Petersburg. Her stated goal was to never throw a party that could be described as ordinary. All of society waited in a state of agitation when she sent invitations. Unlike Mrs. Astor in New York City, whose guest lists must be capped at four hundred due to the size of her ballroom, Masha had no such constraints. She chose to limit her invites, including only those individuals whom she deemed essential to enhancing the occasion. Sometimes that required only twenty or thirty people; other times, thousands. For this particular evening, she had hired singers from the Imperial Theatre to perform excerpts from a new Puccini opera, *Tosca,* that had only just premiered in Rome. It was quite a coup, but, despite the powerful music, her guests could hardly be persuaded to listen to a single note. They were talking nonstop about Nemetseva's murder until their attention was diverted by one among them describing a brazen theft that he had discovered earlier that day.

The victim, Count Grigorii Maratovich Kosyak, a portly gentleman well past his prime, struck me as a singularly unattractive individual. Evidently he was dangerously handsome in his youth (his words, not mine), and still had a reputation with the ladies. This I found incomprehensible, but it could not be denied that his colorful character and brazen sense of humor was an asset to the gathering. He explained to us all that, upon waking at approximately two o'clock in the afternoon—he paused to note a deeply held belief that rising any earlier than this was an affront to all things good and decent— he noticed that his most prized possession, a fifteenth-century icon depicting the archangel Michael, was missing from where it hung above his bed.

"The miscreant who removed it left a note in its place, pinned to the wall, saying that a man of my moral decay had no business owning such a thing. I don't know whether to be insulted or to take it as a compliment. I almost didn't report the theft, as I was afraid certain members of the government might misinterpret *moral decay* as an indictment of my political views, but my wife assured me no one could ever suspect me of revolutionary tendencies."

"If she is not worried, there's no need for you to be," Masha said. "Should the secret police come for you, they'd probably take her as well, and she would never do anything that might lead her to Siberia."

"You are fortunate the piece is gone," Cécile said, frowning. "This habit of keeping pictures of saints in one's home is, to my mind, morbid. Would you live in a church?"

"I most certainly would not, madame," he replied. "Particularly now that I know you do not approve. Perhaps I could leave a note of thanks for the burglar. Does anyone know how I might get word to him?"

"But this is too strange," Masha said. "Last week, a young lady of my acquaintance found an emerald necklace and a note on her dressing table. Subsequent investigations revealed it to belong to the Grand Duchess Maria Pavlovna. The note implored her to wear it at the next imperial ball, as the color would highlight her eyes far better than they would the grand duchess's."

Colin gave me a pointed look and lowered his head to whisper in my ear as he pulled me into a quiet corner of the room. "There can be no doubt this is the handiwork of your old friend Sebastian Capet. Have you had any contact with him?"

"None at all," I said. I had encountered Sebastian Capet, as he liked to style himself, first in London, years ago, when he had caused a sensation by stealing a shocking number of items that had belonged to Marie Antoinette. Later, in France, our paths crossed again. No longer looking for objects owned by the ill-fated queen, he had embarked on what he viewed as a noble mission, painting his illegal activities not as theft but as the righting of wrongs. He was no Robin Hood, stealing from the rich and giving to the poor; his goals were more subjective. If he felt someone owned but did not truly appreciate a work of art, jewelry, or anything else he deemed interesting, he would (as he said) liberate it and give it to someone he judged more deserving. I could well imagine him setting his sights on the imperial collection. He had decidedly mixed opinions of royalty.

"No doubt he will be in touch before long," Colin said. "I shouldn't be surprised to find he'd followed you all the way from London." Sebastian, alas, clung to the delusion that he was in love with me, and over the years had left me a series of notes—always written in Ancient Greek—with roses and other little trinkets. He was not a favorite of my husband's.

"Following someone is too easy, Hargreaves," came a low voice, just behind me. "I should hope you would not think me amenable to using such a tired device."

I turned around to see a man, dressed in the robes of a Cossack and sporting a beard that perfectly mimicked the tsar's.

"They would not let me wear my hat inside, no matter how much I pled. Without it, the look is entirely spoiled." He grabbed for my hand and began to raise it to his lips. I pulled it away.

"What a shame for us all," I said. His disguise, though expertly crafted, did not alter his unmistakable sapphire eyes, and his lazy drawl was all too familiar. "Mr. Capet, I will not—"

"No, no," he said. "Not here, my dear. Here I am Fedor Ivanovich Dolokhov, but you may call me Fedya. I admit to being wholly charmed of the Russians' use of diminutives to reflect the closeness— dare I say *intimacy?*—of relationships."

"Dolokhov?" Colin asked, raising his eyebrows.

Sebastian immediately returned to character. "My mother was a great admirer of Tolstoy's and brazen enough to bestow upon her son a name that conjures up such . . ." His voice trailed and he looked at me, smiling wickedly. "Such complexity."

"Brazen indeed," Colin said. "Although *complexity* is not the first thing that springs to mind when I think of Dolokhov."

"I admit I haven't read the book, only flipped through to find a name," Sebastian said. "Was it a poor choice?"

"Decidedly," I said. "He's reckless and dissolute."

"Quite fitting, I'd say." Colin glowered at Sebastian. The truce between these two, if one could claim such a thing existed, was uneasy at best.

"Too late to change now, at any rate," Sebastian said. "And anyway I'm rather fond of it."

"The man you stole the icon from is here," I said. "This is reckless behavior, even for you."

"I already have a reputation as a fierce warrior," Sebastian said. "And I have offered my services to the count should he find himself in need of defending."

"That's quite enough nonsense for one night. I'm going to fetch more champagne, and I expect you to be gone when I return, Capet." Colin kissed my cheek and slipped away.

I stepped closer to Sebastian and lowered my voice. "Why are you here?"

"I've learned that the recipient of one of my . . . er . . . delicate attentions has met an untimely end. Nemetseva, the ballerina. You have heard?"

"Of course I've heard. I was at the performance that night and discovered the Fabergé egg she was holding." I sighed. "I should have known you were the one who stole it."

"My darling girl, you cannot believe there is anyone better capable than I of removing Fabergé's treasures from the Winter Palace. Have you met another man with the hubris to pull off such a feat?"

"I certainly hope not."

"It was a crowning achievement and ought to have secured my reputation forever," Sebastian said. "I am concerned, however, that people may draw erroneous conclusions about my role in the unfortunate incident that occurred."

"The murder, you mean?" I asked. "I'd hardly call that an incident."

"I know you don't believe I am capable of violence, Kallista—"

"Don't call me Kallista." The nickname, bestowed on me by my late first husband, was now only used by Cécile, who preferred it to Emily, and Sebastian, who steadfastly ignored my pleas that he stop.

"I shan't argue the point now," he said. "I did not harm that poor girl. I admired her greatly—that is why I wanted her to have the egg. But the police may misinterpret—"

"Enough," I said. "I do not think you murdered her. I know you too well to suspect such a thing. If you are concerned that you may fall under suspicion, however, you should leave Russia at once."

"I'm not *that* concerned, Kallista. So far as I can tell they don't have the note I left with the egg. The papers haven't reported anything about it, but I should like to be sure. That wretched husband of yours can find out anything he wants. Would you be so good as to persuade him to inquire—discreetly, of course—about it? I helped you when you required it and humbly beg you to do the same for me."

He had me there. In difficult straits, I had summoned him to my parents' house in Kent a few Christmases ago, when a rare jewel belonging to the Maharaja Ala Kapur Singh disappeared. Not only had Sebastian offered his assistance, he had subtly tormented my mother in a manner that brought me incalculable happiness. Should this admission horrify you, you have never met my mother.

"I shall ask him," I said, "but can make no promises."

"My darling girl, you never disappoint." He bowed low and kissed my hand with a wholly inappropriate flourish. "I shall be in touch again before you know it." He winked, turned to the crowded room, and called for vodka. His Russian, accent and all, was flawless.

The next morning, I collected Cécile, having recruited her as my assistant of sorts, and we went to the Imperial Theatre, where together we nimbly charmed our way backstage. The manager, Mr. Chernov, an imposing man in the prime of life, showed us into his small office.

"I must say again how terribly sorry we are for your loss," I said, sitting in one of the two chairs across from his desk.

"It is a blow, of that there is no doubt. Artistically, of course. Nemetseva might well have been the greatest ballerina of the next century. Her talent and her passion combined as I have never before seen. But she was also a friend, not just to me, but to everyone who worked with her. We will miss her heart even more than her dancing."

"I know you have already spoken to the judicial investigator," I said, "but Madame du Lac and I have taken a special interest in the case. As I have already explained, my experience puts me in a unique position to assist in bringing this terrible criminal to justice."

"We all know not everyone is comfortable talking freely to government officials," Cécile said. "They can be so insensitive to the delicate nature of people's situations. We have all heard stories of their brutality. No one wants to risk saying something that could be misinterpreted."

"It would be a gross miscarriage of justice were Nemetseva's murderer to remain at large because someone was afraid to speak freely," I continued. "I would like to conduct interviews with each of the members of the company, away from the judicial investigators, and away from any chance of misunderstanding."

"I cannot imagine anyone would object to a conversation with you," Mr. Chernov said. "We're hiding no political radicals here. Please, start with me. I will tell you everything I can. I knew her very well. She sent my children gifts on their name days and told me many times that she credited no small part of her success to a well-run theatre."

For half an hour, he regaled us with stories of the dancer's kindness, and while I did not doubt his sincerity, I feared that he loved her too well to have noticed anything negative about her. Even if he had, he would never admit it now that she was dead. I doubted anyone could be so angelic in every facet of her life, but the stagehands to whom he introduced us waxed no less enthusiastic. It was only when we made our way to the costume department that Nemetseva began to seem human.

Nataliya Nikolayevna Zhdanova explained, in the gravest of tones, that she had come to work in the theatre when she was only twelve years old, more than fifty years ago. Her mother, a seamstress, had taught her to sew, and over the years Madame Zhdanova had worked her way up to the position she now held as costume mistress.

"I loved Nemetseva like a daughter," she said before turning and barking a command to one of her underlings, who, in response, brought tea for all of us. "So you know I see all her flaws. A dancer with so much talent can do nearly anything she likes, but not at the start of her career. Nemetseva was too eager."

"Did the more senior dancers feel threatened by her?" I asked.

"No, no. She was promoted to principal more quickly than anyone I can remember, but not at the expense of those more experienced. They will always have their roles, so long as they want them and so long as they can dance them. Her position in the theatre was good, but she wanted to set herself up in society like our Little K, and she is not quite ready for that."

"Little K?" I asked.

"Mathilde Kschessinska," Madame Zhdanova said. "She, too, is a great talent, but other qualities have kept her from being a favorite of Petipa's. She was the mistress of Nicholas II before he became tsar and has long been entangled with any number of grand dukes. She is more difficult than Legnani, whom Petipa loves above anyone."

"And Nemetseva?" Cécile asked. "Is she modeling herself on Little K?"

"I wouldn't go quite so far, but she certainly was not above flirting when she thought it would get her something. Her youth and inexperience could put her in awkward situations, if you read my meaning."

I was not sure I did, but Cécile was nodding vigorously. "There is an art to handling such things. I have never seen a lady adept at it before the age of thirty. Thirty-five, even."

"Ancient by ballet standards," Madame Zhdanova said, a conspiratorial glint in her eyes as she leaned closer to Cécile. "In the theatre, they have to learn more quickly. I do not say I approve, but that is reality. There is a long tradition of the grand dukes and princes falling in love with dancers. They are enchanted by seeing them on stage, of course, but there are other, more practical reasons as well. The physicians who tend to the ballerinas ensure they are healthy in every regard, if you once again read my meaning."

This time, I suspected I did, but felt it preferable to confirm with Colin rather than Madame Zhdanova or Cécile. "Had Nemetseva spurned any of those gentlemen?" A jilted lover, thrown over for Prince Vasilii, might have ample motive for murder.

"Not of which I am aware. There was a boy she cared for when she was still a student. I did not know him at the time, but I heard talk of it when she first graduated and joined the company. If he came backstage, I never noticed. At any rate, he was soon replaced with someone more glamorous. And him by someone more glamorous again."

"Was her behavior out of the ordinary?" I asked.

"Not at all," she said. "Ballerinas flirt. That does not mean they take things further, at least not all the time. The Grand Duke Vladimir Alexandrovich sent her enough flowers to fill a hothouse and did his best to monopolize her attention during intervals. She encouraged him shamelessly, but I did not see any sign of her especially returning his interest."

"What did the grand duke think of that?" Cécile asked.

"You would have to ask him," she said. "I know nothing more, nor is it likely anyone else in the theatre does. If you really want to delve into her private life, you will have to speak to Ekaterina Petrovna."

"The understudy who took over for Nemetseva?" I asked.

"Yes," she said. "They were great friends for years, going back to their days as students."

I noted her use of the past tense. "Did that change?"

"Nemetseva was a star, already promoted to principal. Ekaterina Petrovna is only a *coryphée*, dancing a few solos and hoping to be noticed. Do you suppose they would still be friends?"

"They never stopped being friends."

The interruption came from the door to the costume department. In it stood the man who had danced the part of the Prince in *Swan Lake*. "Nemetseva would have done anything for Katenka. They were closer than sisters."

Madame Zhdanova shrugged. "The most vicious fights I have ever seen were between sisters. Talk to her. See for yourself."

I turned around, wanting to ask the man what else he knew, but he had vanished.

"Don't bother searching out Yuri," Madame Zhdanova said. "He will have nothing else to say."

Ekaterina Petrovna
February 1897

From that fateful day at Irusya's dacha, Katenka had known a happiness she had never before imagined possible. She did not begrudge her friend for diverting Lev's attention from her, but rather rejoiced that the three of them were now almost like a family. Back at school, Irusya could not join them when Lev collected her for Sunday services, but she never failed to send a letter to him via Katenka, and Lev, in return, always had a small gift and note for Irusya.

The girls were busier than ever, preparing for their graduation performance, an occasion that would be attended by the imperial family. Dancing well would mean a glorious start to a career on the Mariinsky stage, and Katenka and Irusya were both expected to shine. They worked hard in class, and harder still when they returned alone to the rehearsal room in the evening. Taking turns, one playing the piano while the other practiced, they worked and worked until they had mastered their choreography.

Because they were both graduating with firsts, they were allowed to choose their pieces. Katenka selected a solo from Riccardo Drigo's *La forêt enchantée,* a work that had been composed more than a decade earlier for the school. It was so well loved that it moved almost immediately to the Imperial Theatre and had been in the repertoire at the Mariinsky ever since. Irusya picked the pas de deux from *La Fille mal gardée*, a piece long associated with the greatest ballerinas. Mathilde Kschessinska, whom they both admired, had danced the same at her own graduation performance eight years earlier, and Irusya told Katenka she did not think she could do better than by emulating Kschessinska.

"She caught the tsarevitch's attention with her dancing that night," Irusya said one night as they stretched to warm their muscles before beginning to rehearse. "I've asked Madame Zhdanova to find me the costume Kschessinska wore. It's blue, which suits me well, don't you think? Sprinkled with little forget-me-nots. Could anything be more fitting?"

"You don't need flowers to avoid being forgot," Katenka said. "Your dancing is sublime on its own."

Irusya was not willing to take any chances. She had selected as her partner for the piece Yuri Melnikov, the best male dancer at the school. He groused about the extra rehearsals upon which she insisted, but he knew he was lucky to dance with her. Her grace, her elegance, and the weightless way she glided across stage en pointe were ethereal. No one doubted that she would someday be named prima ballerina assoluta.

Katenka leafed through the music she had placed on the piano. "You're playing the beginning a bit too fast. Could you slow it down this time?"

Irusya sighed. "Whatever you wish. I take it this means you want to dance first?"

"Your powers of observation are extraordinary, Irina Semenova. I think you are destined for greatness!"

"Focus on your steps, Ekaterina Petrovna, or I will find a cane to beat you with." Their first teacher relied on his cane to encourage his students, though he did stop short of beating them. A little prodding, however, and a quick whack, he considered perfectly within the bounds of acceptability.

At the sound of Irusya playing the opening notes of Drigo's score, Katenka transformed. She stood taller, perfectly poised, and moved her arms in port de bras with impossible fluidity. Irusya danced regally, with great elegance, her body so pliable it was as if she did not have bones, but Katenka infused her every movement with an unmistakable energy and passion. Her adagios strained against refinement while never straying from technical perfection. Some of her teachers implored her to hold her feelings in check, to not reveal so much emotion, but Katenka could no more do that than she could choose to stop breathing.

"Watching you I wonder that anyone bothers to dance when they can never match your skill. What a pity we will have no tsarevitch in the audience to impress. He would be taken with you in an instant," Irusya said.

"I would not wish for such a thing, particularly as rumor says he stays away because of ill health," Katenka said. "Should I try that last bit again?"

"You are already a study in perfection. Let me have a turn."

Katenka wrapped a soft shawl around her shoulders and wiped the sweat from her face before sitting in front of the piano. "Are you nervous at all?" she asked. "Don't you feel that whatever happens at this performance will mark the course for the rest of our lives?"

"I think both of us will be welcomed into the company," Irusya said.

"Yes, but I am convinced there is something profoundly symbolic about this last time we dance as students. If I do well, I shall find success. If not, my road will always be a difficult one."

"What a lot of nonsense. We will both have spectacular careers."

"Until you marry Lev and retire to have a house full of babies."

"It will have to be a very small house," Irusya said. "I have never been much fond of babies."

5

~~~❖~~~

Interviewing all the members of the Imperial Ballet took hours. None of the dancers admitted to seeing anything out of the ordinary. I had started with the principals, some of whom felt Nemetseva had taken roles from them, but they did not show signs of anything beyond ordinary professional competitiveness. From there, I made my way down the ranks, uncovering little things that piqued my interest: a *coryphée* whose bitterness took me by surprise, a first soloist who admitted to sometimes borrowing costumes for private performances at parties without first securing Madame Zhdanova's permission, and a member of the corps de ballet who did not try to hide her disdain for Nemetseva.

"She got promoted because she was good at choosing protectors," the corps girl, Larisa, said. "I cannot admire that. She was good enough to deserve them. I'm not saying she wasn't, but I prefer dancers who don't take aristocratic lovers. Although it doesn't seem like she had one anymore, but she'd already been promoted, so it doesn't matter."

The person with whom I was most interested in conversing, Ekaterina Petrovna Sokolova, was not in the theatre. After getting her address from Mr. Chernov, Cécile and I set off for her house. She lived across town, far from the glamorous surroundings of the Mariinsky. When I had speculated about Colin taking rooms in a neighborhood that would have seemed right for Raskolnikov, this was what I had imagined. The architecture and colors of the buildings matched those in Petersburg's more genteel areas, but here the grand façades were covered in flaking paint, their walls cracked, their windows grimy, and their courtyards filled with all manner of refuse.

Nevsky Prospekt, in front of my hotel, was full of court carriages driven by liveried coachmen decked out in crimson and gold. An atmosphere of bustling chaos pervaded the area. On the wide pavements, the fashionable set strolled, bundled in the most extraordinary furs, beneath which they wore the finest European clothes. Officers dressed in immaculate uniforms and mounted on beautiful stallions charged through the street at speeds that would have left the inhabitants of London aghast. I loved best the proud men, standing tall like Roman charioteers, who commanded the gaily painted troikas, sleighs pulled by three horses. The bourgeoisie preferred carriages, no doubt because they were more European, and workers kept the snow on the streets packed down enough that their wheels would not get stuck in even the worst winter weather. I could not fathom how anyone would choose such a conventional and uninspired mode of transport when one had at one's disposal a troika.

Neither vehicle was to be seen in Ekaterina Petrovna's neighborhood. There were smaller sledges and a few sorry-looking, battered carts pulled by even sorrier looking horses. On the pavements there was no room for a fashionable parade; they were filled with stooped vendors swathed in coarse coats and thick hats, selling a motley assortment of objects and food. They stomped their felt-booted feet on the ground in what had to be a vain attempt to stay warm, and shouted at Cécile and me, trying to entice us to buy something, shooting toothless grins and shaking their heads when we declined.

Ekaterina's building must have been beautiful when first built. It had gracious lines and large windows and, so far as I could tell, had once been painted a charming shade of coral. Now the color looked drab, and many of the windows were broken and badly mended. Inside, we had to climb to the fourth floor to reach the dancer's apartment.

When at last we reached the top, we stood, out of breath, in a narrow, dark corridor. There were gaslights at even intervals along the walls, but only two of them were lit. I knocked on the dancer's door. A lanky young man wearing spectacles and dressed in an unremarkable suit opened it, inquiring as to our purpose. Speaking Russian, I introduced us and asked if Ekaterina Petrovna was home. He replied in French and told us to wait a moment, before closing the door and returning a few moments later to usher us into a large and surprisingly well-furnished flat. A bright Persian carpet covered the floor of the sitting room, where, on a long, leather sofa, sat a delicate young woman, with large, icy-blue eyes, golden hair, and skin so pale that it was almost translucent. She rose to her feet the moment she saw us.

"Forgive me for not coming to the door myself," she said in flawless French. "I am not much for visitors today."

"I offer my most sincere condolences for your loss," I said.

"Thank you. Do take a seat, please," she said, her voice soft. "This is my friend, Dmitri Dmitriyevich Ivchenko. He tells me you have come to speak about Irusya. You may call him Mitya and me Katenka. We know how difficult our names are for you Europeans."

"I admit I have not entirely deciphered the system," I said. Mitya crossed to a table in the corner of the room and poured four cups of tea from a large bronze samovar. He distributed them, each nestled in a gleaming silver *podstakannik,* the traditional Russian way to serve the steaming beverage. The clear glass allowed one to admire the tea's color, and the elaborately decorated *podstakannik,* with its convenient handle, enabled one to drink without burning one's hands.

"Do not bother to try," Mitya said. "We do not expect you to master it."

"What a beautifully furnished home," Cécile said, making an exception of her rule that champagne was the only acceptable libation by sipping her tea.

"Unexpectedly so, *oui*?" Katenka said. "Do not think I suggest you are insulting me by saying this. I know this neighborhood is not desirable, but I prefer large rooms, and my salary at the theatre is not sufficient to fund reasonable space in more fashionable quarters."

"Our great writer Dostoyevsky lived only a few blocks away," Mitya said. "Katenka is proud to make her home here."

"Mitya can make any circumstance seem more palatable," Katenka said, giving him a small, but warm, smile. "It is his special talent. What brings you here? It cannot only be to express your condolences over poor Irusya's death, although I assure you I am most appreciative of the gesture. She was my dearest friend from the time we were small girls."

"Madame Zhdanova suggested that we speak with you," I said. "I have been charged with the task of investigating Nemetseva's death by a party who wishes to remain anonymous. I can imagine this seems strange—"

"No, not strange in the least," Mitya said. "Why would a woman not make a good investigator?"

His question startled me, but pleasantly so. What a refreshing perspective! "Not strange that a woman would conduct an investigation, but strange that anyone is asking for an investigation separate from that being conducted officially."

Mitya laughed. "You don't know much about our judicial investigators, do you?"

"No, but I have been told that not everyone feels they can be relied upon," I said. "It is not much different elsewhere."

"Elsewhere they don't send you to work in a Siberian mine when they don't like your politics."

"Mitya, this is not the time." Katenka spoke with a firmness that surprised me. I suppose I must have expected a ballerina to be as light and quiet at home as she was on stage. Until now, she had confirmed my assumption.

He crossed his arms and leaned back against his chair. "Yes, yes. You are correct."

"What help can I offer?" Katenka asked. Her voice was quiet again, and she looked like a delicate shell in danger of breaking.

"The more I know about Nemetseva, the more likely I will be able to identify people who might have wished her ill," I said. "We have interviewed everyone at the theatre, where it is clear she was well loved. But no one can have had a life so perfectly full of bliss and happiness."

"No, Irusya's life was as complicated as anyone's," Katenka said. "You have seen her dance?" I nodded. "Then you know of her skills on the stage. Not just her dancing, but her ability to act. She knew that the fastest way to become a prima ballerina was to dance and to behave like one from the beginning, and she did just that. I remember on our first day of school, when we were only nine or ten years old, she already carried herself like a prima and treated everyone around her with gracious ease. She never seemed like she had something to prove. She knew how good she was."

"People did not resent her talent?" I asked.

"They would have if she had ever let them see how fiercely competitive she was, but she was too smart for that. She wore a mask all the time, careful never to reveal what was churning beneath it."

"Not even to you?" I knew better than to take everything she said as solid fact. She had just lost her dearest friend and was unlikely to say anything she thought might harm Nemetseva's memory.

"I was apart from the others from the moment I first arrived at

Theatre Street. I was never gregarious like Irusya, and, although I craved success as much as she, I had no skill in anything beyond dance. To become truly great, one must learn more than just technique and artistry. One must be able to charm choreographers and know how to work with them to best show off one's talents. Every person in the theatre contributes to a prima's success. Without their support, one can only go so far."

"But how valuable can all that be?" I asked. "Surely the actual dancing matters more than anything."

"*Bien sûr*," Katenka said. "But it is far easier to join the ranks of the legendary if you can master the rest, too. That, I was never good at. I am uncomfortable putting myself forward."

"Is that what drew Nemetseva to you?" Cécile asked.

"At first, she befriended me because she felt sorry for me. I was shy and unhappy outside of the rehearsal room. I had no talent for artifice, so she knew I was always candid with her. She didn't have to pretend with me, because she trusted that I was her friend unconditionally. I didn't want anything from her, and the only thing she ever asked of me was that I give her the trunk that had stood at the foot of my bed when we were in school. She liked the memory of it."

"We saw you dance, too," I said. "You come to life on stage, Katenka."

"I know what you are implying, Lady Emily," she said. "Irusya never felt threatened by me. There is room in the company for at least one more prima ballerina."

"If she did not consider you a threat, did she consider anyone else in the company to be one?" I asked.

"No." Katenka shook her head. "You have seen her talent for yourself. She had no need to worry on that count."

"What about her personal life? Ballerinas have ardent admirers who sometimes want more than they ought."

"Irusya could flirt all night, leave a gentleman with nothing more than a kiss on the cheek, and he would go away in a state of blissful rapture."

"Surely not all gentlemen are so easily pacified," Cécile said. "We need not bow to propriety here. I am well acquainted with the grand dukes and more Russian princes than I can count. Ballerinas are their preferred mistresses."

Mitya stiffened at her words and his face darkened.

"Do not scold me, sir," she continued. "I condone neither their actions nor their expectations, but it cannot be denied that there is a long tradition in the theatre of romantic encounters. It is not the case only in Russia. I could tell you scandalous things about the Paris Opera Ballet, but I shall spare us both the embarrassment. The dancers here in Petersburg are the best looked after in the world. They are healthy, if you understand my meaning."

Mitya rose to his feet. "Madame!"

Cécile waved her hand. "I know, I know, it is something one ought not say aloud, and I shall speak of it no more."

"We are concerned only with what happened to Nemetseva," I said. "Were any of the gentlemen who sought her attentions disappointed to be rejected?"

"She did not reject all of them," Mitya said, his countenance changing. "She was no angel."

"I know that as well as anyone," Katenka said, her tone sharp. "But she never toyed with anyone's affections. She has been in love, she has been thwarted, and she has loved again. She has hurt and been hurt."

"Whom did she hurt?"

"You must understand we were very sheltered at school. When at last we joined the company and were living on our own, we possessed what seemed to us unprecedented freedom. We still had very little time to ourselves. We take class and rehearse every day but Sunday, when we could do what we wanted. Irusya met a very charming count during the interval of a performance and started spending as much time as she could with him."

"And it ended badly?" I asked.

"As you say," Katenka said. "She was very inexperienced and thought herself immediately in love. But when, a few months later, she met an even more charming man, a grand duke . . ."

"She realized the count was not quite so fascinating," Cécile said.

"Yes. She did not handle the situation as well as she would have today."

"When did this happen?"

"Three years ago, I believe," Katenka said. "I don't remember exactly."

"Not so long ago, then," I said.

"It seems like another lifetime," Katenka said. "So much happened so quickly, especially for Irusya. She started in the company as a *coryphée* right from school, instead of in the corps, and was promoted to principal within a few months."

"And that is unusual?" Cécile asked.

"I entered the company at the same time as her, but in the corps and was only promoted to *coryphée* last month. My performance in *Swan Lake* was well received, and I am likely to be promoted to second soloist as a result, but there is still first soloist to reach before I could be a principal."

"Irusya skipped ranks?" I asked.

"A different set of rules apply to those as talented as Irusya," Katenka said. I detected no hint of bitterness in her voice. "It is because of those things of which I was just speaking. She could do anything, Irusya, and as a result, people would do anything for her."

"Did you see her leave the theatre the night of her death?" I asked.

"No, nor did she mention anything about it to me. We shared a dressing room. That is, she shared hers with me. As a principal, she had her own, but she didn't want me crammed in with the rest of the *coryphées*."

"Did you see her during the second interval?"

"No, but I didn't go to the dressing room."

"Why do you think she left the theatre?" Cécile asked.

"I cannot imagine anything that would have caused her to do such a thing without telling anyone. Not in the middle of *Swan Lake*." Sadness painted Katenka's face, making her look decades beyond her true age.

"But she did leave," I said.

"I cannot believe it was voluntary," Katenka said. "That night was to be her greatest triumph. Nothing could have distracted her from that. Nothing."

"No one has come forward with information that supports the idea that she left against her will."

"Someone is lying. There can be no doubt of that."

Ekaterina Petrovna
March 1897

Other than acquiring an astonishing command of the French language and becoming competent on the piano, skills she believed essential to every ballerina, Katenka did not much distinguish herself in the nondance classes she was required to take every afternoon. But whenever she thought about the wondrous exchange of energy that occurred in the theatre between audience and dancer, she was reminded of something mentioned in her literature class. If a writer could persuade a reader to suspend disbelief, to deliberately turn off any critical voice, then his work would succeed. Dancing was much the same. Having flawless technique and a pleasing line were essential, but it was something else that led the audience to silence their inner critics, and without achieving that, a dancer could never be sublime.

The night before their graduation performance, Katenka and Irusya, unable to sleep, escaped from their room and padded softly through the dark corridors of the school until they reached the small theatre it housed. Irusya had brought a lamp, but it did little to illuminate the space. It flickered between them as they sat on the stage and looked into the auditorium.

"We will never dance here again after tomorrow," Katenka said. "It saddens me."

"You are too sentimental," Irusya said. "After tomorrow, we will join the company and dance at the Mariinsky. We shall never miss this tiny stage. But for now, dance with me, Katenka!"

For the next hour, the girls flew about in an energetic compilation of bits of choreography they knew. They even partnered each other in an improvised pas de deux. Finally, Irusya went to the front of the stage and commanded Katenka to take her place at an imaginary barre.

"We begin with pliés. Counts of two, starting in first position. Two demi, two grand, repeat in second, fourth, and fifth. Finish with port de bras forward, then back, then balance sous-sus."

Laughing, Katenka complied while Irusya, looking very stern, counted and gave corrections. "Shoulders back, Ekaterina Petrovna, and watch your knees. Over the toes, please. Now, tendus from fifth . . ."

They continued like this until it was almost time to rise and have breakfast. A sleepless night ought to have harmed their performances that evening, but they both felt more invigorated than ever. In class that morning, their teacher complimented them both. He had never seen them so focused and precise. Both, he said, were destined for greatness. Just how much greatness would be determined in only a few hours.

January 1900

6

I left the hotel long before my first planned meeting with Prince Vasi-lii, wanting time to take a leisurely stroll along Nevsky Prospekt, the most famous boulevard in St. Petersburg. Winter in Russia made the season elsewhere seem the friendlier sister of an inclement spring day. Some years back, I made the acquaintance of an American writer, Isa-bel Hapgood, who had spent extensive time traveling in Russia. She stressed to me the critical importance of dressing appropriately for the weather. Even for a short trip, she said, it is worth the expense. I shall never forget the tone of condescension in her voice when she confided in me, *"the horror inspired in anyone who is acquainted with the treacherous climate at the sight of tourists in inadequate coats."* The phrase *treacherous climate* stuck with me, and before leaving England I took the time to purchase what she had described as *the requisite furs.*

After taking approximately seven steps out of the warm lobby, I was determined to send Miss Hapgood a note of thanks for her excel-lent advice. The sky, a deep blue entirely different from the shades found in Greece or the Côte d'Azur, had a hard edge to it, almost in-dustrial in its beauty. Dense columns of smoke so thick they looked heavy sliced through its steely hue, and although sunlight dazzled on the snow, its rays offered no warmth. I buried my gloved hands deeper in my enormous fur mitt and turned the corner of Mikhaylovskaya ulitsa onto Nevsky Prospekt.

Some might consider this stretch of road comparable to the Champs-Élysées in Paris or Piccadilly in London, and although they would be correct in some measures, the comparison fails to capture the essential nature of not only Nevsky Prospekt but also St. Petersburg. The broad avenue, named for Alexander Nevsky, the thirteenth-century prince of Novgorod who drove off invading forces from the banks of the Neva (hence his name, *Nevsky*), stretches from the river to the monastery named for the prince. His military victories not only gained him political success but also led to his canonization by the Orthodox Church.

The stretch of pavement just north of the monastery was little more than an ordinary road, full of mundane shops with modest apartments above. Darker quarters spirated from side streets whose inhabitants had little interest in the European playgrounds created for aristocrats north of the Anichkov Bridge. Nicholas I said *St. Petersburg is Russian, but St. Petersburg is not Russia*, and I suspected these edgier areas to be more Russian. I had timed my departure so that I might explore a bit of this side of the city, but now ringing church bells signaled that I had dawdled nearly too long.

I turned around and headed back in the direction of the Neva, passing Gostiny Dvor, a large covered marketplace where one could buy nearly anything, and crossing two more canals, the bridge over the first of which provided an excellent view of the not-yet-complete Church of the Savior on the Spilled Blood. Alexander III had ordered its construction over the precise spot where assassins bombed his father's carriage. Scaffolding covered much of it, but I could see the tops of the onion domes that crowned the magnificent building. This, to me, looked like Russia.

Prince Vasilii was sitting at an upstairs table when I entered the

Literaturnoye Café. He rose to his feet and hailed me, asking if I could join him or if I already had plans to meet someone. Despite feeling his subterfuge to be unnecessary, I managed to reply that I was merely taking a break from shopping and would be delighted to have a cup of tea with him.

"You should try harder to appear sincere, Lady Emily," he said, giving me a half smile as I sat down across from him. "Your eyes give away your true thoughts. I am very glad I am not your lover. Your husband would be onto us before our first kiss."

"That situation would never occur," I said.

"Not as such, but in your work surely there is a certain value to being able to willfully mislead people."

"Yes, there is, and when that is required I have no trouble accomplishing it. In this case, however, I find no need for it."

"Then I thank you for indulging me." He was a vision of soldierly perfection, with his spotless uniform and well-groomed appearance, but his hazel eyes were dull, no doubt from grief. Nothing else betrayed the pain he must be feeling. We talked about stuff and nonsense until the waiter brought my tea and a napoleon pastry. Only after his departure did the prince ask what I had learned.

"Not a great deal, I am afraid," I said. "Nemetseva's fellow dancers and the stage hands at the theatre had nothing but kind words to say about her. I find it odd that she was able to leave the theatre wholly unnoticed in the middle of a ballet, but no one admits to seeing her exit."

"It is impossible that no one saw anything," he said. "People idolize ballerinas here. No one would want to admit to having seen something that eventually led to her death. I imagine guilt is the motivation for the lie."

"A person telling me he observed something out of the ordinary is a far cry from admitting guilt."

"No, but if you cared for someone who had been murdered, and you realized that you saw that person doing something out of the ordinary just before her death, wouldn't you regret not having intervened in the moment? If a stagehand or a dresser who saw her had inquired as to where she was going, for example, it might have stopped her from continuing on. It might have saved her."

He clenched his left hand, which had been resting on the table, until the knuckles were bone white. I placed mine over it. "There is nothing you could have done to stop this," I said. "A casual word from a passerby would not have kept her from going to her dressing room or wherever she was headed. And you, who were not even backstage, certainly couldn't have changed the course of events."

"You see through me too easily." He tipped his head back and looked at the ceiling. "I never went to her backstage, during the interval or otherwise. I feared it would draw attention to our relationship. But if I hadn't been so concerned with my bloody reputation . . ."

"It would have made no difference. Think it through rationally. She left the stage, and instead of chatting up the dukes and princes and whoever else was backstage, she headed for her dressing room, ostensibly to fix a ribbon. I believe that was her true intention, as I noticed one loose on her slipper when I saw her body. Between the stage and the dressing room, she changed her course."

"How can you know that?"

"Because she wound up outside, not far from the stage door, with not so much as a cloak covering her costume. She must have had a very particular reason for going to the door. Either she had planned to meet someone there all along, or she received a message telling her to go there."

"I feel most tormented. It seems there is no hope for finding her murderer." His brows knit together and his countenance darkened. I had braced myself for him to bring up the imperial egg, but his emotion had got the better of him before he did, something for which I was thankful. As I knew Sebastian was responsible for the theft and, more to the point, that he was not involved in the murder, I had come up with several schemes for diverting Vasilii's attention from it. None of them seemed adequate, and I was grateful not to have needed to employ any of them.

I reached across the table and put a hand on top of his. "You must not lose heart. This afternoon I've a meeting with the investigator in charge and will see what he and his colleagues have learned from her body and any other evidence they have gathered. No one can commit so violent a crime without leaving behind some sort of calling card."

"How did you manage to convince him to speak with you?"

"I am nothing if not resourceful," I said. "And I promise you I will do everything I can to bring the perpetrator to justice."

Prince Vasilii might have been less impressed by my meeting with the judicial investigator had he known that my husband organized it. I walked from the café to Palace Square, where Colin was waiting for me under the towering red granite Alexander Column. We hired a sledge to take us to the dingy office in which we met a surly detective.

"It is, of course, my delight to help you," he said, not bothering to mask the dripping sarcasm in his voice. He spoke no English and only a little French, so I had to rely on Russian to communicate. To say he had agreed to the meeting gives the wrong impression; his superior, after a brief word from *his* superior (to whom Colin had spoken the day before), told him to do it, and in imperial Russia, one did not question one's superior. That did not mean, however, one must approve of what one was asked to do. He did his best to ignore me altogether, looking at Colin whenever he spoke.

The slight did not offend me in the least. It allowed me to peruse the case while he talked to my husband. The stark photographs of Nemetseva's broken body warranted close study, but looking at them was difficult, and I felt bile rise in my throat when faced with the full horror of the gashes on her neck and chest. They had not been visible when I saw her body as it lay facedown in the snow. I had been in no position to analyze them and determine the details of the weapon used, but Colin confirmed, through the detective, my suspicion that the blows had come from someone taller than the diminutive ballerina.

Even more interesting was something I spotted on a picture of the bodice of her costume. Much of it was saturated with blood, but a long, dark shape that seemed out of place drew my attention. It did not look to be part of the garment. The detective disagreed with me, insisting it was one of the feathers sewn onto the silk, and that blood made it appear irregular. I pressed and pressed until I frustrated him so much that he slapped his hands on his desk, stood up, and motioned for me to follow him.

We went into a room full of crowded shelves. He pulled a box down from one of them, slammed it onto a nearby table, and flung off the lid. The metallic scent of blood assailed me. Inside was Nemetseva's tutu and the rest of the physical evidence collected at the scene. He removed it, spread it on the table, and then handed me a slim wooden baton of sorts, indicating that I could use it to prod as I saw fit.

It was ugly work. The blood, stiff and brown, had cemented the feathers on the bodice together, but those on one side of the skirt were relatively unscathed. Using the baton, I poked at the area just above the waist. There, caught between tight rows of beading, was a shredded bit of fabric decidedly different from anything used on the costume. The detective grunted, but did not sound displeased. He tugged at it, removing it from the bodice and lay it on the table. It was dark blue velvet, the sort often used in evening cloaks. A few stray strands of fur clung to it.

"She wouldn't have pulled on a cloak unless she intended to go outside." I examined the remaining contents of the box, heavy with sadness at the sight of the little satin slippers, their ribbons crumpled. There was no sign of the note Sebastian had left with the imperial egg or the egg itself. The investigator explained that the latter had been returned to the Palace as quickly as possible. He squirmed when I questioned him about it, making it clear that the theft had caused the security forces in the palace a great deal of embarrassment and that everyone preferred it be mentioned as little as possible. I took this as a rare example of a time when protecting the nobility had good, if unintended, consequences. We thanked him and stepped back onto the icy street, where our sledge was waiting, and ordered the driver to take us to the Mariinsky.

The investigator had told us his men had searched (I use the term loosely) the area around the theatre for clues, to little avail. I was not so naive as to think I would locate the cloak. If it had been discarded somewhere obvious, they would have found it. I had come to study the area around the theatre.

Fresh snow had long since covered the bloodstains where the ballerina had fallen, but we had no trouble finding the exact spot. It was not terribly far from the stage door, at a great enough distance from the front of the theatre that it would have been quiet even during the interval. Anyone who had stepped outside for a breath of air (unlikely on a frigid January night) would have left through the lobby. The stagehands were all accounted for during the time in question, and none of the dancers would have wanted to subject themselves to the cold before going back on stage.

There was a wide snow-covered pavement that stretched from the edge of the theatre to the parallel side street. Across it stood the usual Petersburg apartment buildings. I was staring at their neoclassical façades when the motion of a curtain in one of the windows caught my eye.

"I saw nothing in the records of the investigation to suggest anyone has spoken to the residents of that building," I said, pointing.

"And you would now like me to serve as your translator should you encounter any unfamiliar idioms when you interview them?" Colin asked.

"You do, I hope, know how much I adore you."

He grinned and took my hand. We crossed the street engaged in a lively debate over how best to gain access to the building.

Ekaterina Petrovna
March 1897

"They're here," Irusya said, peeking through the edge of the curtain. "All of them. I can see the tsar."

"Stop looking," Katenka said. "They will see you!"

"Isn't that the whole idea?" Irusya's brown eyes were sparkling. The shawl she carried to keep her warm while she wasn't dancing was dragging on the floor, hanging from her shoulder. "I don't know how I shall stand waiting another moment to begin!"

There wasn't long to go. Katenka pulled her backstage, and they huddled together, pressing themselves up against the wall to give room for the dancers up first to pass them en route to the stage. They were doing a scene from *The Little Humpbacked Horse*, one of Katenka's favorites. Petipa had choreographed it to music from Cesare Pugni and Riccardo Drigo. It was a charming folk tale, familiar to every Russian child, and one that Katenka's mother had told her frequently. She had always liked the idea of a magical horse helping a man win the hand of the lady he loved, and it didn't hurt that the man wound up becoming tsar.

Next up were selections from *Paquita*, which included some lovely solos as well as a mazurka. The latter was danced by students who had excelled at character dancing. They moved brilliantly, stomping their feet and clicking their heels, but would never be great classical dancers. Katenka held her breath as she watched them from the wings, grateful that she did not share their fate.

Irusya danced next. Her eyes flashed like diamonds as she prepared to take the stage. She squeezed Katenka's hand one last time, smoothed her dark hair, and as soon as she heard the first strains of music, she floated out of the wings. Katenka watched closely, knowing Irusya would want to parse every step of her performance when they were home in bed that night. They both knew perfection could not be attained if one did not pounce on every possibility to improve.

No one could have found the smallest mistake in Irusya's dancing that night. The sternest teacher would have had no correction to offer. She was sublime: musical and precise, fluid and strong. She transcended the art, and the audience knew it from the moment she appeared before them. Katenka could feel their energy. It was as if they were all sitting forward on the edges of their seats, unable to breathe until Irusya had taken her final bow.

Triumph was not a word extravagant enough for Irusya's success.

Katenka was waiting in the wings with her friend's shawl. Irusya glowed, not just from exertion but from the innate pleasure that came from knowing she had acquitted herself well. She let Katenka wrap the soft cloth around her and then embraced her, tight.

"You will be even better," she said.

Next came a variation from *Sleeping Beauty* and then the Dance of the Little Swans from *Swan Lake.* Then, at last, it was Katenka's turn.

She stood in the wings, extremely still, poised, full of purpose and confidence. She had mastered her choreography and knew she could bring it to life. She had worked for almost her entire life to reach this moment, and now that it had come, she was ready. She lifted her right arm, pointed her foot, and stepped onto the stage.

Nothing in particular went wrong. She hit all her steps and

landed her jumps gracefully. Her face perfectly expressed the correct emotions at the correct times. Her port de bras were admirable, her arabesque flawless. But something was off. The energy was not right. She could not find her passion. She heard someone in the audience cough, and she knew she had lost them. In this final performance as a student, she had not managed to bring magic to the stage.

Katenka took her bows, curtseying to the imperial box and to each side of the audience, but she hardly heard the applause. She felt numb, knowing technical proficiency alone did not make one great.

Irusya knew it, too. She was waiting in the wings with Katenka's shawl, and draped it over her friend's shoulders, but she said nothing. They leaned against the wall, waiting for the rest of the program to finish, but neither of them felt even the slightest joy. Their paths would diverge after this. No longer would they be two brilliant pupils, their teachers' greatest hopes. One would be a rising star and one a very competent corps dancer.

They might always remain friends, but they would never again be equals.

January 1900

7

Colin rejected outright my suggestion that we pretend to be looking for accommodation in the neighborhood because we were dedicated balletomanes. I explained this would give us the chance to ask pointed and direct questions as to just how much one could see from apartment windows, but he was unmoved.

"Simple, Emily, is generally best. We will tell them the truth about why we are here," he said, and rang the bell of the flat he determined to have the best view of the theatre. A maid opened the door and led us to her mistress, an ancient woman who, even if she had showed the slightest interest in looking out her windows, could not see far enough to make out a single detail on the far side of the street. Above her was a young couple who had gone to a play at the Alexandrinsky Theatre the night of the murder. Below her we found a very eager gentleman, desperate to help. He told us story after story of watching ballerinas come and go through the stage door, but in the end admitted that, although he had been home on the night in question, he had seen nothing, adding that the street had been remarkably quiet until Nemetseva's body was discovered. He had heard the screams that alerted all of us to the murder. "I was sitting here"—he leapt up from his seat and crossed to a chair near the window—"reading. A newspaper, if that matters."

"It does not," Colin said.

"I say it only to communicate that it was not something engrossing. I would have heard any sort of commotion outside. When I realized something serious had happened, I ran downstairs to inquire what it was—we humans are morbid, aren't we?—and when I saw her body . . . I was very much struck that I had been sitting so close, in clear view of so heinous a crime and yet had no idea what was transpiring until it was too late. I found it most humbling. I wish I had more to say."

"Thank you," Colin said and rose, giving me his arm and starting for the door.

"Wait," he said. "Before you go, I do recall hearing someone walking beneath my window—his boots crunched in the snow."

Colin thanked him again and we took his leave. Once outside, my husband shook his head. "He couldn't possibly have heard footsteps. Screams, yes, but the crunch of snow through those double windows? Never."

"Then why did he say—"

"He wants to be involved, wants to help," Colin said. "People like that are often the most useless. It is why I prefer hard evidence to human. Even a good witness, with the best of intentions, is fallible."

We continued to make our way through the building. On the top floor, we encountered a tiny bird of a woman. The deep lines on her face looked like they might have been carved in stone, as on the wall of an Egyptian tomb. She stood a good foot shorter than I, and despite her age, bore no sign of the slightest stoop, although she moved so slowly it hurt to watch her. She told us her name, Agrippina Aleksandrovna Minkovski; invited us inside without hesitation; and insisted on giving us tea from a tarnished samovar, which she served in glasses held in remarkable champlevé enamel *podstakanniks*, their handles fashioned as dragons. In each saucer she placed three lumps of sugar and two small cookies.

"You have come about Nemetseva," she said, lowering herself into a chair next to the window. Her furniture was all quite battered—the upholstery nearly worn away in spots—but the pieces were good quality and had probably cost a great deal when new. Heavy curtains were pulled back from the windows with golden ties, and framed watercolors depicting dancers in old-fashioned costumes covered the papered walls.

"Yes. How did you know?" I asked.

"No one would come to me for anything else," she said. "You do not recognize my name, do you?"

"I'm afraid not," Colin said.

"I, too, was a great dancer, many years ago, but few people remember me now. I am old enough to recall Napoleon's defeat in Russia, although I was only nine. It was the year I came to the Imperial Theatre School."

"It is an honor to make your acquaintance," Colin said. He placed his cup and saucer on a low table and rose from his seat, moving to stand in front of one of the watercolors. "Is this you?"

Agrippina Aleksandrovna smiled broadly and nodded. "It is. My costume for *Zéphire et Flore*. Is it not exquisite? We wore our skirts much longer than they do today."

"You are beautiful," I said, joining my husband. Her white skirts, layer upon layer of tulle, landed a few inches above the ankles, and delicate pale flowers decorated them and the bodice. On her head, she wore a wreath of matching blooms, and a pair of translucent wings peeked above her shoulders from the back.

"And I am en pointe," she said. "I was one of the first at the Imperial Ballet to dance on my toes. Enough, though. What can I tell you about my friend? It is most upsetting to have lost her to such violence."

"You were friends?" I asked. "I'm sorry, I did not know, and offer my most sincere condolences. We came hoping you might have seen something from your window the night of the murder."

"I always watch the theatre," she said. "Even there, I am largely forgot—the youngsters have no interest in our old ways. They have carried the art to new heights, wonderful heights, but they think I can offer them nothing. Nemetseva was different. She knew the history of ballet, and she sought me out when she was only eleven years old and still at school. She had just started dancing en pointe, and her teacher had told her class about my early mastery of the technique. She showed up unannounced at my door with a large bouquet of flowers and begged me to tell her stories from my days on stage. After that, she came every week. I coached her in all of her roles. She was an exceptional talent."

"I am profoundly sorry for your loss," Colin said. As always, his sensitivity struck me. His voice, deep and soothing, had an instant effect on the woman. "We—primarily my wife, actually—are here investigating her murder. An interested party fears the judicial investigators may not be able to solve the crime."

"Your wife is a detective in her own right?" She narrowed her eyes and looked at me, scrutinizing. "This is excellent. But your posture, madame, leaves me aghast. Do not let yourself be corrupted by this modern love of the slouch. It is ugly." She demonstrated and looked not only several inches shorter, but far less elegant than she had. "Now, with me." She pulled her shoulders up and back, straightened her spine, and then lowered her shoulders, keeping her chest open. I did my best to follow. "Much improved."

"I shall endeavor to remember your lesson," I said, never before having considered my posture substandard. When my mother criticized me for slouching, it irritated me. This correction felt entirely different, perhaps because it did not disguise a general disappointment in my whole character.

"Very good. Now, on the night Irusya died, I was watching, as I always did. I no longer go to the theatre—I cannot manage the stairs anymore. But every night my Irusya danced, she would come to the stage door during the interval, open it, and wave to me. It was a ritual of hers. We dancers are often superstitious."

"On that last night, was anything different?" I asked.

"The first interval was normal," she said. "Of course, she hadn't been on stage yet. But during the second, she was holding a cloak around her, which she never normally did."

"Even though she was opening the door to catastrophically cold air?" Colin asked.

"You have never had a *banya,* have you, Monsieur Hargreaves? We Russians love the feeling of cold air against hot skin. But ordinarily she only poked her head out of the door and waved. She'd hardly have time to get cold. That night, she stepped all the way outside, with the cloak, but still in her dancing slippers, which alarmed me, as I feared they would be ruined by the snow."

"What did she do then?" I asked.

"She did not wave to me. She never even glanced up at my window. I do not know where she went. As you can see, from my window one can see the stage door, but only just and nothing beyond. I waited for her to go back inside, but she didn't, so I could only imagine that she had reentered the theatre through the lobby, which seemed most peculiar to me."

"Did you see anyone else?" Colin asked.

"No, she was alone. I worried as I did not see her go back inside and, then, when she did not appear at the door during the next interval . . . She never waved to me again." Her voice, already thin and dry, started to crack.

"Did you tell the investigator what you saw?" Colin asked.

"No, monsieur. They did not come to me. This shows you why your—what did you call him? An *interested party*?—needs you. Our judicial investigators often let the people down. I have heard scandalous stories about them manufacturing evidence, and, furthermore, everyone is terrified they will dig up some tenuous association with a person who holds unacceptable political beliefs and send you to a labor camp in Siberia when all you have done is try to be a helpful witness."

"When did you last speak to Nemetseva?" I asked.

"The very afternoon she died. We had a light luncheon together. She did not like to eat much before a performance, but needed a little something."

"Was she in good spirits?" Colin asked.

"Exceptionally," she said. "She knew what an honor it was to be chosen to dance in *Swan Lake*."

"Did she seem worried about anything?" I asked.

"Not at all, other than the usual nerves that come with debuting in a new role."

"Can you think of anyone who would want to harm her?" I asked.

"A better question to ask is who benefitted from her demise. There is only one person whose position immediately improved: Ekaterina Petrovna. She acquitted herself well and danced beautifully when Petipa called for her to replace Irusya. But she never would have earned that role otherwise."

"Weren't she and Nemetseva friends?" I asked.

Agrippina Aleksandrovna shrugged dismissively. "Friends can sometimes be our worst enemies. They know our weakness and our vulnerabilities. And they know our habits as well. I do not accuse Ekaterina Petrovna of this barbaric act, but I do wonder at how conveniently things have worked out for her. She was promoted yesterday to principal dancer. No one expected she would ever reach that rank."

"She is an extremely talented dancer, is she not?" Colin asked.

"Yes, but she has a difficult time summoning her passion. Her technique is perfect, her line gorgeous—Irusya brought her to me once, before their graduation performance, for coaching. When she fans her passion, she is a brilliant flame, but when it abandons her, she is cold. That she cannot reliably call on it is a terrible flaw. Perhaps now she has mastered it. It is possible. By all accounts, her performance was breathtaking. We shall see how she does from here."

"Do you think Nemetseva somehow held her back?" I asked.

"Irusya was always her most enthusiastic supporter, but after they joined the company, she feared that her friend no longer believed herself capable of great dancing. A crisis of confidence, if you will. Did Irusya's immediate success make things more difficult for her? Was she unable to dance without making comparisons to her friend? This you must ask her. No one else can know."

"Did their friendship wane over the years?" I asked.

"Not so far as Irusya could tell," she said. "It was she who insisted that Ekaterina Petrovna be her understudy for *Swan Lake*. Irusya did everything she could to forward her friend's career." She shrugged again. "Even die."

Ekaterina Petrovna
May 1897

Irusya did not allow Katenka to mire herself in painful regret. Both girls had been invited to join the company, their contracts starting on June 1, and their first performances as professionals would be during the summer season at Krasnoye Selo, in the country outside St. Petersburg. The theatre was neither large nor grand, but the dancers loved their time there, away from the city.

In the weeks between finishing their exams and needing to report for company class, Irusya and Katenka retired once again to Irusya's family *dacha*. Lev, who wanted to be as close to Irusya as possible, arranged to visit a nearby friend, Dmitri Dmitriyevich Ivchenko. Mitya was not so handsome as Lev, but he was a smart, studious young man who seemed constantly at odds with his family, whose old-fashioned political views he abhorred.

Irusya and Lev circled each other cautiously at first. They had not spent much time together in the final weeks of Irusya's schooling. She had been busy with preparations for her graduation performance and her exams. And he, after resigning his naval commission, had accepted a position at a bookstore on Nevsky Prospekt.

He would never have been allowed to leave the navy if his grandfather were still alive. Misfortune had struck after the old man died.

Having lost their mother only a few months earlier, Lev and Katenka were shocked to discover the family had no money left. The apartment overlooking the Neva near the Admiralty had to be sold to pay their grandfather's debts. Katenka's salary in the corps de ballet was enough only for her to rent a modest flat in an undesirable neighborhood. She filled it with the pieces of family furniture they had not been forced to sell. Lev arranged to sleep in the back room at the bookstore, explaining that this would enable him to save money for the future.

A future, Katenka knew, he intended to share with Irusya.

"Do you still love my brother, even though he is an impoverished bookseller?" she asked her friend as they rowed in a small boat on Lake Ladoga.

"I love him all the more for it," she said. "I did so adore his uniform, but he is even more handsome to me now. Noble poverty becomes him. Besides, it's only temporary. He has grand plans of opening his own shop once he saves enough. And you know I am in no hurry to change my current arrangements."

Irusya had taken a first-floor flat near the theatre, overlooking the narrow Moika River. Although her salary as a first soloist was nearly double Katenka's, her parents, wanting to see her grandly settled, had purchased it for her. Over the summer, they were having it decorated, and Irusya had ordered suites of brand new furniture to fill the rooms.

"What does he think of your sumptuous accommodations?" Katenka asked.

"He finds them shockingly bourgeois," Irusya said, pulling her oars. "I told him it's a perfectly ordinary home for a prima ballerina, and he laughed, but I know he likes seeing me so well quartered."

"He adores you," Katenka said. Irusya did not reply, only looked to the horizon, her gaze unfocused. "Don't go moody on me." Katenka splashed water at her. Irusya returned the favor, and by the time they returned to the dock, where Lev and Mitya were waiting for them, both girls were soaked.

"What an appalling site you two are," Lev said, helping Irusya out of the boat and shaking his head.

"No worse than you'll be soon!" Irusya cried and pushed him into the lake. He bobbed up and down, laughing as he grabbed his hat before it could float away from him, and swam to the dock. Taking Irusya by the ankles, he pulled her in next to him. Katenka, still in the boat, looked to Mitya, who was wiping water from the lenses of his spectacles. After he returned them to his face, he steadied her as she stepped out of the boat.

"I think it best we flee before we suffer the same fate," he said, dropping her hand. He pulled a book out from under his jacket, no doubt placed there to protect it from any stray splashes, and walked to the end of the dock without so much as offering her his arm when she caught up with him. As they moved away from the water in the direction of the house, Katenka turned to look back. Lev and Irusya were floating happily next to each other, their hands clasped together.

"They are so happy together," she said.

"This is bound to be their best time," Mitya said. "I expect much will change now that you are both in the company. You are entering another world, a world far removed from that of a humble bookseller."

"It's the same world we've been in from the moment we started at the Imperial Theatre School."

"No, you were like little fairies then, flitting between the glamour of the stage and the hard work of the classroom, never belonging entirely to either. Now, the stage will control you both."

"What an odd thing to say." Katenka frowned. "You make it sound quite dreadful." She was doing her best to tease him, but Mitya never noticed her efforts at flirtation.

"I do not mean to denigrate your chosen path," he said. "It is just a world apart from my own."

"And what is that?" Katenka asked.

"My primary concern is the plight of the working class. Do you know how little money the average worker has to support his family?"

"Probably more than I. My salary is a scandal. I can't even live near the theatre."

"A terrible burden, I am sure. But can you afford food? Are your children starving?"

"You know perfectly well I have no children." She never knew how to react when Mitya grew even more serious than usual and started talking about politics.

"That is hardly the point." He stopped walking and turned to face her, taking both of her hands in his. She liked the feeling of them, strong and coarse, and his touch sent her heart racing. "Let me make it easier to understand. You receive a small salary, yes? Irusya's is much bigger?"

"Yes, she has earned a higher rank in the company than I."

"Is her role more important? Can ballets be performed without the corps?"

"No, but of course her roles are more important. There are fewer dancers capable of performing them. It does not trouble me that she is paid more."

"Fair enough. But do not you, also, deserve to earn enough to live comfortably?"

"Yes, I suppose so, and I will, if I work hard enough to get promoted."

"What about those who can't earn enough, no matter how hard they work? Is their plight fair? Most of the residents of Petersburg are working themselves to the bone for a pittance while the bourgeoisie spend fortunes on a single evening's entertainment. Is that fair?"

She shrugged. "No, but that is life. Some are more fortunate than others."

"Wouldn't it be wonderful if that wasn't life? Wouldn't it be wonderful if everyone could live well? What if the bourgeoisie shared some of their wealth?"

Katenka laughed. "You are a dreamer, aren't you? I wouldn't have guessed. You always seem so serious, with your books and ideas, but now you are talking about fairy tales." She looked down, blushing, then forced herself to meet his eyes. "I like you all the more for it."

He dropped her hands. "You will never understand, Katenka. The dream of a better world is ours for the taking, if only we can find the courage to create it." He turned on his heel and stalked up the path.

Katenka chided herself for saying the wrong thing. Lev spouted this sort of nonsense on occasion, but she ignored it, and he never forced her to listen. Perhaps Mitya was too serious. She liked him, but after this conversation, she would not feel a loss when he returned to Petersburg.

St. Petersburg, 1900

8

---·◈·---

Finished with Agrippina Alexandrovna, we returned to our sledge and, snuggled under warm blankets, watched the snow fall as the driver steered us back to the hotel. The noble buildings on Nevsky Prospekt, newly dusted white, looked straight out of a fairy tale. When we reached the door to our rooms, Colin paused after putting the key in the lock. "I am very much looking forward to having you all to myself. We have two hours until we are to meet Cécile downstairs for dinner, do we not?"

"Yes, but we have to dress," I said.

"I can assist you with that." He kissed me softly. "First, though, I shall have to remove your coat." He took my muff, unfastened my coat, and then unlocked and opened the door. Inside, he slipped the coat from my shoulders. "After the coat, of course—"

Sebastian, in his full Cossack regalia, a ridiculously tall hat on his head, interrupted him. He was sitting on our settee, a spread of *zakuski* on the table in front of him, along with an icy bottle of vodka and three glasses.

"Please, please, no more! I ought not be subjected to such a scene! It is outrageous!"

"Outrageous?" Colin asked, stepping toward him, his dark eyes flashing. "Outrageous is you breaking into our room and violating our privacy. How dare you, sir?"

"Oh dear," Sebastian said, draping his arms across the back of the settee. "It's no wonder I can't lure Kallista away from you. You're a vision of manly strength when you're angry. How am I to compete?" This question did not merit the courtesy of a reply. "At any rate, I am here to follow up on a request I made of your charming wife at Masha's the other night."

"I examined the police evidence myself," I said. "They do not have the note you left Nemetseva."

"How intriguing," he drawled. "I shan't be able to rest altogether easy until I can be certain of its fate. You will keep me abreast of any further developments, won't you?"

"I suggest you abandon whatever delusions you may have about enlisting any more assistance from me or my wife," Colin said. He removed his fur hat and ran his hand through his rumpled curls before flinging his overcoat onto a chair. "It would behoove you to leave the premises before you irritate me further."

"There's no point in my leaving now," Sebastian said. "I've already changed your dinner reservation to accommodate a party of four, and I don't want to sit in the lobby for two hours on my own. Now have some vodka. It will warm you up. Kallista looks positively frozen."

He handed me a glass, but Colin refused the one he offered. Sebastian shrugged and downed the contents in a single gulp before picking up a salted cucumber from the platter on the table and munching on it.

"I feel as if I am forgetting something," he said. "Something with the bread. Is one meant to sniff it before taking the shot? I can't remember. Perhaps it doesn't matter." He squinted and scowled, looking at me. "What on earth can you mean by wearing that hideous brooch? A silver lizard covered with demantoids?"

"It was a gift from the boys," I said. "Nanny let them select it. It may not be to my taste, but that is nothing compared to the joy I felt seeing their little faces beaming when I opened it. It is beautiful because it reminds me of them."

Sebastian groaned. "Motherhood has not improved you, Kallista."

"That's quite enough, Capet," Colin said.

"Very well," he said. "I have no interest in charming domestic scenes. I shall leave you now and see you at dinner. Madame du Lac always enjoys spending time with me. I won a friend when I returned her earrings all those years ago."

"She might have liked you better if you hadn't stolen them in the first place," I said. He did not reply, but bowed with excessive flourish and backed out of the room.

"I'd like to have him barred from the dining room." Colin went to the door, locked and bolted it.

"He'd only come in some other disguise," I said. "And he does amuse Cécile."

"I suppose you are right, but I promise you I shall not be civil to . the man unless I am in an extremely good mood." He shot me a knowing look and took me in his arms.

"Several methods of achieving such an end spring to mind. What a pity we don't have time to explore them all."

We were a quarter of an hour late coming down to dinner. Colin was resplendent in his evening kit, and his mood could not have been better. Cécile and Sebastian were already seated when we arrived in the hotel's restaurant. At the far end of the long, rectangular room an art nouveau stained-glass window boasting a noble image of the god Apollo in his golden chariot covered most of the wall beneath the tall, vaulted ceiling. Below this stood a small stage, where a string quartet was playing. There was an arched mezzanine gallery on one side, under which were private tables, the bases of the arches separating them from each other, which could be curtained off from the main restaurant. Cécile and Sebastian, eschewing privacy, had chosen a table in the center of the room, directly in front of the stage.

Colin took the chair next to Sebastian. "Might as well settle in for a cozy chat, Capet. You're stuck with me as your dinner partner instead of my wife." Sebastian frowned, but said nothing. All things considered, the meal went better than could have been expected. Several ladies approached, addressing Sebastian as Fedya and inviting him to a variety of dinners and parties. He basked in their attention.

"I had no idea the Cossacks were so popular with the ladies, Capet," Colin said.

"I have never better enjoyed a disguise," Sebastian said.

"I cannot decide what to do with you, Monsieur Capet," Cécile said. "Part of me wishes to reform you; the other would prefer to provide you with a list of items I think you should steal."

"What a fascinating idea, Madame du Lac." Sebastian's sapphire eyes shined even brighter than usual. "A challenge!"

"You would have to accept my rules, and they would differ from yours," she said. "Take that lady three tables over. The one in the aubergine gown, the sight of which is enough to tell you everything you should know about her taste."

The color did not enhance her complexion, but more alarming was the dangerously low-cut bodice held in place by small, lacy straps that could only be hanging on to her shoulders as a result of miraculous intervention. Her ample bosom—which she clearly felt she was showing off to her advantage—dwarfed her diamond and amethyst necklace, part of a spectacular parure.

"I have been watching her. The man next to her is her son. Across from her is his wife, whom she has been subjecting to nonstop criticism. Notice how the young lady has very little jewelry. I should like to see her with the amethyst parure instead of her mother-in-law."

"It is an admirable start, Madame du Lac," Sebastian drawled, "but you are not considering what would happen to the young lady should she receive the jewels in question. The toad of a mother-in-law would suspect her of being responsible for the theft. Our innocent friend would feel terrible and no doubt return the parure without even trying it on. It is best if one leaves several degrees of separation between parties in schemes such as these."

"I see your logic," Cécile said.

His sapphire eyes flashed. "Perhaps you could give me two lists: one of items you think should be taken and one of people you think deserving of a little something special. We could look at the two together and determine how best—"

"I cannot believe you are encouraging him, Cécile," I said, interrupting.

"You don't like the idea, Kallista?" Sebastian asked. "Say the word and I shall abandon it without regret."

"I haven't the slightest interest in how you choose to spend your time," I said. The waiter approached, not with our next course, but with a package for me. I removed the plain brown paper to reveal a pink enameled card case, very similar in color to the lilies of the valley imperial egg. Inside the case was a scrap of paper, folded small. On it, written in a faint hand, was a single sentence in English:

I shall never rest in peace until you stop him from hurting another innocent victim.

Ekaterina Petrovna
May 1897

"But are you in love with him?" Irusya had been asking the question over and over. "He's not quite handsome, is he, our Mitya, but there is something about him. An intellectual intensity that is surprisingly attractive." They were on the lawn outside the dacha, having just finished a picnic lunch. Irusya was on the swing, sitting in exactly the spot she had occupied the first time Lev kissed her.

"Why does it matter if I'm in love with him?" Katenka said.

"We need to know if we should worry about you becoming entangled with a man of such radical political beliefs," Lev said. His tone alone told her he was teasing, and if she had any doubt, his laughter would have confirmed her suspicion. "I don't want to see my sister arrested."

"Stop tormenting me. He's your friend, Lev."

"Indeed, and I admire him above any man I've ever met. That doesn't mean I want him for you."

"He hasn't the slightest interest in me," Katenka said.

"I like his spectacles," Irusya said. "They lend him an air of gravitas. But his lips are his best feature."

"I did not know you were taking such close notice of him," Lev said. "Should I be jealous?"

"You need never be jealous," Irusya said. "I shall adore you forever, my little revolutionary."

Katenka studied her brother's face. She gave very little thought to his politics and certainly had never considered him to be a revolutionary. "Do I need to worry about you?" she asked.

"Never." He grinned. "I don't like it when you worry, and it isn't good for your dancing."

Katenka pressed her lips together and didn't reply. She began to pack the remains of their lunch into a large wicker basket. "Look at the clouds," she said. "I should get this inside before it starts to rain."

"You aren't going to use the weather to distract us from the matter at hand," Irusya said. "Katenka, are you in love with Mitya? I shall not stop asking until I get an answer."

"You shall grow hoarse before you are satisfied," Lev said. "My sister is implacable and will admit to nothing."

"I despise you both," Katenka said, and kicked at her brother to get him off the blanket they had spread on the ground. She picked it up, shook it out, and folded it. "Not everyone is so fortunate in matters of the heart as the two of you are."

Irusya jumped off the swing and flung herself dramatically on the ground. "It is just as I feared! He has broken her heart!"

"He has not broken my heart."

"Has he insulted your honor?" Lev asked. "Must I challenge him?"

"He has done nothing of the sort," Katenka said. "And you, Lev, who count him as your closest friend, should know better than anyone he would not behave dishonorably."

"See how she defends him?" Irusya, still lying on the ground, rolled onto her stomach and propped her chin with her hands. "She does love him."

"I see your mother coming, Irusya," Katenka said. "Shall I go distract her, so the two of you can run off to the garden without drawing her attention?"

"Oh, yes, please," Lev said. "I don't think she approves of me, Irusya. She keeps asking why I'm still staying at Mitya's when he has already returned to Petersburg. I expect to be banned from calling here any day now."

"Go, Katenka!" Irusya leapt to her feet in one graceful movement and took Lev by the hand, running as she pulled him toward the lake.

By the time Irusya's mother had reached Katenka, the two lovers had leapt into the small boat at the dock and rowed a good distance from shore.

"Your brother is very energetic," Mrs. Nemetseva said. "I suppose he would have to be to keep up with our Irusya. I do hope she lets him down well. I don't dislike the boy, but he must know they will never be a match."

"Our family backgrounds are not so different," Katenka said. "It is true we have fallen on hard times since our grandfather died, but—"

"My dear child, do not think I meant to insult your excellent family. Your grandfather was a hero, and your mother a model of good breeding. But I know my daughter. She is impetuous and ambitious. This love will not last."

January 1900

9

After reading the message that accompanied the parcel, I passed it to Colin and scowled at Sebastian. "Is this from you?"

"No, no it isn't, but I'm ashamed to admit it." He reached across the table in a vain attempt to grab the card case from me. "What does the note say?" Cécile had all but torn the paper from Colin's hand, and Sebastian now rose from his seat and read it over her shoulder.

"This is brilliant. Messages from beyond the grave!" he exclaimed. "I know Fabergé has the most exclusive clientele, but I had no concept of the true scope of his reach."

"Give the paper back to me," I said, and Cécile complied. "Obviously it was not written by a ghost."

"Very odd that it's in English," Cécile said.

"Not so odd," I said. "I am, after all, English."

"Not many people in Petersburg speak the language, Kallista. Nemetseva certainly didn't." Cécile always did have a soft spot for a good ghost story.

"Whether she did is irrelevant," Colin said. "She did not write the note."

"*Bien sûr*," she said. "But whoever did isn't concerned with authenticity, then, is he?"

"It's a soft, feminine script, just what one would expect from a ballerina." I held the paper up to the light, looking for a watermark.

"Have you had occasion to make a study of the handwriting of ballerinas?" Colin asked. I raised an eyebrow but did not reply. He might rely entirely on hard facts, but I did not shirk from making use of my intuition. In theory, my husband agreed with my methods, but we applied different standards to determine what we deemed appropriate.

"I wonder if it was written in English to encourage us to think that in death we can all speak every language," Sebastian said. "May I please see the case? It looks to be an exquisite piece."

"No, you may not," I said. I slipped it into my beaded evening bag. "What can the sender hope to accomplish by giving this to me?"

"Perhaps he—or she—thinks you are taking too long to solve Nemetseva's murder and wishes to spur you on," Cécile said. "You know ordinary people, Kallista. They do not understand the intricacies of what it takes to conduct a thorough investigation."

"It is a warning," Sebastian said. "Someone else is going to come to harm. Your villain is searching for his next victim and only you, Kallista, can keep him from striking again."

Normally, I did not agree with Sebastian, but I had to admit he could be correct. Until I knew more about Nemetseva's death, I could not dismiss the notion that the murderer might pursue someone else. "We cannot allow there to be another victim," I said, feeling my forehead crease.

"Do you plan to keep the case?" Sebastian asked. "If not, I have several ideas about what to do with it."

I glared at him with such ferocity he did not dare reply.

Despite Sebastian's strenuous protests—made in three different languages; he never could resist showing off—we refused to let him accompany us for the rest of the evening. The soirée after dinner was too lackluster to merit description. The ball at Yusupov Palace, however, would have dazzled even the most jaded individual.

The palace faced the Moika River and was only a few blocks from the Mariinsky Theatre. Its bright yellow façade, with majestic columns, glowed over the snowy street and frozen river and its interiors were as ornate as any in the world. Louis XIV would have envied the Yusupovs their residence. The current prince, Felixovich Sumarokov-Elston, was not the family's heir; he had married her. Zinaida Nikolaevna Yusupov, an elegant beauty with black hair and olive skin, was the sole heiress of the fortune, rumored to be greater than that of the Romanovs. Her refinement, social graces, and kindness, combined with a genuine modesty, endeared her to everyone she met. She was an excellent hostess, and although I had seen enough gilded ballrooms and gleaming chandeliers for a lifetime, I could not deny that she knew how to throw a spectacular ball.

Her orchestra, playing waltzes, mazurkas, polkas, and more, was the equal of any to be found in the world's great concert halls. Fresh flowers from her hothouses defied the cruel Russian winter to fill the ballroom with the scent of roses. Champagne flowed freely into crystal glasses, and piles of caviar—black beluga and the smaller, golden starlet—seemed to be replenished as if by magic. No matter how many people dug in with thin, mother-of-pearl spoons, more always appeared.

Soon after we arrived and were ushered up a majestic staircase to the ballroom, Colin abandoned Cécile and me with a pretty apology. He was here to work; we would have to amuse ourselves. Cécile had been well acquainted with our hostess's mother and had told me the story of how Zinaida's parents had allowed her to choose her husband. She had been courted by countless royal princes and important members of the court but was impressed by none of them and fell in love with an officer in the imperial guards. Although they must not have been delighted by her choice, her parents did not stand in her way. I could not imagine my own mother having given me such freedom.

Cécile sought out Zinaida, and we spent a pleasant interval conversing with her. My friend asked her permission to show me the rest of the house, as she felt I would be particularly interested in one of its famous rooms, and Zinaida, who was even more charming than her reputation suggested, acquiesced at once. Soon we were wandering through a corridor decorated as if it were a villa in Pompeii. Delicate paintings in the ancient style framed the space around sections of the terracotta-colored walls. Within each hung a painting depicting scenes from classical mythology: Daphne and Apollo, Artemis and Acteon, Zeus and Leda, Zeus appearing as a swan. The astute reader may wonder why I use the Greek names rather than the Roman, given the context. As my passion for ancient Greece is well known, I ask to be indulged.

We descended to the ground floor and entered an astonishing space. Elaborate mosaics covered every inch of the walls and ceiling of the Moorish drawing room. The niches into which candles had been set, casting a flickering, golden light, reminded me very much of those I had seen in Constantinople.

"This is magnificent," I said.

"I thought you would appreciate it, Kallista," Cécile said. "Now that you've seen it, we should return upstairs. We cannot avoid dancing forever. Zinaida would not stand for it."

"I have no intention of trying," I said. I took a last look around the room and had just stepped into the corridor when I heard my husband's voice. He was nowhere to be seen, in the room or out. Cécile gave me a quizzical look, and I took her hand and pulled her in the direction of the sound. It seemed to be coming from behind a wall.

We pressed our ears to it and strained to listen. It was Colin, of that I had no doubt. He was speaking Russian, and from his tone I could tell he was angry; nothing else made him so preternaturally calm. A second speaker, a woman, interrupted him, and he reprimanded her sharply. At least that is how it sounded. I could not hear well enough to understand the words.

I was leaning against the wall and suddenly felt it begin to move. The panel concealed a hidden door. I motioned for Cécile to stay silent and pushed it open, just enough to reveal a plain, narrow servants' staircase. Their voices were coming from below. Inching forward, I peered over the banister, careful not to be seen. The woman, dressed in the uniform of a maid, had a look of terror on her face. She was shaking her head, as if in disbelief. I returned to the corridor and pulled the wall panel shut.

"Monsieur Hargreaves is most fierce when he scolds, even if he does it quietly," Cécile said. "I should not like to be interrogated by him."

"We should go back to the ballroom. We didn't come here with the intention of spying, but it would be difficult to convince Colin of that if we are caught in a compromising position." We retraced our steps and had just reached the gallery at the top of the grand marble staircase in the front of the house when we noticed a commotion in the street. Shouts overwhelmed the strains of a waltz coming from the ballroom, and the liveried servants at the door disappeared outside.

Cécile and I followed. The road in front of the palace was crammed full with the carriages of Prince Yusupov's guests. All of the drivers were looking across the river. There, perched on one of the stone pedestals dividing the long iron rail that skirted the embankment above the frozen river, stood a slim, pale figure, perfectly balanced on her toes. She wore a ballerina's costume, the bodice covered with beads and feathers, all in white. In her hands, she held a long, red sash, the color of fresh blood, which she was waving above her head with hypnotic fluidity.

"Nemetseva!" someone cried. At the sound, the dancer stopped, lowered herself from point, placed one foot delicately behind the other, and curtseyed. Then, in a flash of red and white, she was gone. Two of the drivers leapt from their carriages in pursuit, but by the time they reached the bridge that crossed the river and made their way to where she had stood, all they found was the red sash.

In the meantime, news of the apparition had reached the guests in the ballroom, and they had started to pour from the house. The air was too cold for most, but a few of the heartier gentlemen raced across the river, eager to see the scarf for themselves. I looked around for Colin, but he did not appear. My teeth were chattering—my azure silk evening gown offered no protection from the cold; further investigation would require a trip back inside. Pulling Cécile behind me, I went to the cloakroom and retrieved our coats and boots. As soon as we were adequately bundled, we joined the growing crowd across the river.

I elbowed my way through the gentlemen (although I am not certain the word *gentlemen* could be applied to the men in question; some of them had the audacity to elbow me back) until I reached the one holding the scarf. He was loath to relinquish it but had no palatable alternative. Cécile, a commanding presence next to me, looked as if she might strike him should he not comply, and I do not think he wished to deal with the aftermath of that.

The crowd began to disperse, their evening kit incapable of standing up to the cold wind and the heavy snow that had started to fall. There was no sign of the mysterious ballerina. She must have disappeared into one of the buildings along the street, but I did not go in search of her. If friends had provided a hiding place, we would not be able to locate her. All she need do was change out of her costume, wash off her makeup, restyle her hair, and she would be unrecognizable. I folded the scarf carefully and put it in my bag, feeling the Fabergé card case against my gloved hand.

Back inside the palace, the atmosphere in the ballroom was explosive. Far from being concerned by the incident, Zinaida's guests were delighted. Half of them insisted it was Nemetseva's ghost. The other half didn't much care what the explanation was; they enjoyed the excitement regardless of its source.

The orchestra started to play the waltz from *Swan Lake*. I felt this was in poor taste and was about to say as much to Cécile when Colin appeared and slipped his arm around my waist.

"May I have this dance?" he asked.

"Do you know what just happened?" I asked.

"The ghostly ballerina? Yes. I suppose she came here directly from the Grand Hôtel de l'Europe after dropping off the card case for you. She seems rather efficient. I am almost impressed."

"It's rather disturbing," I said.

"Dance with me." His eyes held mine with an intensity impossible to ignore. I have never, from the earliest days of our courtship, been able to deny the power waltzing with him held over me. I rested one hand on his shoulder, gave him the other, and we began to move across the floor.

"The dancer looked very sad," I said, nearly breathless from the speed at which we were spinning. "It could be one of Nemetseva's friends."

"Ekaterina Petrovna?"

"No, she might have changed the color of her hair with a wig, but her features were all wrong. It was not she." I frowned. "Is your evening going well? Getting everything accomplished you need to accomplish?"

"You know better than to ask me about my work."

I felt a slight pang of guilt at not telling him that I had heard him in the stairwell near the Moorish drawing room. "I was not asking for specifics, just inquiring as to your success or lack thereof."

"Things are moving at a desirable pace," he said. "I am satisfied with my progress."

I stared into his eyes, lost for a moment in the depths of their liquid darkness. I could never hide anything from him. "I must tell you something . . ." I hesitated for an instant, just long enough for our conversation to be interrupted. A uniformed gentleman—a high-ranking officer of some sort—stopped us dancing and whispered something to my husband. Colin's eyebrows drew together, and I saw a hint of displeasure cross his handsome face.

"Forgive me. I must abandon you mid-waltz. Duty calls. Find Cécile and return to the hotel. There has been a murder belowstairs, one of the servants, and I am called to the scene." He did not pause long enough even to kiss me before weaving his way through the other dancers and disappearing from sight. No one watching him would have thought anything was amiss. He drew no attention to his departure.

Cécile was dancing with a tall gentleman in an expensively tailored suit. She seemed to be enjoying his attentions, and I saw no need to take her away from him before absolutely necessary. I had no objection to being kept out of Colin's work, but the murder of a servant was not something I could ignore. It had occurred during a function to which I was invited. Why should I leave when the ball was still going on without any sign of disruption? Obviously no one felt the guests were in danger, and no harm could come from us staying as well.

I always endeavor to be candid, and must, therefore, admit that I had only one purpose: I wanted to know if the murdered servant was the same girl I'd seen speaking to my husband on that hidden staircase.

Ekaterina Petrovna
July 1897

Although she had enjoyed her respite at Irusya's dacha, the feeling of failure that had plagued Katenka from the night of the graduation performance had not faded. She had managed to relegate it from her thoughts while she was at Lake Ladoga, but now that she was back with the company, the pain had only intensified. Irusya's success thrilled her, and she felt genuine pleasure at the news that her friend had won a plum soloist role in *Don Quixote*, the ballet opening the summer season in Krasnoye Selo, but the demons that had taken residence in her thoughts would not let her enjoy learning her role in the corps de ballet.

This did not stop her from executing her steps with flawless precision. Katenka worked hard and earned her placement in the front row, but she could take no happiness from the recognition of her skills. Front row or not, she was languishing in the corps.

Summer rehearsals were conducted in Petersburg, as the small theatre in the countryside did not have adequate facilities for the company to remain there in residence. On the morning of performances, the dancers would gather at the Baltic Station to catch a train to Krasnoye Selo.

The new company members buzzed with anticipation as they

boarded the train, eager for their first professional performance. The more seasoned dancers gave them wry smiles and tried to remember their own early days. When they reached their destination, many of them paused for lunch at a restaurant across from the theatre, but Katenka was too excited to eat. Afterward, they were assigned to dressing rooms, and Katenka watched as Mathilde Kschessinska, who had one of the best, supervised the hanging of filmy fabric over her walls and directed the placement of bright flower arrangements. Not that she needed to bring her own flowers. She would be showered with them at her curtain call, but she always liked to prepare for performance in a beautifully appointed room.

During the first interval of the opening night, Katenka hung back when a handful of grand gentlemen—princes, she imagined, or perhaps even grand dukes—left their boxes to join the dancers for conversation on the stage. She was too shy to speak to any of them, although one man, old enough to be her father, did compliment her on her pirouettes. As she had performed no pirouettes, she knew his pretty words were nothing but pretense, and she understood well his motives. She rebuffed him at once and decided to go to the dressing room she shared with the others girls in the corps.

She passed Irusya on her way across the stage. A dashing young man in a guards' uniform was praising her to the skies. Katenka smiled, glad that Irusya's dancing was appreciated, but her happiness faded when her friend grabbed her by the arm.

"Ekaterina Petrovna is my dearest friend," she said, pulling Katenka to face her companion. "Katenka, you must meet Count Anatole Emsky. He is a great fan of the ballet and a connoisseur of Petipa's choreography."

Katenka made a small curtsey. "It is a pleasure to make your acquaintance," she said, her voice soft.

The count nodded at her. "Yours as well."

"Katenka is a brilliant dancer," Irusya said. "Before long you shall see her dancing in all the best roles."

"I look forward to it," the count said.

"You are very kind," Katenka said. "Please forgive me, but I must get to the dressing room. One of my ribbons has come loose." She could feel the count's eyes on her as she left the stage and hoped she wouldn't see him again. None of this sat well with her. She did not like being expected to be a witty conversationalist between acts, and she had no interest in entertaining noblemen with a taste for ballerinas. As a student, when she and Irusya had roles in the company's productions, they had watched the dancers flirt with their admirers, thinking it all looked so very grown up and glamorous. Now it seemed sordid and distracting, taking the focus away from the performance. She would have preferred to stretch backstage and mark her choreography, concentrating on her work before she returned to the stage. The interval should not be a soirée.

Perhaps, had conversation come more easily to her, Katenka would have felt differently about it all. Her golden hair and pale blue eyes attracted a good deal of attention. During the second interval, two princes asked if they might look for her in the park when they were next out driving. She had not known how to reply to either of them, and had looked for Irusya, hoping to summon her assistance, but she was at the front of the stage basking in the count's open admiration of her.

After the final curtain, Lev and Mitya surprised the girls, waiting for them at the stage door. Katenka embraced her brother fiercely while Irusya teased Mitya about his suit, which she viewed as wholly unsuitable for an evening at the theatre.

"Have you nothing better to concern yourself with than my inadequate wardrobe?" Mitya said. Katenka expected he would reprimand Irusya more severely, but he seemed to be in a fine mood that night, and he took her criticism in the spirit intended: the harmless ribbing of a good friend.

Petersburg's famous white nights, the stretch of weeks when the summer sun barely set, were not yet over, and the sky remained bright long after the ballet had ended. The city's citizens would pay for the extra hours of sun in the winter, when the golden orb would all but disappear, but they made the most of the light, staying out almost until morning. The four friends roamed through the village's pretty gardens, stopping to buy ice cream. Lev and Irusya lingered behind, wanting some semblance of privacy, leaving Katenka with Mitya.

"Lev is doing very well at the bookstore," Mitya said in a careless tone, as if a beautiful, bright midnight ought to be wasted in discussion about one's brother's employment. Katenka felt tears smart in her eyes and wondered if he ever thought about anything that mattered.

"I am delighted to know it," she said.

"I tell you only so you know that he will soon be in a position to propose to Irusya."

"That will make her very happy."

"Will it?" he asked.

"Are men all so daft as you?" Katenka turned to face him and spoke in a tone she did not know herself capable of. "Of course she will be happy. She has loved him since she was fifteen years old. Or perhaps you haven't noticed that? Do you notice anything, Mitya? Has even the brilliance of the white nights escaped you?"

He stood before her, flabbergasted. "I did not expect this sort of reaction. I thought you were happy about their relationship."

"I never thought you were stupid, Mitya. I believed you to be an intellectual, but now I wonder that I ever held you in such high regard when you have no ability to see what is right in front of you." Katenka could not entirely understand why she felt so full of rage, but she knew she wanted to direct all of it at Mitya, whether he deserved it or not. She raised her hand to slap him, not caring whether her action was just. He grabbed her by the wrist, his eyes wide, and searched her face.

"Katenka . . . can it be that you . . ." His voice trailed. "You speak of the midnight and remind me of the magic that exists in our northern summers . . ."

"You are talking nonsense," Katenka said, looking away from him and directing her gaze to the hard pavement beneath their feet.

"*Then came a moment of renaissance, / I looked up—you again are there, / A fleeting vision, the quintessence / Of all that's beautiful and rare,*" he said, quoting Pushkin. Without giving her time to reply, he took her face in his hands and kissed her.

Behind her, she heard Irusya whoop. "It's about time, Dmitri Dmitriyevich! I thought I would die waiting!"

January 1900

10

The instant the waltz finished, I tore Cécile from her partner almost before he had thanked her for the dance. Sometimes, propriety is an unnecessary inconvenience, and I had already waited long enough to find out who had been murdered. Cécile understood the urgency as soon as I explained the situation. We needed to get belowstairs, and the only access of which I was aware was the hidden staircase near the Moorish drawing room. Perhaps this was the Russian equivalent of the green baize door?

We descended the narrow staircase, at the bottom of which was a long, well-lit passageway. At the end of that we reached a junction. Following the sound of voices, we turned left and soon came to the servants' domain. There, a group of individuals—all of whom, by the look of their stained aprons, must work in the kitchen—stood, huddled, their voices agitated and loud. How I wished I could understand them, but their dialect was incomprehensible to me. Further down the hall, I could see three men in livery; they might know some French. We approached them. They looked horrified to see us (the staff never do like their part of the house to be invaded by those they would prefer stay upstairs) and asked if we were lost. I inquired as to the identity of their murdered colleague, but either they did not understand my question or they chose not to answer, as they replied by pointing us to another staircase and offering to escort us back to the ballroom.

I heard Colin's voice and cringed, just a bit. I had been foolish to think I could get a glimpse of the victim without his knowledge, but I had not come this far to leave unsatisfied. Cécile agreed to press on. Colin and a gaggle of military officers and policemen were in a large servants' hall. We managed to pass the open door without being spotted. I grabbed by the lapels the next liveried footman I saw and demanded, in French, to be taken to the dead girl.

This bold strategy proved more effective than asking politely. The young man did not look happy, but he led us to a small cellar room with a single table standing in its center. On it was a body covered with a crisp, white bedsheet. Gingerly, I lifted it, and saw the face of the girl who had been talking to Colin. Her neck, bruised and swollen, told me the brutal manner in which she had been dispatched. I silently said a quick prayer for her and thanked the footman.

Colin did not return to the hotel until nearly six o'clock in the morning. I managed to fall asleep, but my slumber was far from peaceful. I tossed and turned, dreaming of the maid and Nemetseva, their dead faces haunting me. Colin shook me awake, more gently than I deserved.

"I should know better than to expect you would do as I asked," he said. "Why did you insist on seeing the body?"

"How did you know?"

"I questioned every servant in the household. More than a few of them mentioned seeing two ladies from the ball belowstairs. Who else would it be?"

I propped myself up on my elbows and pulled the bedclothes around me. "You must forgive me," I said. "I had to see for myself." I confessed everything to him, passionately imploring him to believe that I hadn't set out to search for him on the hidden stairway.

"I do not doubt you," he said. "I wish, Emily, that I could tell you more, but you know I cannot. Suffice it to say that Anna had been an important source for me. It is a blow to lose her."

"I'm very sorry. Did you know her well?"

"Well enough," he said. I could read the strain in his face. His forehead crinkled, and his eyes were dull. "She was a valuable asset."

"She was so young," I said. "I never considered that someone like her would be engaged in such dangerous work."

"The world is not an easy place for many people," Colin said. He had flung his jacket and white tie across a chair and was unfastening his stiff collar. "She was a girl of principle, who allied herself with people searching for nonviolent means of achieving their goals. Now . . ." He sighed, deflated.

I did not prompt him to continue. "You don't need to say more."

He sat on the edge of the bed. "She trusted me because I convinced her she could. And now . . ." He took my hand. "We both have chosen taxing work. In order to do it efficiently, we cannot allow ourselves to be consumed by the emotion of it. Have you had any further word from your ghostly ballerina?"

"No, but I am told dancers generally sleep quite late."

He smiled. "Would that I could emulate them." I could not remember when I had seen him so tired. Ordinarily, it seemed he could work endlessly without sleep, but now his eyes closed and he dropped off almost at once.

Not wanting to wake him, I slipped out of the bedroom and silently closed the door. I took a long bath, dressed slowly, and read a hundred pages of *War and Peace* before heading downstairs. St. Petersburg was not a city for early risers. The sun would not come up until nearly ten o'clock and would set by a little after four. The dining room, ordinarily lively, was still half-empty, but my fellow guests were buzzing. The story of the mysterious apparition across from the Yusupov Palace had spread overnight, and it was all anyone was talking about. A German lady, to whom I had never been introduced, came to my table, apologizing for her lack of decorum.

"I cannot resist," she said. "I am told you were at the ball. Did you see the ghost?"

"I did see it, but can assure you it was not a ghost. It was a living and breathing dancer," I said.

"Why on earth would any ballerina risk her health by appearing so scantily clad in the dead of winter? I'm telling you, it had to be a ghost. Everyone is in agreement."

I shook my head. "A ghost who left behind a scarf?"

"Did you see the scarf?" she asked. "I've heard it was wrapped around her neck like a bloody gash. Just where Nemetseva received her deadly wound."

"I did see it, but it was not around her neck. She was holding it above her."

"That's not what I heard. Are you certain?"

"Quite certain." A waiter appeared with my scrambled eggs and caviar.

"I was told there were bloodstains on the scarf."

"There were not."

The truth held no interest for this woman. She returned to her table. I overheard her saying that I must have been extremely frightened by the event, as I had not noticed even the most obvious details. People will always find a way to justify the things they want to believe, and a ghost is far more alluring than an actual person.

I had sent word to Cécile to expect me, and she was ready when I collected her in a troika. The clouds visible overnight had disappeared the moment the snow had stopped, and the sun, more silver than gold in the brilliant blue sky, was blinding. Snow in Petersburg was nothing like its counterpart in England, where it fell heavy and wet. Here, it was light and dry, dry enough to make practical the thick felt boots worn by the working class in the city. We climbed out from under our fur blankets when we reached the Mariinsky, the snow creaking beneath our own, insufficiently warm, leather boots.

Inside, we headed straight for Madame Zhdanova's realm. Bent over a swath of bright red satin onto which she was sewing small, glittering beads, she hardly looked up when we entered.

"Give me one moment, *mesdames*," she said. With deft hands, she fixed a handful of beads into place and then cut through the thread with a pair of tiny scissors. "I am surprised to see you again. I do not suppose either of you is in need of a tutu. What do you seek from me?"

"Information," I said. "Last night, a ballerina appeared on the embankment across from the Yusupov Palace—"

"I have already heard the story."

"She was wearing a costume very like those worn by the dancers in *Swan Lake*. Are any of them missing?"

"It is unlikely," she said. "But I am happy to check for you. Follow me." She led us to a corridor near the dressing rooms, where a long row of swan tutus hung from a metal bar, and started to count. She paused once, about a third of the way down the line, before going back to the beginning and starting again. This time, she made it nearly to the end before stopping and pulling out an empty hanger. She pushed apart the hangers on either side, and one slightly crumpled garment fell to the ground. She picked it up, laid it over her arm, and went back to counting. "They are all here."

"Is there something unusual about that one?" I asked, indicating the one she was holding.

She shook it out, put it back on its hanger, and held it at arm's length to better inspect it. "It is a bit smashed, but that may be from falling off its hanger. However . . ." She flipped up the tulle skirt and looked closely at each of its layers before turning her attention to the silk bodice. "Some of the feathers have been torn away as well, but that is not unusual."

"Could someone have taken it outside?" Cécile asked.

"We account for every costume at the finish of each performance and inspect each to see what needs repairs or cleaning. We have not done *Swan Lake* again since Nemetseva's death. It is possible that in the commotion we were not as thorough as usual."

"If these costumes haven't been used since then, would it be possible for someone to have slipped a tutu from the rack and borrowed it for an unauthorized purpose?" I asked.

"It is not beyond the scope of possibility," she said. "Though I do not like the thought of it."

"Can you tell me which dancer wears the tutu that had fallen off the hanger?"

"It was Ekaterina Petrovna's. She wore it in the corps before she stepped in to replace Nemetseva."

"What did she wear then?" Cécile asked.

"Odile's tutu is brighter, as you see." She pulled from the rack a brilliantly colored piece, all luminescent blues, greens, and gold. "For the final act, the dancer wears the one she did in the second act, but we did not have Odette's tutu, as Nemetseva was wearing it when—" She stopped. "Forgive me. You must leave me to my work. I've a great deal to do."

On our way out of the theatre, we saw Yuri Melnikov, Nemetseva's partner, leaning against a wall in the corridor, a look of perfect ennui on his face.

"I should like very much to have a word with him," Cécile said.

"You suspect him of something?" I asked. "I found him perfectly useless when we interviewed him."

"Non, *chérie,* it is not that. He is quite alluring, *non*? Getting to know him better could prove most fascinating."

"Despite his inadequate age?" I asked. She had always insisted that no man below forty could be interesting.

"A dancer, *chérie*, is a different beast altogether. He is more than just a man."

Ekaterina Petrovna
August 1897

Irusya teased Katenka mercilessly after Mitya kissed her. Katenka didn't mind; if anything, she liked it, because it confirmed that she hadn't dreamed the entire thing. The next morning, Mitya sent her a note, saying he had some business to attend to but that he would return in a week to be in the audience for the company's production of *Sleeping Beauty*.

The theatre at Krasnoye Selo was not so large as that at the Mariinsky, which meant each ballet had to be pared down. The sets were less elaborate, and the stage held fewer dancers. Given her lack of seniority, Katenka feared she might not be chosen among those in the corps for the performance, but in this matter her worries were for naught. Again she was placed in the front row. Irusya was the Diamond Fairy in the first act and Little Red Riding Hood in the third.

After the ballet ended, Lev and Mitya met the girls backstage. Lev was carrying a large bunch of wildflowers for Irusya, and Mitya handed Katenka a beautifully illustrated volume called *The Blue Fairy Book*.

"I know you have not studied English, but this is an excellent selection of stories retold by a Scottish poet, Andrew Lang. It includes a version of *The Sleeping Beauty*. Someday, I hope, you will be able to read it."

Irusya whacked Mitya on the arm. "As if she needs more work! Study English when we've so much new choreography to learn? You are the least romantic man I have ever met."

"Irusya is wrong. It is the most romantic gift in the history of romantic gifts." Katenka's eyes brimmed with tears. "Thank you."

Back in their dressing room, Katenka chided Irusya for taking too long to change out of her costume. "It's as if you're getting ready for a ball," she said. "We are only going for a walk. There's no need to cover yourself with jewels."

"Wearing a single bracelet hardly constitutes covering oneself with jewels," Irusya replied as she clasped around her slim wrist a delicate bracelet made from rubies and gold fashioned to look like flowers.

"I have not seen you wear this before," Katenka said, examining it when Irusya held her arm out to her. "It is exquisite. Is it new?"

"It is just a trifle," she said. "A gift from the count."

"Anatole Emsky?" Katenka asked.

"Yes, he wanted something to mark my debut in *Sleeping Beauty* and gave it to me last night when he saw me in the park. He told me he expects I will be dancing the Lilac Fairy in the autumn and that it won't be much longer till I am Aurora. How I long to dance the *Rose Adagio!*"

"What does Lev think of his attentions?"

"Why should he mind? He knows that all dancers have their admirers and wouldn't want me to turn down such a lovely gift. It doesn't signify anything."

Katenka felt her lips press into a firm line. Gifts always came at a price. Sometimes a price not worth paying.

St. Petersburg, January 1900

11

I was due to meet Prince Vasilii at the Literaturnoye Café at two o'clock and brought Cécile with me. We arrived early, which gave us time for a satisfying luncheon before our appointment. Sebastian had been at it again. The patrons of the café were buzzing about the theft of a silver tea set taken from one of the grand duchesses. The burglar had left in its place a scathing note criticizing her inability to pour from the pot without spilling. Vasilii arrived precisely on time, his spotless uniform and perfect posture beyond reproach. But although every detail of his appearance was correct, his eyes had no luster, and his complexion was sallow. He looked as if he had not slept in days and ordered a bottle of vodka almost before he had sat down. Concerned, I inquired as to his health.

"I am finding that burying one's feelings takes a not insignificant toll," he said, his baritone husky. "I ought never to have hidden my relationship with Irusya. I should have married her. Would the scandal of allying myself with a dancer have destroyed my family? I would not wish this crushing feeling of regret on anyone. Please tell me: Are you closer to finding the wretch responsible for all this?"

"I am doing all that I can," I said. "Are you acquainted with Agrippina Aleksandrovna?"

He smiled. "I have heard many stories about her but have not been fortunate enough to meet her. My Irusya relied on her for so many things and even braved the cold to wave to the old woman from the stage door during performance intervals. I wish I could call on her and thank her for all she did."

"Why can't you?" Cécile asked. "I do not mean to sound harsh, Prince Vasilii, but what do you stand to lose now, if one old woman learns of your affair?"

"Nothing," he said. "My misplaced pride has all but destroyed my life, yet I continue to cling to it. Why? Because to stop now would be to admit my catastrophic mistake. It is too late now to make any difference, so I shall go on as I began."

"Don't be morose, young man." Cécile frowned. "I cannot stand such dramatics from anyone of your age. You cannot be much above thirty, if you are even that, which means your life has barely begun. Although you cannot fathom it now, someday this will all be in the ancient past, a bittersweet memory that adds a layer of depth to your character."

"You must despise me," he said.

"No," Cécile said, "but I shall be glad to meet you again when you have recovered from this blow."

"As shall I." He smiled, but the sadness did not fade from his eyes. "In the meantime, I've been meaning to ask you, Lady Emily, about this ghostly ballerina the entire city is talking about. Who is she and what can she possibly mean to accomplish?"

"These are questions not easily answered," I said. "It may be that she is a friend of Nemetseva's who is mourning her loss and has chosen to use her artistic talents to facilitate her grieving process. Or it could be someone who wants to draw more public attention to the case."

"You don't think she was issuing a warning of sorts?" the prince asked. "To the murderer, perhaps, to let him know that his crime will never be forgot, that it will haunt him forever."

"Vasilii, I'd never have suspected you to be susceptible to such romantic rot." Colin appeared at our table and motioned for the waiter to bring another chair. He kissed Cécile on both cheeks and squeezed my hand. "Promise me that you won't try to convince my wife the dancer is an actual ghost."

"You should know better than to suggest such a thing is possible," I said. "It's a lovely surprise to see you."

"Have some vodka, Hargreaves," the prince said, filling a glass for him. "You know we Russians never allow an opened bottle to be left unfinished."

"Thank you," he said, taking the glass and draining it in a single gulp. Vasilii refilled it immediately and then did the same to his own. "I find myself with a few hours to spare and knew I could find you here. I've news. A man has confessed to murdering Anna Salko."

"The Yusupovs' maid who was killed during their party?" Vasilii asked.

"Yes," Colin said. "The newspapers will report in their next editions. He is a known revolutionary, connected to the League of Struggle for the Emancipation of the Working Class. Went to the Peter and Paul Fortress under his own volition and asked to speak to the warden before giving him every detail of the crime."

"I have no doubt his colleagues will find a way to make the poor girl's death somehow shore up support for their organization," the prince said. "They're experts at manipulation."

"They have every right to be unhappy with the situation workers face in Russia, but I do not agree with their methods for trying to change it," Colin said.

"The guillotine was far quicker," Cécile said.

"And more barbaric." Colin poured more vodka for him and the prince. "One group within the league purports to be seeking—at least initially—nonviolent solutions to what they view as the problems facing the Russian people. I suspect this man belongs to another faction."

"I'll never believe any of them would shy away from violence," Vasilii said. "None of these groups is above reproach, whatever they might want the public to believe. But we ought not subject the ladies to such discussion."

"I should like to return to our previous topic," I said. I pulled the Fabergé card case from my reticule and passed it and the note that accompanied it to the prince. "Have you seen this before?"

"No," he said, holding it gently in his palm and then opening it. "I have seen many such things, but not this one specifically. But this note—it is my Irusya's handwriting. It is as familiar to me as my own." For an instant, the golden flecks in his hazel eyes glowed, but then his hand started to shake and tears pooled, ready to fall. "We must do everything possible to stop this man, Lady Emily. He cannot kill again."

"I plan to go to Fabergé as soon as we are finished here to determine who purchased the case," I said. "That may give us the lead we've long needed."

"Forgive me if I sounded fierce, Lady Emily," the prince said. "It is maddening to know that this villain is still wandering the streets of Petersburg. I let my emotion get the best of me."

"There is no need to apologize," Cécile said. "Kallista is never put off by fierceness in any context. I do, however, have a suggestion to make. Now that you have joined us, Monsieur Hargreaves, perhaps you could go to Fabergé with Kallista instead of me. I cannot face another round of grueling interrogation and propose that I stay here with the prince. Champagne might rescue his spirits."

Colin raised his eyebrows. "*Grueling interrogation?* I hardly think that will be required in Fabergé. Nonetheless, I will happily take your place on the expedition."

"I knew you would, my good man. You are the finest gentleman I have ever met, incapable of ever letting down a lady. I can think of no greater pleasure than knowing I can wholly rely upon you."

"I thank you for the compliment," Colin said, "but remind you that you need not flatter me. My devotion to you shall never falter."

Vasilii drained what little vodka remained in the bottle. Despite the quantity they had ingested, neither her nor Colin exhibited the slightest sign of intoxication. Still, Colin fortified himself with a large cup of coffee before we bid farewell to Cécile and the prince and set off for the House of Fabergé. It was located on Bolshaya Morskaya, a short walk from the café, so we saw no sense in hailing a troika. The snow had started falling again, more heavily than ever. The city looked magical, feathery flakes blanketing everything with a fresh, white coat. It was past four o'clock, so the sun had already disappeared below the horizon, making it feel much later than it actually was. Shop windows glowed golden, and snow danced against the illumination of flickering streetlights.

Peter Carl Fabergé had grown up in the center of St. Petersburg, and his sense of the aesthetic must have been molded by the beauty of its neoclassical architecture. His work, wildly popular with the wealthy nobility in his native Russia, made up most, if not all, of the imperial gifts given by the Romanovs. It was coveted by royalty all over the world. The king of Siam was an avid collector, as was our own princess of Wales, who had received numerous Fabergé pieces from her sister, Empress Alexandra Feodorovna. Whispered rumors claimed Monsieur Fabergé preferred the dowager empress Maria Feodorovna to her daughter-in-law Alexandra, but that did not stop him from providing the latter with some of his most exquisite pieces, many ordered by her husband. Apparently, once, after having made his annual request for an imperial Easter egg for his wife, the tsar inquired as to the subject chosen for the piece. Fabergé responded by saying, "Your Majesty will be content."

Rows of glass vitrines displayed a colorful range of objects inside

117

Fabergé's shop: picture frames, parasol handles, table clocks, cigarette cases, writing utensils, small egg pendants, boxes, bracelets, cuff links, bookmarks, and some of the most exquisite fans I have ever seen. The colors of the enamels, ranging from deep blues to soft pastels, and the skillful manner in which Fabergé's artisans employed the guilloche technique created objects that seemed to glow from within.

"I see I shall have to take matters in hand," Colin said. "You are already distracted. I shall inquire as to whether Mr. Fabergé is available to speak with us. In the meantime, you may browse."

Of course, I was not distracted; I never lose sight of the importance of my work. That does not mean, however, that I was incapable of appreciating the beauty around me, and I admit to being ever so slightly disappointed by how quickly Monsieur Fabergé invited us into his office.

After introductions and the usual pleasantries, I explained the situation and showed him the enameled case I had received, asking if it would be possible for him to tell us who had originally purchased it.

"Ordinarily, this is not something I would be comfortable doing," he said. "I respect the privacy of my clients. Your situation, however, is unusual. Excuse me for a moment and I will see what I can uncover."

"I shouldn't mind having an egg of my own," I said, when Colin and I were waiting for him to return. "It would make a fitting remembrance of our time together in Russia."

"I'd rather find you a nice Greek vase," he said. "No, that would never do. You're far too fastidious about vase painters. Ancient jewelry is more my forte. I did well with your wedding ring, did I not?" He took my left hand and touched the ancient band of gold and lapis lazuli on the fourth finger.

"Indeed you did," I said, feeling my cheeks flush as I met his eyes. "I agree to leave all purchases of ancient jewelry to you, as you have proven yourself a master at it, but in return you must allow me to indulge myself in the occasional egg."

Monsieur Fabergé returned. "Your card case was purchased six years ago by the Countess Lagunova. She died two years later, and all her possessions were sold at auction to cover unpaid debts."

"Do you know which house handled the sale?" Colin asked.

"I am afraid I do not. I wish I could be of more help."

"We could hardly ask for more," I said. "We are most appreciative."

On our way out, I lingered in showroom. I was severely tempted by a lovely blue-and-gold egg but instead purchased a charming fan, its guard sticks covered in pink enamel embellished with diamond-studded flowers and a laurel festoon. It opened to reveal mother-of-pearl sticks and silk leaves painted with tiny flowers in gold paillon borders. Who was I to resist such beauty?

The next morning, from our suite, I telephoned all the major auction houses in the city until I identified the one who had handled the sale of the Countess Lagunova's estate. The card case had been part of a larger lot that included nearly a dozen other small items. The high bidder was a man who ran a shop in Gostiny Dvor. Colin had left early for undisclosed purposes and Cécile and Masha had planned to go to the Hermitage—Cécile wanted to see the collection of eighteenth-century French art—so I went on my own to visit the establishment. On the way, I reflected that not so long ago, society had considered a lady going anywhere unescorted to be scandalous, and I had more than once been judged harshly for my habit of walking alone. Now, on the cusp of a new century, much had changed. I was feeling quite pleased with myself, hoping that my own example had influenced this shift, but when I reached my destination and showed the proprietor the card case, my sense of satisfaction disappeared. Although he recognized it, he had no memory of the person to whom he had sold it.

Frustrated, I returned to the hotel, where I buried myself in *War and Peace* until it was time to dress for the evening. The party that we were attending was hosted by Masha's dearest childhood friend, and it was so crowded that I never in the course of the evening managed to meet her. I wished I could have stayed home with my book. Colin agreed with the sentiment and pulled me into a convenient alcove.

"I say we make our escape," he said. "There's no point staying any longer. No one could possibly notice that we've gone."

"I would notice." Sebastian had crept up next to me. "Have you heard about my latest coup? I liberated a divine sable coat from a countess who trod on my foot at a ball. Gave it to a young lady I met walking near the Neva last week. Her own coat was all but threadbare, and I am certain she was on the verge of freezing. I signed the accompanying note Anatole Kuragin. You recognize the reference, I hope?"

"When Kuragin was planning his elopement with Natasha Rostova, a friend warned him that he must have a sable coat for her. Anything of lesser quality might not keep her warm enough, and he would risk her abandoning her plans to run off with him," Colin said. "I hadn't realized you were looking to get married."

Sebastian pulled a face that would have wilted a lesser man. "Of course not. A wife would be nothing but a burden to my lifestyle."

"If you're reading the book, you ought to do more than skim it," Colin said. "Emily would be far better impressed by literary references that made sense. Furthermore, you're posing as a Cossack, yet you belong to no regiment. Someone is bound to discover the fraud."

"Nothing matters more to the aristocracy than having an honorable family," Sebastian said. "And I am always careful to have all necessary explanations at the ready. In my current guise, I tell anyone interested that my father is an eccentric man who supplies the emperor with a regiment made up of his own men and led by me, his son and heir. I never mention specifically what part of the Russian army it belongs to, but instead distract anyone exhibiting signs of excessive curiosity with stories of our family being staunch supporters of the Romanovs. My great uncle helped stop one of the assassination attempts against Alexander II and, no doubt, would have prevented his death had he been present when the fatal bomb exploded at the site where is now being constructed the Church of Our Savior on the Spilled Blood. Once they've heard all that, they never doubt Nicholas would be only too glad to accommodate whatever my father asks."

"I could hardly follow your train of thought," I said. "Can you possibly believe you are deceiving those who know the emperor?"

"I have met the emperor himself twice since my arrival here—I saw him just last week at the Alexander Palace." Sebastian could not have looked smugger if he tried. "He told me how much he admires my dear pater."

"You told these lies to the tsar?" I asked.

"Bold lies are always better than timid ones," Sebastian said. "People are far more likely to believe them."

Colin was shaking his head. "I do not know whether to admire or despise you, Capet."

"Do whichever you find most amusing, Hargreaves," Sebastian said. "Neither shall trouble me."

Ekaterina Petrovna
August 1897

Katenka considered that summer's production of *Sleeping Beauty* a turning point. The morning after the performance, as they were leaving company class, Irusya received an enormous delivery of flowers from the count. While it was common for members of the nobility to shower ballerinas with attention, to have a gift delivered to rehearsal space was unusual. More than a few eyebrows were raised, and Mathilde Kschessinska pulled Irusya aside and spoke to her for nearly half an hour.

"What did she say?" Katenka asked. She had waited for her friend outside the theatre, basking in the sunny day and allowing herself, for the first time, to contemplate Mitya—and his kiss—without censoring her thoughts.

"It was nothing." Irusya's tone was unusually sharp. "She asked me a series of practical questions about my goals. I told her I hope, someday, to command the stage the way she does."

"Petipa does not much like her," Katenka said.

"That doesn't matter," Irusya replied. "Her talent forces him to use her, even if they don't get along."

"I mention this only to suggest that she may not be the best person from whom to seek advice. Why don't you talk to Pierina Legnani? She admires you."

"That is true," Irusya said. "But Mathilde understands the pressures that come from royal attention."

"Are you feeling such pressures?" Katenka asked.

Irusya thrust the flowers at her friend. "The count grows more attentive with every passing day, and I can no longer ignore the fact that he would like a closer friendship than that we currently share."

"What does Lev say?"

"This doesn't concern Lev."

"Of course it concerns Lev! He loves you."

"And I love him." They were walking now, away from the theatre and toward the park. "But is it reasonable to believe we will always be together? We were so young when we met, at least I was, and we inhabit very different worlds. I will always adore Lev, but I have to think about my career, and he cannot help me with it."

"You are too talented to require the count's assistance."

"You are kind to say so, but I am of the mind that it would be foolish to reject anyone's help. There are many dancers in the company, Katenka. They will not all be principals."

"So you mean to throw over my brother?" Katenka asked.

"No, I don't want to do that . . ." She looked away from her friend. "It's just that, well . . . I don't know what I want to do."

Later that evening, after another well-received performance, Katenka took the train back to Petersburg and walked alone to her flat. The count had invited Irusya to a party, and she had accepted with obvious satisfaction written on her face. Katenka hated to think what would happen next. She had been so happy only twenty-four hours earlier. How could things change so quickly?

After the close of the summer season, the company had a short break before they would begin performing in the capital, and, again,

Irusya invited Katenka to her dacha. The holiday had not ended so badly as she had feared it might. Mitya had declared himself to her, and the count had not come between Irusya and Lev. His engagement had been announced less than a week after he had begged Irusya to let herself grow closer to him. By the time the girls had arrived back in St. Petersburg, everything had returned to normal.

In class, she and Irusya had always claimed places next to each other at the barre, but now that their ranks were so different, Katenka was relegated to a less desirable spot with the rest of the corps de ballet. After that, the girls did not work together again, as Irusya was rehearsing soloist roles, and Katenka was not.

Miraculously, though, she no longer felt plagued by regret and hardly ever thought about her graduation performance. She was dancing every day in the greatest ballet company in the world. Working in the corps proved more difficult than she could have imagined and required a different mind-set from that of the roles she had learned while still in school, but she delighted in the challenge. Petipa himself noticed her diligence, and gave her the occasional compliment. Perhaps her position was not so dire as she had first believed. She would earn promotions, even if it took longer than she had originally hoped.

The autumn season was opening with *Sleeping Beauty*, and just as the count had predicted, Irusya had been cast in the role of the Lilac Fairy. The afternoon before the first performance, Irusya invited Katenka to lunch at her elegant apartment. When Katenka arrived, expecting an intimate chat with her friend, she was surprised to find Pierina Legnani, Mathilde Kschessinska—the only two prima ballerina assolutas in the world—and four other senior ballerinas in the company already there, including Olga Preobrajenska, whose turnout was the envy of all the other dancers. They were all gracious to Katenka, but as the lowest-ranking dancer present, she could not help but feel out of her depth.

Irusya made a point of trying to make her feel welcome, but the deliberateness of her actions only served to make Katenka more uncomfortable. Legnani, who had taken the seat next to her, leaned close during the soup course.

"You are in possession of a great talent, my child," she said. "Right now, it appears to be your master, as if you do not believe yourself capable of controlling it. You must learn how to make it serve you. Do this, and you will be one of the greatest dancers to ever grace the stage of the Mariinsky."

Katenka meditated on those words for the rest of the afternoon. She had not understood precisely what Legnani meant, but was too in awe of her to ask for any explanation. By the time she stepped onto the stage that evening, she was consumed by the notion of being controlled by her talent. Was not talent a good thing? She was thinking of this when she made a sloppy landing on a jump in the first act, and again in the third when she nearly missed her partner's hand in the grand dance celebrating Princess Aurora's wedding.

She had never given a worse performance. Now, not only had her emotions failed her, her technical prowess had gone missing as well.

Legnani had not performed that night, but she had been watching, and she came to Katenka backstage, finding her fighting back tears in a corner of the corps' dressing room.

"Tonight you accomplished nothing beyond proving the truth of what I told you this afternoon," she said. "You need to do more. Study with Cecchetti. He will teach you all our Italian tricks. I shall tell him to expect you."

12

I did not often have the opportunity to observe my husband while he was working. Generally speaking, he was abroad and I at home, but my time in Petersburg gave me daily reminders of the toll his duty took on him, physically and mentally. He had collapsed into our bed yesterday after having been awake for more than thirty-six hours and looked more haggard than I had ever seen him. I could not help but worry about him.

My own investigation was proving both challenging and frustrating. I had decided to speak to Katenka again, but wanted to meet her somewhere other than her flat or the theatre, and invited her to join me for luncheon at the Polish Café, which the concierge at the Grand Hôtel assured me was quite popular with ladies. Even better, it was less than a block away from the hotel, just on the other side of Mikhaylovskaya ulitsa.

Katenka arrived precisely on time, dressed in a simple but elegant gown that would have been fashionable five years ago. Not that its age mattered; she carried herself with such grace and moved so fluidly that no one could fault her appearance. No sooner had we sat down than two ladies from a nearby table bent their heads together, whispering and staring before rising to approach her.

"We saw you in *Paquita* last night," the shorter of the two said. "It was a triumph."

"We have already booked tickets for *Cinderella*," the other said. "It is a scandal that the theatre kept you hidden for so long. It ought not to have taken a murder to get you the roles you should have been dancing years ago."

Katenka smiled, but I could see it was forced. Her pale blue eyes looked strained. "We all must wait for our time to come. I do hope you enjoy *Cinderella*."

I waited until after they had returned to their seats to speak. "It must be difficult having your success tied to the loss of your friend."

"I hate it," she said. "It is all so difficult, but Irusya would never approve of me wallowing. If she were here, she would implore me to move to better accommodations, to start lobbying for even more roles than I am currently getting, and to insist on more private coaching."

"And will you?"

"I shan't move house. I don't like disruption and I don't think Mitya would approve of me adopting a more bourgeois lifestyle."

"Is that so?" I studied her face. She had blushed slightly when she said his name. "I met Agrippina Alexandrovna the other day. She told me that Irusya made a habit of waving to her from the stage door during intervals. Were you aware of that?"

"Yes, of course," she said, and opened her menu.

"I wonder that you didn't mention it when we spoke before? Had I not found her myself, I would be missing critical information about the night of the murder."

"I should have. I see that now. Do forgive me; I'm afraid I've been rather scatterbrained of late and too upset to get much sleep. I am glad you found her and learned what you did."

She gave every appearance of being sincere, and while I did not hold the omission against her, I would not forget it. In the meantime,

I had other questions for her. "What does your family think of your promotion to principal? They must be delighted."

"My parents died years ago, as did my grandfather," Katenka said. "Before I graduated from school. I wish so much they were here to see me. Grandpapa particularly adored *Cinderella*. He was at the first performance of Petipa's production, when Legnani shocked everyone with her thirty-two fouettées."

"Have you any siblings?"

"I have one brother left, Lev. The rest we lost to cholera." She returned to studying the menu. "Will you start with soup? I'm going to have the borscht."

"Tell me about him. Where does he live?"

"After the soup, a cutlet, I think. I can't remember the last time I had one. They were my favorite when I was young."

"You're still young," I said. "Does your brother live in Petersburg?"

"I'm afraid we've fallen out of touch. I have not spoken to him in more than a year. Last I heard, he was in Moscow."

Katenka's acting skills would have fooled most people, but I could see tension in the fine lines at the corners of her eyes. She smiled beguilingly, and made pretty conversation for the rest of our meal, even insisting that we share a cream-laden pastry to finish, but none of this hid from me her reluctance to talk about her brother.

"I ought not to have eaten so much," she said after we had collected our coats from the cloakroom. "I will pay for it tomorrow in class. It was a lovely meal, though; thank you. I have enjoyed myself immensely."

We stepped out of the door and onto the pavement, crowded with shoppers bustling toward Nevsky Prospekt at the end of the block. "I hope to see you dance again while I am here," I said. "Which upcoming production is your favorite? I shall get tickets to that."

She bit her lower lip, looking suddenly very young and vulnerable. "I am afraid I am not the best judge of what you would like. You should choose whatever you prefer. My opinion doesn't matter."

"Of course it does. If—"

A shout—really more of a bark—from a nearby man interrupted me. He had stopped a few feet away from us on the snow-covered pavement and was looking across the street at the Grand Hôtel, which stretched the entire length of the block along Mikhaylovskaya ulitsa. I followed the direction of his gaze to one of the narrow balconies gracing some of the first-floor rooms of the hotel. There, stood a dancer, costumed as if for *Swan Lake,* on her toes, her arms stretched above her, waving a long red scarf.

In an instant, everyone on both sides of the pavement was watching and calling to her. I heard many cries of *Nemetseva*. Next to me, Katenka, her face a mask of fear, crumpled into a heap on the snow. I knelt next to her, patting her cheeks in an attempt to get her to regain consciousness. Soon, a crowd had circled around us, and someone passed me smelling salts, which brought her around as soon as I waved them under her nose. She insisted on rising to her feet and looked immediately back to the balcony. The dancer had disappeared.

I went in fast pursuit, crossing the street and running back to the hotel lobby and up the stairs to the first floor. Trying to gauge how far along the corridor the room from which the dancer had accessed the balcony would be, I knocked on the first door in a location I thought might be favorable. No answer. I tried to open it, but it was locked. Katenka had followed me, and, taking my lead, started knocking on more doors.

An elderly German gentleman opened one of them. I explained as quickly and efficiently as possible what had happened and asked if we might see his balcony. Katenka headed straight for it the instant he let us in, leaving me space to make a quick search of the rest of the suite.

Not surprisingly, I found no trace of our mysterious dancer, and Katenka saw nothing on the balcony. We thanked the man and returned to the corridor, where one of the housekeepers was unlocking the door to another suite, her cleaning supplies on a cart. She told me that this was the last room she needed to clean on the floor and agreed to let me search it before she set to work.

Neither the dancer nor anyone else was in the room, but a red scarf, silk like its twin I had found across from the Yusupov Palace, was draped over the handle of the French doors that led to the balcony.

"Who was staying here last night?" I asked.

"A woman and her daughter from Paris," the housekeep said. "They were with us for nearly a month. This morning they overslept and very nearly missed their train. I saw them rushing out. They were in quite a state."

"Do you know what time that was?"

"Quite early, certainly no later than nine."

So they were gone in plenty of time for our dancer to have used the suite to stage her performance. "Is it usual that a room would still not be cleaned by this time of day?"

"New guests may not check in until four o'clock, so we begin with the rooms already occupied and move to the empty ones after lunch," she said.

I wondered if our dancer had a connection with anyone in the hotel. If not, she had left to chance that her scheme would work, for she could not otherwise have known which room was likely to be vacant. More important, what was her purpose? As she had on her pedestal on the Moika Embankment, our dancer had caused a sensation, and I did not doubt that she would dominate all conversation on Nevsky Prospekt for the rest of the day.

Katenka did not look well. I ordered a carriage and accompanied her home, amazed at how easily she climbed what to me felt like the unending flights of stairs to her flat. Inside, she sank onto her settee, leaned back, and flung an arm over her eyes.

"What do they want from me?" she asked.

131

"Who?" I asked.

"These people. I feel so harassed." Her voice was barely audible. "Her presence must be meant as an indictment of me." She removed her arm from her eyes. "Many of Irusya's most ardent admirers are unlikely to accept me—or anyone—as her replacement. What if some of them blame me for her death? I received a letter yesterday, saying I would never be as good a dancer as she."

"May I see it?" I asked. Could Katenka be in danger? I did not think any of Nemetseva's admirers were likely to harm her, but I had to consider that if the murderer was a jealous dancer, Katenka could be the next target.

"Mitya burned it. He said it was nothing more than an incoherent rant."

"He was probably right," I said. "Public figures are always vulnerable to the base thoughts of a critical public. You cannot be the first dancer to have received a nasty letter."

"No, I am not. But this woman on the balcony—who is she and why is she tormenting me?"

"This is not the first time she has made an appearance, and the previous incident occurred when you were not present, so it hardly seems likely that she means to rebuke to you."

"I suppose you are right," she said, rising and crossing to the samovar. She poked its coals and peeked into the small teapot. "Will you have tea? It will not take long for the water to boil."

"I shouldn't stay," I said. "Unless you would prefer not to be left alone?"

"No, thank you. I do appreciate you bringing me home, but I should like to rest. Irusya's funeral is tomorrow, much later than it ought to have been, but I am told this is to be expected when one meets such a violent end. I am to dine with her parents tonight and can hardly bear the thought of facing them."

"Would you like me to contact anyone for you? Is Mitya nearby?"

"No, he's quite busy these days. He will accompany me to the funeral, but otherwise I am content on my own. Thank you for all your help today."

I took my leave from her and had made my way down the first flight of stairs when I heard someone approaching me from above. It was Katenka, her face damp with tears.

"May I have the scarf you found today?" she asked.

"I'm sorry; I must keep it," I said. "I need to compare it to the first one I found. When the investigation is over—"

"No, that's all right," she said. "It wouldn't make any difference, would it? I don't know why I even want it."

"Perhaps I shouldn't leave you on your own," I said. "Let's go to your flat and have some tea."

"No, please. I need to be alone."

Without another word, she turned and went back up the stairs.

Ekaterina Petrovna
November 1897

Enrico Cecchetti, a brilliant dancer in his own right, had started teaching in 1890 and was now the Imperial Theatre's second ballet master. Katenka had rarely worked with him, but she knew many of the company's best dancers trained privately with him. Why would he want to waste time on a lackluster corps dancer? But she dared not ignore Legnani's advice, and four days later found herself headed to Cecchetti's studio, more nervous than she had ever been in her life.

Now, after nearly three months of private coaching, Katenka was convinced Cecchetti despised her. This belief, coupled with the fact she had run through nearly all of her money, led her to tell him that she could no longer study with him. The Italian raised his eyebrows.

"You need me, Ekaterina Petrovna," he said, his posture still that of a dancer. "If you are too foolish to see this, I cannot be of any service to you."

"I am afraid, sir, you misunderstand me," she said. "It is a question of funds. I am only in the corps. I cannot afford you."

He leaned his head to the side and studied her. "I understand all too well," he said. "My parents were both dancers. I was born in a dressing room. Did you know that?" He did not pause for her to answer.

"I will continue to work with you, once a week, regardless of your ability to pay."

"Thank you, sir, I cannot begin—"

"That's quite enough," he said. "We will waste no more time. Where did we finish last week?" He sat at the piano and began to tap out a melody. Katenka stood in the center of his studio, prepared for the choreography she knew accompanied the music, hardly able to concentrate, but knowing that, somehow, she must. She could not squander this opportunity.

After a grueling two hours with Cecchetti, Katenka rushed home. Irusya was coming to dinner, and for the first time in months the two friends would be together, away from the rest of the company. Pierina Legnani had fallen ill that autumn, leaving Mathilde Kschessinska to fill most of her roles. This created an opening for other dancers to shine, and Irusya was one of the first to benefit. This was a boon to her career but left her with almost no time to socialize. The following night, she would make her debut as Swanilda in *Coppélia*.

"I am so fraught with nerves, Katenka," she said as they sat, eating. "There is no place I would rather be than here with you right now, having this abominable sausage. You really must learn to cook better if you are going to live without servants."

"Someday, when you are a principal dancer, you will look back on these days with great fondness. You will grow tired of overblown French meals and beg your cook to make you something plain, but he will refuse, and you will fling him out of his kitchen, roll up your sleeves, and make a good, Russian meal."

Irusya wrinkled her nose and they both laughed. "Tomorrow night, Katenka, after the ballet, will you come with me to a party? It's hosted by the Grand Duke Vladimir Alexandrovich. There will be champagne and dancing—"

"And overblown French food?" Katenka asked. "I don't think so, Irusya." But Irusya could always persuade her to do anything, and, almost without realizing it, Katenka agreed to go. Feeling deflated, she got up to clear their dishes and pulled a box out of a cupboard. "You will be glad to learn that I did not make any pastry."

"How on earth did you afford this?" Irusya asked, opening the package to reveal a pair of spectacular napoleons filled with cream and raspberry preserves.

"I traded two hours of dance instruction for them," Katenka said. "The bakery owner has a daughter."

"You are most resourceful, my friend. Is there nothing you can't achieve?"

Katenka looked down, and the atmosphere turned in a heartbeat. They both knew what she couldn't achieve, and not even years of private lessons with Cecchetti could change that.

January 1900

13

~~~⋅⋅◦❊◦⋅⋅~~~

Colin's work kept him from accompanying me to Nemetseva's funeral, but Cécile agreed to go in his stead. She collected me in Masha's carriage, and we made the trip to the far end of Nevsky Prospekt and the Cathedral of the Holy Trinity at Alexander Nevsky Monastery. The interior of the cathedral was neoclassical and lit from large windows beneath its dome and a large chandelier, but no light could cut through the gloom consuming it today. There were no chairs inside Orthodox churches, so the mourners had to stand for the entire service, packed close together, crammed so tightly it felt as if we were all swaying in unison. We held the candles we had each been given upon entering, and their flames, bobbing along with the crowd, contributed to the somber mood.

Tchaikovsky's funeral, at the much larger Kazan Cathedral in the center of Petersburg, had drawn enormous crowds. Those who could not get a seat inside—the church could accommodate only six thousand; rumor said sixty thousand had requested tickets—lined Nevsky Prospekt for a glimpse of the composer's coffin. Nemetseva was not so famous as he, but Holy Trinity was stuffed full nonetheless. Her fellow dancers, slim and elegant, unmistakable even in ordinary clothes, stood closest to the altar, along with Nemetseva's family and Katenka. Cécile and I hovered in the back, trying to avoid being crushed. I searched for Prince Vasilii but did not see him.

Able to understand only parts of the service, which was conducted in Russian, I nonetheless found the haunting chants unique to the Orthodox faith profoundly moving. Their beauty reached deep into my soul. At the end of the service, all those who wished to stepped forward to the coffin and kissed the icon placed on top of Nemetseva's body. I had no desire to see the dead girl again. Once this ritual was complete and the coffin closed, those going to the burial processed from the church to the waiting grave in Tikhvin Cemetery, where the ballerina would rest among other great Russian cultural figures, Tchaikovsky and Dostoyevsky included.

Snow had been falling steadily all morning, and the wind picked up as we exited the church. Cécile, shivering with cold despite her furs, returned to the carriage, but I braved the weather and stood near the grave site as the bearded priest intonated a final prayer and the coffin was lowered. Mourners tossed coins into the grave, and the woman standing next to me, small and sturdy, dressed in felt boots and an ankle-length sable coat, shook her head.

"It is a bad death," she said. "Nothing good comes after a bad death. All those close to her will suffer, not just from their loss, but from the misfortune that plagues the living after such a death. Destruction and misery will follow."

"The ghost!" someone cried, and we all turned as one at the sound. I could not see well through the crowd and pushed my way ahead— gently and decorously, I hoped; this was a funeral, after all—until I saw her, standing en pointe atop a convenient gravestone, from which the snow had been removed. She was in the same white costume she had worn before and waved a familiar-looking crimson scarf.

She had chosen her stage to be at some distance from her audience, no doubt to ensure she could easily disappear before anyone might reach her, and the scene unfolded precisely in this manner. Several gentlemen and a handful of dancers ran forward, shouting for her to stay where she was, but with a graceful leap, she descended from the stone. A group of larger grave markers had surrounded her, and now she vanished behind them.

Knowing she would have made her escape before the mass of mourners surging forward reached the spot where she had stood, I followed at a reasonable pace, wanting only to secure the scarf she had left behind. I had to grapple with a burly gentleman who wanted to keep it as a souvenir, but, needless to say, I won the battle. Nothing else could be learned here as the mob had trampled the snowy ground that might have provided a trail of footprints along her escape route. I returned to the carriage. After holding the door open for me, the driver presented Cécile and me with a flask of vodka and two enameled glasses.

"I do not want it," Cécile said. "But Masha swears it is the only thing that will keep us warm."

I drained my glass in a single gulp. "I agree with her," I said. "I feel better already." Cécile, looking skeptical, followed suit and admitted that the subsequent warming sensation was nothing short of miraculous. The driver, smiling, now gave us a well-insulated vessel filled with steaming-hot, strong coffee. Although I generally despise coffee, in that moment I loved it dearly.

"I was thinking while I waited for you," Cécile said. "If I were the ghost of a ballerina, I would not limit my appearances to such mundane surfaces as balconies and tombstones. I would hover right above my open grave and dance there, where no one could deny my presence. The fact that this ghost is apparently earthbound suggests to me she is human."

"I'm not sure that your reasoning is altogether sound," I said, "but I agree with your conclusions. She is a person, not a ghost."

"It hardly matters what she is," Cécile said. "The news of this return of the apparition will already be spreading through the city. It's all anyone will be talking about by noon tomorrow." On that point, I had no doubt she was right.

As instructed, the driver dropped me at the Mariinsky Theatre before returning Cécile to Masha's. It was locked, but I gained entrance through a back door whose lock I picked with the small set of tools I always kept in my reticule. I knew the dancers and backstage workers would have all been at the funeral. If our mysterious ballerina had taken her costume from Madame Zhdanova's workshop, she could easily return it now without drawing attention.

The costumes for *Swan Lake* were no longer in the corridor outside the dressing rooms but had been moved back into the costume shop. I wished I had taken note of how many Madame Zhdanova had counted when I had last seen her. As I had not, all I could do was carefully inspect each one for signs of recent use.

Nothing seemed out of place, but it was possible I had beat the dancer back from the cemetery. It was also possible that she would not come here at all, but I thought it worth waiting to see. I looked around the room, pondering the best place to hide. A tall cabinet full of bolts of fabric would have made a snug spot were it not lined with shelves that made it impossible for me to cram myself in. In the end, I draped a mannequin with a piece of heavily embroidered velvet and crouched low behind it, close enough to the *Swan Lake* tutus that I would be able to observe anyone near them.

Colin has often told me that his work for the palace involves long periods of time doing nothing, and he views this as the most challenging of his tasks. Taking action, even in dangerous circumstances, is preferable to remaining inert. Never have I felt more sympathy for him than in those endless hours I spent on the floor of the Mariinsky costume shop.

At least it felt like endless hours. My knees were stiff and my legs cramped. I was too hot at first and then too cold. I shifted my position, trying and failing to find one that would be less overtly uncomfortable. Giving up, I began to silently recite *The Iliad* in ancient Greek. This kept my mind occupied but did not distract me from my physical discomfort as much as I had hoped.

An eternity later, I heard the door of the workshop open, followed by two sets of footsteps, one light, one treading harshly on the wooden floorboards.

"You should never have come here."

I recognized Katenka's voice.

"And you should be at the funeral reception right now." The man's voice was wholly unfamiliar, and while I was situated to be able to observe the *Swan Lake* costumes, I was not in a position conducive to watching anyone in the front of the room. A large worktable blocked my view.

"I can't face any of them," Katenka said. "I want to go home."

"Then why did you come here?"

"Why did you follow me?" she spat back, sounding hardly like herself.

"You wouldn't speak to me in church or at the cemetery," he said. "What did you think I would do?"

"You're always telling me it's dangerous for me to be seen with you. What did you think I would do? Go, go from this place now." Her voice strained almost to the point of breaking. "This ghost is haunting more than just the theatre, and I cannot bear it. You have no idea how tormented I am, and you have made it clear again and again that I cannot rely on you. So leave me, once and for all. I do not want to know where you go. I don't want to have any information to hide when I am eventually asked. Because I will, eventually, be asked."

Her companion stamped his foot and groaned. "I cannot do what you wish," he said. "I have my work, too." I heard a rustle of fabric; he must have embraced her. Then more heavy footsteps and the sound of the door opening and slamming shut. Katenka began to cry.

I debated my options. Should I confront her? If I did, she was unlikely to reveal the identity of her companion. Furthermore, she would know that I was now aware of his existence. She might even be anticipating me as one of those who would ask her those eventual questions to which she referred. On the other hand, her heart-wrenching sobs revealed her current vulnerability. I might be able to comfort her and convince her to confide in me.

In the end, I took too long in deciding. Katenka, still weeping, left the room. I counted to thirty in Greek and then followed, but saw no sign of her in the corridor. Stepping quietly, I began to systematically search for her.

She had gone to the stage. Her shoes sounded louder on its boards than ballet slippers, but she was moving with exquisite grace, dancing something I recognized from the end of *Swan Lake,* silhouetted against the glow of the electric chandelier above the audience seats. She had not turned on any stage lights. After executing a series of *pirouettes* I would have thought impossible in her dress, she collapsed, sobbing.

I would not disturb her private grief. Her wounds were too raw, too fresh. The time for questions could wait.

Ekaterina Petrovna
November 1897

No nobleman would hold in his home a *soirée* that included ballerinas on the guest list—dancers were not socially acceptable unless they came to perform—so the grand duke had arranged the use of a private room in one of the city's finest restaurants for his fête. A table laid heavily with an assortment of hors d'oeuvres stood in the center, and waiters circulated with magnums of Roederer champagne, bottled sweeter than that found in the rest of Europe, especially for the *goût russe*. A small orchestra played in the corner, and some of the guests were waltzing, though there was not really space for it.

The chamber was crowded and vibrant, sounds of laughter and the babble of excited conversation filling the air, but Katenka wished she had not allowed Irusya to take her to this party. She was having an abominable time, but not for the reasons she had expected. The gentlemen were all extremely polite, if a bit too friendly, but they never veered toward the inappropriate.

All the while, she was surreptitiously watching Irusya. Her performance in *Coppélia* had been nothing short of a triumph. Petipa took the unusual step of announcing her promotion to principal dancer from the stage during the curtain calls. Now she stood basking in attention not of the grand duke, as Katenka had expected, but of a younger man.

Irusya, whose complexion was glowing prettily from a combination of excitement and champagne, smiled wickedly as she pulled her friend to her. "Prince Nikolai Danilovich Ukhov, may I present the dearest companion of my youth, Ekaterina Petrovna Sokolova?"

He gave a neat bow and kissed Katenka's hand. "It is a great pleasure, Ekaterina Petrovna. Please call me Kolya, as I know we shall be good friends. Our Irusya is most charming. I do not know how I shall ever tear myself away from her."

Katenka forced a smile. "There is no one I love better in all of Petersburg."

Kolya leaned close to her, put an arm companionably around her shoulder, and whispered—a false whisper, deliberately loud enough that Irusya could hear. "I find myself holding her just as dear."

Katenka's heart was pounding in her chest. She knew she should not care so much. Irusya could love whomever she wanted; Katenka had no control over her. But her heart ached for her brother, who she knew would suffer if he lost Irusya.

"I'm afraid I must return home," Katenka said. "This evening has exhausted me."

"I will call for my carriage and escort you myself," the prince said.

"You are kindness itself, Kolya," Irusya said, shocking Katenka by addressing him so familiarly. "And will you take me home, too?"

"Of course, *douchka*," he said. "I would never leave you to find your own way home in this weather."

Douchka? Little Darling? Katenka was even more shocked, so stunned, in fact, that she hardly noticed Irusya bustling her toward the cloakroom without even pausing to say goodbye to the grand duke. Before she knew it, she was sitting in the prince's carriage, across from him and Irusya. They were leaning close together, their shoulders touching.

"Irusya's flat is not far from here," Katenka said. "If you turn at—"

"We shall drop you first," Kolya said. Katenka knew better than to reply. She sat in silence for the rest of the trip, watching him and Irusya steal knowing looks at each other. When they reached the front of her building, Katenka all but fell out of the door, saved from landing in a half-frozen puddle by the prince's liveried footman who had stepped down from his perch to assist her.

She watched the carriage until it disappeared. The sleet, which had been falling for hours, started to turn to a wet, heavy snow. Her feet were soaked and her teeth were beginning to chatter, but she could not force herself to go inside. Instead, she ran all the way to Nevsky Prospekt, not stopping until she reached the store in which Lev worked. It was closed, but she knew he would be there, in his tiny room in the back, hardly large enough for a narrow bed. She banged and banged on the door until he opened it, concern writ on his face.

Seeing him, she burst into tears. "I must tell you something," she cried, and flung herself against his chest. He put his arms around her and embraced her.

"Come, Katenka, you are soaked and frozen. Mitya is here and some of our other friends as well. We will see you warm and comfortable."

They were gathered, not in Lev's little room but in the shop itself, next to a warm stove around which they had pulled wooden chairs. An empty bottle of vodka and a second, half-empty, along with a jar of salted cucumbers, sat on the floor in the center of their circle. Each man held a shot glass. Only Mitya rose when Katenka entered, the other men nodding to acknowledge her and mumbling greetings.

Mitya handed her a glass of vodka. "Drink this. You must warm up."

She obeyed, but not even the harsh liquid could break through the cold paralyzing her chest. Yes, she was wet; yes, the temperature was freezing. But neither had caused her chill. She wanted to speak with Lev privately but did not see how she could. He had disappeared with her wet coat and hat for a moment but had already returned, carrying the worn blanket from his bed. He wrapped her in it.

"What are you doing wandering the streets at this time of night?" he asked.

"I needed to talk to you, but now is not the time. You are busy."

"We are," Mitya said. "We are dreaming of a new country. If that doesn't warm you, I don't know what will."

How could he be so infuriating? Could he not see how upset she was? Katenka bit back the reprimand on her lips and shook her head. "I am afraid I am not suited to politics," she said. "I should go."

"You must warm up first," Mitya said. "You'll get sick."

"No, I have class early in the morning and should have been in bed hours ago. I will find a droshky," she said.

"I will hail one for you," Mitya said.

"No," Katenka said. "Let Lev, please. I need to speak with him privately."

Mitya frowned. "He can come to you tomorrow. I will do it."

"No," she said, more sharply, and Mitya turned on his heel and went back to his seat without another word. Lev looked confused but followed her to the door. He did not let her step outside, where the snow made it impossible to see even to the far side of the street, until he had a droshky waiting for her.

"You must talk to Irusya," Katenka said as her brother handed her into the small carriage. "She is losing her way, and I fear you will lose her in the process."

"I saw her this afternoon and things could not have been better between us," Lev said. "You are concerned over nothing."

"I have seen something." She stopped. "I do not think you can trust her any longer. She—"

"Say no more, Katyurushka. You are upsetting yourself unnecessarily. I am going to propose tomorrow and then you will have nothing left to worry about." He shut the carriage door and waved as the droshky pulled away. Katenka, tasting bile in her throat, fell against the hard back of her seat, tears soaking her cheeks.

14

I walked back to the hotel, contemplating the conversation I had overheard. Katenka sounded so unlike herself, frightened and afraid. Who was the man who had followed her into the theatre? If I confronted her about it, would she answer me truthfully? My instinct told me she would not. By the time I reached our suite, I had decided I would have to take a different approach with her. I unlocked the door and found Colin inside. He looked far less tired than he had of late, rather refreshed, in fact, and the warmth of his greeting—not to mention the relish with which he removed my coat—told me his work had taken a turn for the better. I said as much to him.

"You are correct," he said. "I am hopeful that we may be in a position to disrupt the activities of the violent faction within the league."

"Do you really believe the others are not violent?"

"They won't shy away from violence should it become necessary, but they are intent on starting their campaign in a peaceful manner."

"That is noble of them," I said.

"Perhaps," he said. "Or it could be nothing more than a strategy to strengthen their support should they later adopt another approach. They will be able to say they tried to seek change without violence, and no doubt attract more support from the public as a result."

"But as for the others—'

"I should say no more, Emily."

"Then I shall press you for nothing further." I called downstairs for tea and a tray of cakes and told him about the funeral and its aftermath while we waited for them to arrive.

"Again with the ghostly dancer," he said. "The masses are captivated by the ridiculous notion that the great Nemetseva has refused to leave the city until her murderer is brought to justice. The newspapers are full of it, and it's all I hear on the streets."

"She shouldn't be called an apparition, let alone a ghost. It's perfectly obvious she's a living, breathing person." Logic had very little influence in these sorts of situations. Time and again I had watched people choose to believe something utterly irrational but emotionally satisfying instead of accepting a difficult truth. I pulled the crimson scarf from my bag and passed it to my husband. "Is there any way we could determine where the scarves came from?"

Colin inspected it and asked me to bring him the others. He laid the three of them out on a long table in the sitting room of our suite. They were identical in dimension and color, and looked as if they had been cut from a single piece of cloth, expertly hemmed to ensure the ends would not fray.

"I doubt we can source either the material or the scarves themselves," he said. His dark curls tumbled onto his brow as he bent over the table. "This sort of thing can be found in any larger store. The quality is not striking, although the silk isn't bad. The stitches are machine worked, not done by hand."

"Which might suggest they were purchased rather than made at home?" I asked.

"Not necessarily," he said. "Plenty of people have a sewing machine at home. Furthermore, there are more than a few of them in the costume department of the theatre." He had draped my coat over a convenient chair and now went to hang it in the wardrobe. "I'll leave your gloves on the table as you never think to look for them in your coat. It's most amusing, how—" A slip of paper fluttered to the floor as he pulled them out of the pocket. He held it up between two fingers. "Something you need?"

"What is it?" I took it from him, unfolded it, and read aloud. "*Beware the evil hail that follows a bad death.*" The handwriting was a perfect match for the note that had accompanied the Fabergé card case. I paused and tried to remember everything I could about the woman standing beside me at the grave who had talked about bad deaths. "I wish Cécile had stayed with me. She knows many more people here than I. Even if she didn't recognize the woman, she might have known some of the others around me and could have asked them."

"The concept of a bad death leading to subsequent disasters is quite common in Russia, so there's no reason to consider her the only possible culprit. Anyone could have slipped it into your pocket," Colin said. "You said the church was quite crowded."

"It was," I said, frowning. "And I was distracted both there and in the cemetery, trying to watch for anyone engaged in suspicious behavior."

"But you saw nothing that triggered your intuition?"

"No. I was surprised Prince Vasilii was not present, but I suppose he would not have thought it appropriate."

"We were both in the same meeting at the Winter Palace this morning," Colin said. "It was not something he could have missed, regardless of the reason. There are rumblings of revolutionary activity, and we believe there may be someone inside the palace involved. Vasilii's tasked with trying to root out anyone deemed disloyal."

"Poor man," I said with a sigh and then looked at my husband, feeling most grateful that we had never had to keep our love secret. I stood in front of him, took his strong hands in mine, and looked directly into his eyes. "Are you at leisure for the remainder of the day? Or have you another meeting that cannot be missed?"

"You are well aware, Emily, how serious my work here is," he said, touching my cheek lightly. "There is never a moment during which I could not be applying myself to some task. However, if you were to alert me to something even more pressing that requires my immediate attention . . ."

I stood on my toes, threw my arms around his neck, and kissed him.

"Yes, quite, well . . . that does seem even more pressing," he said.

"Vital urgency," I replied, still kissing him. "The tsar himself would have you arrested if you didn't tend to it without delay."

"Is that so?" He was backing me up toward the bedroom. "Ambivalent though I am about monarchs in general, I am never one to shirk my duty . . ."

"You could spark an international incident if you ignored this," I said. "What would Her Majesty say if she learned that her most trusted agent had offended the tsar?"

This made him snort. "My dear girl, don't ever mention the queen again in such circumstances. Promise me." He took my face in his hands. I could feel his breath on my cheeks. Just then the sharp sound of a knock caused me to start and Colin to scowl. "This is unconscionable." He straightened his jacket, adjusted his tie, and went to the door, opening it to reveal a most distraught Prince Vasilii.

"Forgive me, Hargreaves," he said. "I ought not to have come unannounced. I was hoping to speak with your wife." He handed Colin a slim wooden box. "This was on the floor outside your door. I presume it was meant for you."

Colin took the box, ushered him in, and poured whiskies for them both before sitting. I declined a glass of my own, preferring instead to wait for the tea, which had not yet been delivered.

"A productive meeting this morning," the prince said. "I am most grateful for your support."

"It is nothing," Colin said, picking up the box from the table on which he had laid it. He opened it and shut it almost immediately, hearing another knock on the door. The tea had arrived. My husband asked Prince Vasilii about military maneuvers during the Napoleonic Wars while the tray was delivered. Only once the staff member had left did his tone take a more serious bent.

"You both should see this." He opened the box again and turned it toward us. Inside was a long, sharp dagger encrusted with dried blood.

"Nemetseva?" I asked, rising and covering my mouth with my hand. No matter how many times I faced it, the grisly evidence of violent death at human hands pierced my very soul. I would never be inured to it.

Vasilii stood as well, unsteady, all color draining from his face.

"It's a naval dirk," Colin said. "There are no markings on it that might indicate to whom it belongs, but it is possible I can determine something about its origins. Did you see anyone else in the corridor when you approached our room?"

"No, not that I remember," he said. "I cannot claim to have been paying any particular attention. Foolish of me to be so unaware of my surroundings."

"You had no reason to think you should be on alert," I said.

He gripped the back of a chair and closed his eyes. "I cannot bear to see it." The poor man looked as if he were about to faint. Hearts can mend, but I wondered if he would ever recover from this blow. Humans have an amazing capacity to adapt to even the worst circumstances; that does not mean they are left unscathed.

"Was anything else in the box?" I asked.

"This." Colin passed me a small slip of paper, folded into a small square. On it were two words: *Help me.* After reading it, I showed it to Vasilii.

"It is my Irusya's handwriting," he said. "I know it as well as my own. I know I ask a foolish question, but there is no possibility, is there, that she is still alive?"

"There is not," Colin said, his terse words and clipped tone allowing no possibility for false hope. "Bring me all the notes you have received, Emily."

We compared the three messages, each written on the same heavy linen paper in the same delicate hand. "We shan't get anywhere trying to source the paper," I said.

"It's all so hopeless." Vasilii's eyes were moist with tears. "I thought I would call on you in the hope that you had made progress in the case. I never expected to be faced with—" He closed his eyes and pressed his hand over them. "Her blood is still on it. It is too much to bear."

"You ought never to have seen it," Colin said. "Go home and do whatever you must to free yourself from the image. We will take care of everything. Emily will bring this vile criminal to justice."

"Thank you. I apologize, Hargreaves, if we started off on the wrong foot," the prince said. "I am prone to handle very badly matters in which I feel my pride is threatened. I ought not to have asked your wife to meet me without you."

"Nothing to worry about, old boy," Colin said.

"Had I known you better, I should have acted differently." His lips curved into an ironic smile. "Or if I had been less stupid. There is much I regret. I wish I could better express how grateful I am to you both. I am overwhelmed, truly."

Colin walked him to the door and then we were alone again, but the mood had shifted too far for us to return to our pleasant interlude.

"He reminds me very much of Prince Andrei in *War and Peace*," I said. "There is an admirable nobility in him, but so much pride and almost a bit of awkwardness."

"Things ended very badly for Andrei," Colin said. "I should find someone else to compare Vasilii to if I were you."

After discussing the most efficient way to attack the rest of the afternoon, we decided to divide our forces, so to speak, Colin going to the Admiralty, headquarters of the Imperial Navy, located just across from the Winter Palace garden, while I went to Nemetseva's flat near the Mariinsky. First, though, we stopped at the office of the judicial investigator handling the case and got from him the key to the apartment. Second, I collected Cécile, knowing two sets of eyes are always preferable to one.

Nemetseva's home contrasted with Katenka's in every way. Its location, on the Moika, halfway between the Yusupov Palace and the theatre, was both fashionable and convenient. Located on the first floor, with high ceilings and a pleasant view of the river below, the rooms were large and full of light. Irusya's taste could not be faulted. She had chosen elegant Empire-style furnishings that were both beautiful and comfortable. Photographs of her in ballet costumes adorned the walls, as did a number of unremarkable paintings. Along with her bedroom, two sitting rooms, a small library, and a dining room, there was a modest-sized ballet studio, with mirrored walls and wooden barres. The kitchen, pantry, and servants' rooms ran along a narrow corridor at the back of the building. I had hoped to speak with her staff, but a neighbor told us none of them had come into the flat since the murder, and the layer of dust forming on every surface confirmed her statement.

"What is to be done with the place?" Cécile asked, flicking from her glove a bit of dust. "Do her family plan to clear it out?"

"Apparently her mother wants it to be left as it is," I said.

"Morbid."

"Quite," I said, "but her grief is still raw. Let's start in the bedroom and see what we can find." As I had expected, Irusya's clothing reflected her elegant style. All of it was of the latest cut and fashion. She had two large jewelry boxes full of a variety of pieces, from simple and modest to extravagant.

"That must be from a most ardent admirer," Cécile said, pointing to a large ruby brooch.

"Vasilii?" I asked. "How rich is he? Do you know?"

"He has more than enough to live three or four extremely prodigal lives."

A spacious en suite bathroom connected to the dressing room, a man's shaving cup, razor, and brush next to the sink. Obviously they belonged to the prince. I cannot say I was shocked; I understood the nature of their relationship. But seeing physical evidence of their intimacy touched me unexpectedly. How tragic that they had not been able to live a normal life together, as man and wife.

Moving out of the bedroom, we went to the larger of the sitting rooms. A cabinet there contained a profusion of the trinkets Vasilii had mentioned, although I am not certain the word adequately described the objects presented to the ballerina as gifts. There were a handful of humble offerings, but most impressive were the numerous Fabergé flowers, perfectly enameled—and, sometimes, bejeweled— copies of nature's best: pearl lilies of the valley, blue cornflowers, a single white anemone with a rose-cut diamond in its center and nephrite leaves, and tiny violets in a rock crystal vase that looked almost real until one noticed their gold stems.

"Surely these cannot be from random admirers," I said.

Cécile shrugged. "The Russians love Fabergé, and they love their ballerinas. To the very rich, these are trinkets, as Vasilii said."

The library held only a few books—Pushkin's poetry, several volumes of fairy tales, and an assortment of popular novels. More interesting were the albums full of photographs. There were more pictures of scenes from ballets, but most fascinating to me were those showing her and Katenka at what must have been a summer house near a lake. The girls sat next to each other on a wide wooden swing that hung from the branch of a large tree, both wearing wreaths of wildflowers. Another showed them in a boat, holding their oars at the ready. Many captured picnics on a broad lawn, and in these were two other individuals.

"That's Mitya," I said, pointing to a young spectacled man. "But who is the other?"

"Who is asking?" The voice came from the doorway, behind us. I recognized it from when I had crouched on the floor of the Mariinsky costume shop. Every fiber of my being shrieked to attention. The man who had argued with Katenka was standing not five paces from us, a shocking look of anger on his face, a face identical to that in the photograph I was holding.

Ekaterina Petrovna
November 1897

Katenka managed, just barely, to go through the motions in company class that morning, but she moved as if pushing through a dense fog. She was grateful she did not have a lesson scheduled with Cecchetti that afternoon and relieved that she would not be performing that evening. Disappointment had consumed her when the cast was announced, as she had always loved Petipa's *Cinderella*, but now she saw the omission of her name as a stroke of good fortune. She would not have to leave her flat again until tomorrow, which suited her well. She did not want to see anyone.

Except Lev. He was the cause of all this worry. Irusya had the night off, too, because she had danced *Coppélia* the night before, and Lev was planning to propose to her that evening. Katenka had tried to warn him and even went back to the bookstore on her way home from class, but he would not hear her, claiming that he knew Irusya better than she when it came to certain matters.

In the end, she gave up. She could not force him to listen, let alone force him to believe her, and now she was left pacing, waiting for that terrible, inevitable moment when he would come to her, heartbroken.

Each hour seemed to last for days. Nothing provided her solace. She rested her hand on the back of a chair and started methodically practicing battement tendus. In a way, they were the simplest step in ballet—sliding the foot in a perfect line while keeping the toes on the floor. She repeated the step, over and over, en croix, to the front, then to the side, then to the back, again to the side, first with one foot, then the other.

Her muscles knew the motion so well she could execute perfect tendus with little thought, and the familiar exercise soothed her. Six o'clock passed, then seven. By nine, fear began to gnaw at her. If, through some miracle, Irusya had accepted Lev's proposal, they would have raced to Katenka's long ago to share the news with her. She had assumed Lev would come on his own in search of consolation had he been rebuffed, but perhaps she had been wrong.

Bundling herself up against the snow, Katenka started for the bookstore. She did not have enough money for a droshky, so she walked, and the cold wind felt as if it would tear apart the seams of her coat. When she reached the shop, Lev was not there, but she found Mitya sitting near the stove with two of the other men she had seen there the night before.

"What brings you here?" he asked, in a tone she did not recognize. He did not stand to greet her.

"I am looking for my brother," she said.

"He's gone, and not likely to be back anytime soon," Mitya said. Now he rose and took her by the arm, wrenching it as he dragged her to the back room. Lev's cot had been stripped of its linens, and all of his possessions were gone. "Did you know she would do this to him?"

"I tried to tell him, but he would not listen." Tears smarted in her eyes.

"Is this the way it is with you dancers?" he asked. "Loyal only until someone richer comes along?"

"That is a hateful thing to say." Katenka met his angry glare. The eyes behind the lenses of his spectacles were hard and cold. "I would never do that."

"I want to trust you, Katenka."

"You can, always," she said. "I thought you knew that."

"Lying is a delightful thing for it leads to the truth."

"You used to quote Pushkin to me."

"You object to Dostoyevsky?" he asked. "These are dangerous times, and we risk everything if we do not choose our friends carefully."

One of the men stepped into the doorway. "Can we go outside?" she whispered.

"No," Mitya said. "I will come to you tomorrow, at your flat, if that is agreeable to you. We will speak then."

Her heart was pounding. What was happening? It was bad enough that she couldn't find Lev, but now to have Mitya lashing out at her as well? How could she endure that? "I've class in the morning and rehearsals until four."

"I will be there at five."

But he wasn't. She waited until eight before giving up on him. And still she'd had no word from Lev.

January 1900

15

The stranger facing us was tall and extremely broad, with square shoulders and a ruggedly handsome face framed with unkempt honey-colored curls. I ought, perhaps, to have been frightened by the menace emanating from his icy-blue eyes, but I was not. Something in his appearance—the well-cared-for but worn suit visible through his open overcoat, perhaps—tugged at me.

"I am Lady Emily Hargreaves," I said in Russian. "I take it you are a friend of Nemetseva's."

He sneered when I introduced myself and replied in surprisingly good French. "I am not interested in your bourgeois title."

I shrugged. "I'm not either, particularly, but I see no need to completely abandon good manners. Who are you?"

"That is none of your concern." He pulled himself up to his full, and not inconsiderable, height, stepped into a wide stance, and moved his tight fists to his hips, as if to intimidate us.

Cécile sighed. "*Mon dieu*, you dramatic young men! I have neither the time nor the inclination to coax you along." She pulled one of the pictures from the corner fasteners glued onto the photograph album's pages and flipped it over. "The names are written on the back.

We know you are neither Irusya nor Katenka, and as we're already acquainted with Mitya, that leaves only Lev."

"Lev, of course," I said. "You're Katenka's brother." I tried to remember everything he had said to her in the costume room at the Mariinsky. Mostly, though, I recalled the fear and pain in her voice, coupled with its unexpected force.

"Who I am is of no consequence to you," he said. "I have come to collect something that belongs to me."

"How did you enter the premises?" I asked. "I locked the door behind us."

"I, too, have a key." He removed it from his pocket, waved it in front of me, and crossed purposely to a battered wooden chest, which he pulled open. It was the only piece of furniture in the flat that did not seem to fit. One side was covered with haphazard-looking notches, carved with a knife that must have been dull. After riffling through the contents, he pulled out a bundle of envelopes tied with a pale-pink satin ribbon and slipped it underneath his coat.

"You cannot come in here and remove things," I said, grabbing—unsuccessfully—for the letters. "There is an ongoing investigation into Nemetseva's death."

"An investigation that has nothing to do with my personal property," he said. "Good day, ladies." Making his final word sound like a vile insult, he turned on his heel and left the apartment. I pursued him as fast as I could down the stairs, but did not catch him before he disappeared down a side street. The cold air burned my lungs, and I began to feel chilled as soon as I stopped running. Unable to determine where he had gone, I returned to the apartment to complete my search, beginning with the chest from which he had removed the papers. It was full of postcards and programs from the ballet, opera, and theatre.

On the desk in the smaller of the sitting rooms I found blank sheets of paper identical to that used for the notes I had received. A cursory examination of the blotter on the desk did not reveal anything related to them, nor anything else of use. I had hoped to find something that would better illuminate the ballerina's life, Irusya's apartment, so beautifully appointed, contained little of a personal nature. Cécile and I retreated to Masha's, where Colin planned to meet us later, and soon were ensconced in her exquisite blue drawing room.

Masha and Cécile fell into animated conversation—something about two former lovers having a scandalous public argument over which of them should keep the dog they had once shared. I admit to not paying attention. The pictures in Nemetseva's flat suggested she had a close relationship with Katenka's brother. Had they been more than friends? Why hadn't Katenka ever mentioned this? If I asked her about this now, would she still claim to have had no recent contact with him?

I had considered professional jealousy a viable motive for Nemetseva's murder, but had found no evidence of anyone hurt by or begrudging of her success. Agrippina Alexandrovna had—rather forcefully—suggested that Katenka alone benefitted from her friend's murder, but I had uncovered nothing indicative of a violent or bitter streak in her. Furthermore, she could not have committed the crime herself, and I had a difficult time believing she would have hired someone else to take on the task for her. If nothing else, she couldn't have afforded to do so. Perhaps I needed to adjust my focus. Nemetseva's private life might prove more illuminating.

"Masha, what do you know about Nemetseva?" I asked. "Did she have spectacular fallings-out with lovers?"

"I remember a brief flirtation with Anatole Emsky that ended as soon as his engagement was announced."

"She didn't throw him over?" I asked.

"No, not at all." Masha laughed. "If anything, she was the one disappointed, although I cannot imagine it had a lasting effect on her. As I said, it was extremely short-lived. I shouldn't be surprised if the man never got so far even as kissing her." This contradicted what Katenka had told me. I distinctly remembered her saying that Irusya had ended the relationship and that she had done it badly. "Later there was a prince—Nikolai Danilovich Ukhov—with whom she fell deeply in love. It was rather sweet, if a bit indiscreet for my taste. She was so young and so infatuated it was impossible for her to hide her feelings."

"Did it cause a scandal?" I asked.

"Not as such," Masha said. "It did, however, sate Petersburg's appetite for gossip. They conducted the affair in plain view and ended it when the prince married. She managed her heartbreak with dignity—never spoke of it—but everyone agreed that afterward she infused her dancing with a deeper level of emotion. From then on, I've heard nothing about her private life. There was a flirtation with the Grand Duke Vladimir Alexandrovich later, but it was never serious on either side. The man is old enough to be her father and categorically devoted to his wife. They were never anything more than friends, amusing each other."

Masha's story explained why Nemetseva valued discretion in her relationship with Vasilii; she would not want to act out another affair in public after such a devastating outcome. It also made me wonder about the ripples caused by her heartbreak. How much did Nikolai Danilovich's wife know about her husband's previous love? If anything had transpired to bring it to the forefront of gossip again, Masha would have heard and mentioned it, but what if the wife discovered something on her own? Something that might inspire a jealous rage. Recalling the police evidence that the murderer had to be considerably taller than Nemetseva, I decided it was unlikely that the prince's wife had struck the fatal blows, although I admit to being rather taken with the idea. My imagination was getting the better of me.

A footman in a powdered wig and elegant emerald green-and-gold livery entered the room and announced my husband's arrival.

Colin followed close on the man's heels, his face red with cold. "It's bitter out there," he said, warming his hands in front of Masha's large fire. "Any luck at Nemetseva's apartment?"

I told him what we had found and how Lev had interrupted us. "He wouldn't confirm his identity, but it is obvious he's Katenka's brother."

"That's rather in line with what I learned about the dagger this afternoon. I consulted a man I've known for some time and whom I trust absolutely. He is an adjutant attached to an admiral," Colin said. "He recognized the weapon as one given to officers as part of their uniforms and dated it from somewhere between eighteen seventy and eighteen eighty. He confirmed my suspicion that there is no way to identify to whom it belonged, but when I told him it may be the instrument of Nemetseva's death and asked if he could think of any naval connections she might have, he surprised me. He said that Katenka's father had been a navy man and that he had known him quite well when they were both early on in their careers. He never met his daughter, but recognized her name when he read an interview with Nemetseva in which she mentioned how close she and Katenka were."

"What became of the father?" Cécile asked.

"He died in a naval accident when Katenka was young," Colin said. "It's entirely possible that she—or, more likely, her brother—would have kept his dagger."

A chill passed through me. "You don't think—"

"My, my, my," Masha said, her lips curling and her dimples deepening. "Perhaps we do have a crime of jealousy here, the desperate attempt of a dancer to win her moment on the stage."

"Katenka could not have organized it more brilliantly," Cécile said. "She triumphed in *Swan Lake*. No one who saw her will ever forget that performance, not only because of Nemetseva's death, but because it was the first time Legnani had allowed someone to take a role that she all but owned."

"And now our shy Katenka is a principal dancer," Masha said. "Rising to the rank in a blaze of glory."

"That old ballerina you spoke with—what was her name?" Cécile asked. "She told you, did she not, that she saw Nemetseva come out the stage door in a cloak? A hooded cloak. What if it wasn't Nemetseva but Katenka, bent on a murderous errand? Perhaps the old woman didn't notice because she was expecting to see Nemetseva."

"You are letting your imagination run away without your common sense," Colin said.

"I appreciate your enthusiasm, Cécile, but must agree with my husband. If it had happened that way, Agrippina Alexandrovna would have seen them both exit through the door, and, at any rate, Katenka couldn't have killed Irusya herself," I said. "Regardless of anything else, she wouldn't have had nearly enough time to get cleaned up and back on stage. But her brother—"

"*Oui*, Kallista," Cécile said. "Her brother. She may have persuaded him to do the dark deed on her behalf. He would not have required any payment, and it would explain why she denies having any contact with him."

"Jealousy is a powerful motive," I said. "Irusya and Katenka were best friends, but their fortunes took markedly different directions, one living a life of pampered luxury, the other residing only a few steps away from squalor."

"No dancer is pampered," Masha said. "They work astonishingly hard and suffer a great deal of pain."

"Yes, *bien sûr*," Cécile said. "But you understand Kallista's meaning. One girl was a success; the other was not, until she managed to eliminate the competition."

"It is a viable theory," Colin said, his voice serious. "But to prove it requires evidence. Hard evidence, not rampant speculation. And you must tread carefully. Murder is a dangerous game."

That evening, back at the hotel, I focused on Katenka. Could she be behind her friend's death? In so many ways every sense revolted against the idea, but I could not deny the possibility. Her quiet beauty and passionate presence on stage were at odds with the image of her as a murderer, but those two same characteristics were also at odds with each other and did not take into account the hints of strength and conviction I had observed in her. She reminded me of St. Petersburg. The city was cosmopolitan and sophisticated, but there was an edge to it, something verging on the barbaric that reminded me of the horrid bits that always lurked in fairy tales. Instead of this being a liability, it somehow managed to become something else altogether, bringing to the city a gravitas or layer of depth or something—I could not quite put my finger on it—beyond that I had felt anywhere else. Its endless complexities tugged at me, pulling me in and luring me into its darkness, filling me with trepidation at what it might lead me to unearth.

Ekaterina Petrovna
February 1898

After that terrible day in November, Katenka went more than a month without hearing from either her brother or from Mitya. She returned to the bookstore, but the owner confirmed that Lev had left his job and moved out, leaving only a note for her and no forwarding address. In it, he begged her not to look for him and explained that he realized now he was not meant for an ordinary life. Marrying Irusya would have kept him from his true, noble purpose. And that purpose, he insisted, could prove dangerous, so he would remain silent until he felt it safe to see her again.

As for Mitya . . . he had no right to be angry with her because of something Irusya had done. She wrote to him twice but received no reply, and she felt her heart begin to harden.

The one person she would have preferred not to see, the one person who had catalyzed all this misery, she could not avoid. The morning after she had rejected Lev, Irusya arrived late to company class, leading Petipa, in his extremely bad Russian, to reprimand her and state, in front of everyone, that having succeeded in carrying one performance as Swanilda was not enough to secure a career. Irusya stared at the floor and nodded. Katenka tried to catch her eye, but her friend never looked in her direction.

After class, Katenka had called to her, but Irusya pretended not to hear; it was not until the following day that the two spoke.

"I am ashamed of myself, Katenka," Irusya said. She had arrived, unannounced, after midnight, at Katenka's flat, where they had spent so many happy hours. Everything felt different now as Katenka listened to her talk, and she wondered if she could ever feel close to her again. "It's not that I don't love him. You must understand that. I don't think I shall ever love anyone else in quite the same way. But . . ." She dropped her head back and sighed. "There is so much I want from my life, Katenka. I could never have made your brother happy. I realized that a while ago, and I have tried to tell him as much, but he wouldn't listen. He can say whatever he wants now, but someday he would come to regret not having a regular life, with a family. I don't want a house full of children and to become old and fat watching them grow. I want to dance and I want to travel the world. I want to be on stage in London and Paris and Milan."

"Lev would never have kept you from that. He adores you."

"Right now he thinks he would not want to hold me back, but I know he is wrong."

"You cannot know what is in another's heart."

"But I do know, Katenka, what is in my heart," Irusya said. She took her friend's hand. "I love him, but he cannot make me happy. It would be unfair to marry him. Unfair to myself. You probably despise me for admitting it, but it is the truth. I do not want to be the wife of a Petersburg shopkeeper. I do not want to have to entertain his wretched political friends twice a week and pretend to be interested in whatever nonsense they're talking about. Can you forgive me for that?"

Katenka sat in silence for a while, staring at her friend. Yes, she had to admit Irusya was still her friend. Her only friend, now that Mitya was gone. She had no right to be angry at Irusya, who answered her brother's proposal with candor and honesty. Her words had been brutal, but they were also the truth. "You don't need my forgiveness,

Irusya. You've done nothing to offend me. You are my dearest friend, and I want nothing more than for you to find your happiness. I would be dishonest if I said I hadn't hoped that would be with Lev, but if it isn't, I can't force you to feel something you don't."

"I do worry about him, you know," Irusya said. "Have you heard anything from him?"

"I have not. He left without a word." The lie came easier than Katenka expected. She might still consider Irusya a friend, but that friend had broken Lev's heart. She did not deserve any news about him.

Now, three months later, she and Irusya were sitting together again, but not in Katenka's apartment. Things had become easier between them, but they never felt quite the same again. Perhaps that was inevitable. Tonight, they were at a party, much like the one at which everything had changed. At least that was how Katenka viewed it. She divided her life between the time before Irusya fell in love with Kolya and the time after. It might sound ridiculous; she knew that, but she did not care. On that night, she lost her best friend, her brother, and Mitya.

Not precisely *lost*, perhaps, but that was how it felt. The three most important relationships in her life shifted unalterably as a result of the transfer of Irusya's affections to Kolya.

Katenka had danced in *Le Corsaire* that evening, but the fatigue consuming her did not come from the performance. Not seeing Mitya backstage still gutted her, leaving her insides twisted and hurt. Her heart had not hardened as much as she hoped it would. When she had performed the same role in October, he had waited for her with a book of Byron's work, knowing the ballet had been based on one of his poems. No one had waited for her backstage tonight.

Ambushed in her dressing room by a desperate Irusya, Katenka had acquiesced without so much as a fight to attend Kolya's party. What did it matter anyway? She had nowhere else to go but home, a place that before had always offered comfort. Yet since Lev left, every piece of family furniture—the objects she had fought to save after her grandfather died—served only to remind her of long-ago happiness she would never again have. She shook her head, wishing she could force herself to engage with her surroundings, but the effort was fruitless. She was standing in front of the buffet table, staring blankly at the food without even picking up a plate. Someone touched her shoulder.

"You look as unhappy to be here as I. They tell us it is an honor to be invited." Sofya Guryevna Pashkova, a fellow corps dancer, slipped her arm through Katenka's. "Yet I am not sure why we believe them. I don't particularly enjoy the company of princes. I do, however, enjoy their caviar. Look." She had in her hand a small tin, into which she scooped a heaping portion. "They never notice, and even if they did, I don't think they'd mind. It doesn't occur to them that we can't afford it on our own. Come home with me and share my stolen feast?"

The girls were giggling conspiratorially as they thanked their host and headed for the cloakroom, but Katenka stopped when she heard familiar voices coming from a nearby dark alcove. Sofya went ahead to collect their coats, but Katenka stayed, pressing herself against the wall so she would not be seen.

"I cannot be your first, *douchka*," Kolya was saying. "I would never do that to you. It would not be fair."

"I don't care about fair," Irusya replied.

"You would eventually and then you would despise me. Come, let's go back and have more champagne. Your beauty has addled me enough tonight; you must grant me a reprieve."

"I love you," Irusya said.

"And I, you, *douchka*. And I, you."

Katenka frowned, surprised at Kolya's words. Maybe he was not so bad as she feared. Sofya had returned with the coats and told her their host had offered the use of his carriage, which meant they did not have to pay a driver themselves. It was a much-appreciated gesture.

"Perhaps the parties aren't so bad," Katenka said, once they were at the little table in Sofya's sitting room. "We were brought home in style—"

"And warm!" Sofya added. "The blankets in the prince's carriage were tremendous, weren't they? Would that I had a coat made out of them!"

"And we have the most delicious caviar I have ever tasted." Katenka spread more of it on a thin slice of black bread. "I am so grateful you reached out to me. I've never been good at parties and thought I was the only one who does not enjoy running with the fast set. Why did we never speak at school?"

"I thought you despised me," Sofya said. "You hardly talked to anyone. Now I know it's because you're shy, but then I was much younger."

"You always seemed so poised. I think I was afraid of you."

"Afraid of me? Absurd! You are the one who was at the top of our class."

"Until I failed miserably at our graduation performance," Katenka said.

"You're the only one who remembers that," Sofya said, filling Katenka's glass with more wine. Good Russian wine, not French. "A performance of yours that is—forgive me—lackluster is still miles ahead of what the rest of us can do on our best days. You lack only confidence. You used to have it when we were in school, and someday it will return to you. In the meantime, I am happy to have you in the corps with me. I know that anytime I lose my place, all I have to do is look to you and I'll have a good guide to follow."

Sofya's attitude was so different from her own. Katenka felt refreshed and more relaxed than she had in as long as she could remember. "Don't you want to get promoted?"

Sofya shrugged. "Yes, of course, but I know I shall never be a prima ballerina. I should like some solo roles, but really nothing more. I earn enough to get by and am fortunate to have this apartment. It's not much, but I can afford it, and I am most content. I love the ballet and I get to dance every day. What more could I want?"

Katenka stayed at Sofya's that night, sleeping on the narrow settee in the sitting room. When she woke up the next morning with a headache, she was glad to remember that it was Sunday, and there would be no company class. She pulled back the curtain covering the window. It had snowed overnight, and the city looked so clean and perfect beneath its fresh, downy blanket. Its brightness revived her. Today, she decided, would be the start of a new way forward.

16

After my run-in with Lev, I was determined to speak to his sister, but I decided not to give her any warning. The following morning was Sunday, so she would not have class, and she was unlikely to go out early in the day. Colin accompanied me, and we found her at home, still in her dressing gown, just finishing a breakfast of black bread with butter and a small bowl of porridge. She insisted on giving us tea and apologized at her state of dishabille.

"I'm afraid the ballerina's life is not suited to early mornings. I see you, Mr. Hargreaves, raising your eyebrows," she said, bestowing upon him a charming smile and then looking away quickly and lowering her voice. "You are quite correct to think that eleven o'clock is not early morning, but it feels that way when you've been at the theatre until after midnight and don't get to sleep before two or three o'clock. When I am not up so late, I like to go to church, though I have not done that so often as I should like to recently."

"You are quite right to chastise me," Colin said. "I can imagine you are utterly exhausted after a performance. Forgive me if I seemed judgmental."

Katenka turned to me. "People always forgive him, don't they? He is so handsome; how could they not?" She blushed as she spoke.

"Now, what can I do for you? I don't think you've come in search of breakfast."

"We've come to ask about your brother," Colin said. "What can you tell me about him?"

"Very little, I'm afraid. I have not seen him in years." She accompanied her lie with an emphatic shake of her head. "He was my closest companion when I was a child. My father died when I was quite young, and my mother never really stopped mourning him. Our grandfather lived with us. He was very strict and very formal, but he loved us very much. Lev is older than I, and always looked out for me. We grew apart after I graduated from school. He had been working at Melnikov's Bookshop on Nevsky Prospekt, but after he quit his position, he moved. It is not so easy to stay close when you are not in the same city."

I took note of the fact that she did not ask why we were inquiring about her brother. "But he returned for Nemetseva's funeral, didn't he?" I asked.

"Not so far as I know. As I said, we have not kept in touch."

"You haven't seen him?" I asked. "Even at the funeral."

"No." She did not look at me as she answered.

"I cannot understand why you are lying," I said, "and I know you are lying. I met your brother yesterday at Nemetseva's flat. Why did you never mention his connection to her? He had come to collect the letters he'd written her." This last point had me on shaky ground, but it seemed a reasonable guess. If I was lucky, Katenka might confirm my suspicion.

"I don't understand why any of this matters. You cannot think he had something to do with her death." A rough edge crept into her voice. "Lev is not violent. He would never—" A flush of bright crimson erupted on her neck and worked its way to her forehead.

"No one is suggesting your brother is violent," Colin said, leaning close to her and speaking in the kindest, most sympathetic tone. "It is important that we know everything we can about Nemetseva's life. It is the only way we can hope to bring her murderer to justice."

"Do you know why Lev removed the letters from Nemetseva's apartment?"

"Of course not," she said. "As I said, we have not been in contact for some time. Yes, I did see him after the funeral. I should have told you the truth about that, but I . . . I . . . you must understand that things in Russia are not always so simple as they are in other places. Lev wanted to sever any connection between us to protect me. From what, I don't know, but I am doing my best to honor his request."

"These have been extremely trying times for you." Colin's voice, so perfectly soothing, could coax anyone to trust him. "I did not realize how concern for your brother has compounded your suffering. Do you know what he is involved in? I may be in a position to help him."

"That's very kind, Mr. Hargreaves," Katenka said, looking in his eyes and holding his gaze. "I don't know any of the details of his situation, but I am confident that he would never engage in behavior that could be viewed as underhanded or immoral. You must believe me. He is a good man. He had nothing to do with—" She covered her eyes with her hand. "Forgive me. I am overcome. This has all been too much for me. Lev would never involve himself in anything that could lead to him requiring help."

We thanked her and left the flat. Her duplicity had convinced me that I could not dismiss her as having played a serious role in the murder. Colin, however, had a different impression. He believed her when she claimed to be out of her depth emotionally.

"Her best friend is dead, and, even if she had nothing to do with it, she's bound to feel guilty because her career has improved as a result. I shall see what I can learn about her brother through official channels. Most likely he's some sort of political activist, which would explain Katenka's reluctance to give us any information. She may, in fact, know very little. The bookstore at which he works is a haven for any number of individuals the government considers to have unacceptable ideological positions. Radical views are not appreciated here, and holding them can be as dangerous for one's family as for oneself."

"Lev was in love with Nemetseva," I said. "He came to collect the letters he had written to her so that he would not now be suspected of killing her."

"Your mind works in the most extraordinary fashion. How did you reach that conclusion?"

"What other sort of letters would he be after?" I asked. "You can't suspect that Nemetseva, whose entire life was ballet and her aristocratic lover, was involved in politics, revolutionary or otherwise."

"I wouldn't be so quick to assume that." He flagged down a droshky and held my hand as I stepped into it. "Politics can seep into the most unexpected places."

"The only politics with which Nemetseva would be concerned are those in the theatre and those on the outside that affect the theatre. Any sort of governmental upheaval could threaten the stability of cultural institutions, the ballet included."

"A valid point," Colin said, "but let's find out more before we start anticipating a revolution."

He dropped me at the hotel and continued on to the Winter Palace, where his work would keep him occupied for the rest of the day. I collected the key and our mail from the front desk. There was a thick letter from Anglemore Park. Eager for news of the boys, I ripped it open and started to read as I climbed the stairs to our suite. There was something from each of them. Henry's portion was a dictated litany about what he viewed as the intellectual deficiencies of his brothers, his evidence being their complete lack of interest in copying Egyptian hieroglyphs from a book that was his own current obsession. Richard and Tom had drawn pictures, Richard's of a small boy on an extremely large horse, and Tom's showing three boys fishing in a red pond. Also enclosed was a lengthy update from Nanny on everything they were doing.

I was so distracted by her missive (she wondered if Henry, always alarmingly precocious, should be sent to school before he turned eight) that I almost didn't notice the all-too-familiar form, a tall Cossack hat on his head, slouched against the wall just outside our door. I did see him, though, and made no attempt to hide my displeasure at being ambushed by him.

"Don't glower at me," Sebastian said. "You seemed upset last time when I let myself into your room, so I thought you would prefer this. I've been waiting a brutally long time for you to return; you might show a little compassion."

"I might if I had asked you to come," I said, folding the letter and returning it to its envelope. "Why are you here?"

He glanced about furtively. "I don't like to speak about such matters in public."

"Fine," I said. "You may come to the suite, but if you're looking to brag about your latest criminal activities, you needn't bother. I've heard all about them already and have no interest in any lurid details you might share." At current pace, I worried that Sebastian might make off with the better part of the fortunes of the entire Russian aristocracy.

"You know how rich and profligate they all are," he said. "This city is the perfect playground for me. But I won't bore you with the details as it would only give you ammunition should you ever try to turn me in to the authorities. I must say, Kallista, you are looking most fetching. The cold air agrees with you. It's as if St. Petersburg has turned you into a snow princess. I should like to see you in white fox. It would suit you."

"I do wish you would refrain from speaking to me like that," I said. I unlocked the door, which he made a great show of holding open for me before following me inside. I hung up my coat and my muff, discarded my hat, and pulled off my gloves. "Where is your overcoat?" I asked.

"I left it in the cloakroom downstairs. I would not let the horrid little man have my hat, though, no matter how much of a fuss he made."

"You'll be shocked to hear that I'm not altogether unhappy to see you," I said, lowering myself onto a chair opposite the settee in our sitting room. "It saves me the trouble of having to track you down." Although I knew his theft of the imperial egg was not connected to Nemetseva's murder, I had wanted to ask him about what he had observed when he left it for her.

His jaw dropped. He had been walking toward me and stopped so suddenly that his hat flew off his head. He caught it neatly and regained his composure. "This is most welcome news. Shall I send for some vodka, or would you prefer champagne?"

"We shan't need either," I said. "Sit on the settee and tell me, in as much detail as possible, exactly how you got the imperial egg to Nemetseva and why you decided to give it to her."

"You know I don't like to divulge specifics of my methods. They are, in effect, proprietary secrets."

"Talk. Now." I leaned against the back of the chair and crossed my arms.

He sighed. "I never could deny you anything. *Why* is the simplest part of your question, so I shall begin there. Nemetseva was an artist of unparalleled skill and the lilies of the valley egg an example of supreme craftsmanship. All ballerinas appreciate flowers, so Nemetseva was a natural choice to receive it. I know the empress enjoys her trinkets, but she has so many that they are all but lost to clutter. Have you ever seen her private rooms?"

"I have not and there is no need for you to describe how you stole the egg. I shall allow you to defend your proprietary secrets."

"You are kindness itself, although I will say it was shockingly simple.

Security in the palace is preposterous; a child could gain access with minimal effort. I had hoped for more of a challenge." Moving with supreme insouciance, he draped one leg over the other. "It would have been too tedious to leave it in her flat while she slept, so I chose to place it in her dressing room during the performance of *Swan Lake*. What use is my occupation if it does not stimulate even the slightest excitement? Although even that was not so difficult as I had hoped. There's a shocking crush of people backstage. Nemetseva didn't dance in the first act, so I hovered in the vicinity of her dressing room, waiting for her to finish her preparations. Naturally, I had made discreet inquiries as to her habits and had learned that once in her costume and makeup, she liked to go to a practice room to warm up. As soon as she did this, I went into her dressing room. I placed the egg—and the note I'd written—into the pocket of her cloak."

"You put it in the pocket?" I crinkled my brow. "So we have no way of knowing whether she found it before or after she went to the stage door after the second act, or even if she found it at all. It might have fallen out of the cloak during the murder. Did you notice anything unusual in the dressing room?"

"Only that she shared it with two other dancers. I should have thought a prima ballerina would merit a private space, but there were three chairs set up in a row along the counter beneath the mirror that runs the length of the wall. A jumble of hairpins and brushes and makeup and I know not what else was at each of the stations."

"Who were the other dancers?"

"I don't know her name, but one was in the corps. I could tell from her costume. I must have seen twenty other girls dressed the same. The other was Ekaterina Petrovna, who so gloriously completed the role of her dead friend."

That Katenka was there came as no surprise, but it did make me consider one thing: Could she have managed to dance so well when she took Nemetseva's place if she knew her friend was dead?

It seemed unlikely, and this gave me the strongest evidence of her innocence so far. Still, though, I had many doubts about her.

"Can you recall any other details?"

"I may have nosed around a bit."

"Don't make me prod, Sebastian."

"You take the fun out of everything," he said. "There were point shoes and ribbons and needles and thread. Nothing out of the ordinary. Or so I thought, until I found that one of our ballerinas had a stash of some sort of political pamphlets, calling for workers to unite and organize."

"This was sitting out in the open?" I asked.

"No, no, it was in a bag shoved in a corner underneath a coat in what seemed to me a very bad attempt to hide something in plain sight. That's what made me interested in looking through it. Why bother to cover something of no consequence?"

"Could you tell if it belonged to Nemetseva?"

"There was nothing in or on the bag that identified its owner, but the coat was not hers. She had worn a blue velvet cloak—fur-lined, quite spectacular—to the theatre that evening. Naturally, I would never have put the egg in it if I weren't certain it was hers."

"Can you recall anything more about the text of the pamphlets?" I asked.

"I have no affinity for politics," he said. "I read only enough to know I'd be bored going on. That's all there is to say, Kallista. May we have our vodka now?"

Not wanting to spend more time with him than strictly necessary, I refused to call down for vodka and instead offered him some of Colin's whisky. Delighted, he accepted with gusto. He had earned his reward, and now I would have to discover which of the dancers had a penchant for politics. Or confirm, really. I had little doubt my suspicions would prove correct.

Ekaterina Petrovna
June 1898

When Lev and Mitya had first abandoned her, Katenka thought she would never recover from the blow, but her ability to adapt surprised her. First, she noticed that she no longer woke up every morning with an ache in her heart. Then she realized that she didn't even think about them every day. After that, her dancing began to improve. Cecchetti was the first to notice. "You are more focused," he said. "This is good."

Petipa complimented her as well but did not give her any better roles. She knew she would have to work harder still and, almost more important, prove to him—to them all—that she could be relied upon to perform consistently at this higher standard. No one wanted to risk giving a solo to a dancer who might wilt under the pressure.

Now that she was no longer struggling artistically, she began to enjoy herself more on stage and in the classroom, and this, more than anything else, enabled her to soar. Finally, the passion and the steps began to connect, and she started to understand the words Pierina Legnani had spoken to her, all those months ago at Irusya's luncheon. For the first time, she felt in control of her talent.

She did not see much of Irusya outside class anymore. They were both busy rehearsing and taking private lessons, and Irusya spent most of her evenings with Kolya and his set. She always invited Katenka, but Katenka rarely came, half wishing Irusya would stop asking her.

"Will I see you tonight?" Irusya asked, taking Katenka by surprise in the corridor after class. "I'm throwing a party for the end of the season. You can bring Sofya," Irusya said. "I should like to get to know her, too. I miss you, Katenka. I don't want us to grow apart."

Guilt stabbed at Katenka. She had been telling herself that Irusya had pushed her away, taken up with her new friends, but the truth was that it was Katenka who had caused the breach. As much as she hated the idea of going to the party, she could do nothing but accept the invitation. No sooner had she done so than she realized that, despite everything, she remained incapable of refusing Irusya.

It proved easy enough to persuade Sofya to join her, although she admonished her friend not to take any of Irusya's caviar home with her. This made Sofya laugh and state unequivocally that she was not so uncouth as to steal from a friend. For a while, they had sat with a group of dancers, talking about ballet, but before long the others had been lured away by gentlemen.

Kolya had spoken briefly to Katenka when he first arrived, but ever since had been firmly at Irusya's side, with eyes for no one else. Irusya, too good a hostess to let him monopolize her, and, if Katenka knew her at all, which she did, fond of making him just a little jealous, pushed him away good-naturedly. They bantered with each other, and when Katenka saw the affection in Irusya's eyes, she began to forgive her friend for having broken Lev's heart.

The apartment, crowded with guests, had grown quite warm, so she decided to slip into Irusya's bedroom, wanting to throw some water on her face. If nothing else, it would bring her back to reality. When she cracked open the bedroom door, she heard voices. Irusya and Kolya.

"Stay with me, just this once. No one will know," Irusya said.

"I was not joking, *douchka*," Kolya was saying. "We can take things between us only so far. I love you and I respect you, but I will not put you in a position you will eventually come to regret."

"You would not say that if I had had other lovers before you," Irusya said.

"That would be another situation altogether," he said. "But it is not the situation we are in. Stop pouting. It will make you lose your beauty, and I could not bear that."

Katenka was surprised Kolya was holding her friend at arm's length, but there had been stories—rumors, nothing more—that the emperor, when he was tsarevitch had made similar statements to Mathilde Kschessinska. Mathilde, as everyone knew, had somehow overcome her lover's concerns. Katenka had assumed for months that Irusya had done the same. Perhaps she did not know Irusya quite so well as she had thought. She went back to Sofya, told her they had stayed long enough, and together they walked the whole distance back to Katenka's flat, drinking in the beauty of the white night. Slowly, they climbed the stairs up to the flat.

"I would much rather face these steps every day than live in Irusya's apartment," Sofya said, as they started up the third flight.

"That reveals a predilection to madness I had not expected to find in you," Katenka said.

"No, no madness at all." Sofya paused to catch her breath. This made Katenka laugh. "You are more used to the stairs than I am! I should not be breathless otherwise. I only have two flights to reach my own flat. But I am quite serious about what I said regarding Irusya. I do not envy your friend her bourgeois trappings. They are pretty and comfortable, but they keep her from seeing what is important."

"Now you sound like my old friend Mitya," Katenka said. They had nearly reached her flat. "Mitya."

"Yes, I heard his name the first time," Sofya said. "Who is—"

"Mitya!"

Katenka raced to her door, in front of which Mitya was sprawled, unconscious, on the floor.

January 1900

17

Colin did not return to our room until the next morning, and he devoured the letters from Nanny and the boys as soon as I showed them to him. His reaction to Sebastian's visit was somewhat less enthusiastic, but he did not begrudge him the whisky I had given him and admitted to being impressed that Sebastian had spotted the pamphlets in the dance bag in Nemetseva's dressing room. Although he had been up all night, he was alert and full of energy. He had a break in his schedule and suggested we take the opportunity to ice-skate while discussing my next steps in the investigation of Nemetseva's murder.

We reached the Angliyskaya Embankment, named for its proximity to the British embassy, and descended the stairs to the patch of ice that had been cleared of snow and smoothed for skaters. Taking seats on one of the benches set up against the tall granite walls built to contain the wide river, we fastened our skates and soon had joined the lively crowd gliding on the ice. The neoclassical buildings lining both sides of the Neva and the bridges spanning it formed an incomparable backdrop, but after we had taken only a few turns around, the tenor of the skaters changed.

People careened by, losing their balance as they tried to stop too quickly in order to look across the river, to the embankment in front of the Menshikov Palace. There, on the top of the wall, stood our ghostly ballerina, waving a crimson scarf. The ice became a scene of pandemonium as skaters crashed into each other. Some set off to cross the river, hoping to catch her. Others rushed to remove their skates and ran up the stairs and toward the nearby Nikolaevsky Bridge, racing to reach the dancer before she disappeared.

Colin held me firmly by the arm. "There is no point chasing," he said. "She will have her escape route well planned."

I agreed but suggested that we remove our skates regardless and make our way to the other side via the bridge. When we reached the halfway point of the bridge, the dancer leapt down from her perch. There was a not-insignificant crowd of people around her, but they parted to let her through. She was gone when we arrived.

"Where did she go?" Colin asked in both Russian and French. The mood of the people was shocking. They were quiet and subdued, most of them staring at the ground.

"Why does it matter?" one man asked. "She cannot rest in peace, wherever she may go." Someone else mumbled something about bad deaths. A woman said they had all seen the gory gash on the dancer's neck as she glided past them. Another man insisted she was floating above the ground.

"Did anyone try to stop her?" Colin asked.

"You don't touch the dead," the first man said. "Not when they've come back from the grave."

"I can assure you that is not the case," Colin said. "This is a woman—who is very much alive—pretending to be a ghost. You were all within arm's reach of her. Surely you saw that she is living and breathing."

"I did not see her breathe," the woman said, and several other people shouted their agreement.

"When she crossed the street, where did she go?" I asked.

"She didn't go anywhere," she said. "She vanished, just as you'd expect a ghost would." She crossed herself and hurried away. The rest of the crowd, murmuring anxiously, followed suit.

Colin and I separated, each canvassing different roads that led away from the river, asking everyone we encountered if he had seen the ballerina. We had agreed to meet, when finished, in front of the gray granite Rumyantsev Obelisk that stood in the center of a small park next to the Cadets College housed in the Menshikov Palace. Colin was already there, stamping his feet to keep warm, when I approached the monument.

"No luck at all, I'm afraid," I said. "No one admits to having seen her."

"I had the same result," he said.

"She could have stashed a coat, hat, and boots in a doorway," I said. "As soon as she pulled them on, no one would recognize her."

"I don't remember anyone saying they saw the bloody gash before," Colin said. "Is she escalating her performance? And if so, why?"

"This was a bolder gesture," I said. "She appeared in broad daylight in a crowded place with no easy way to disappear. When she was on the hotel balcony, all she had to do was step back inside. At the cemetery, she had chosen her location carefully so that she could make her escape before anyone reached her."

"And across from the Yusupov Palace, she could vanish into one of the buildings long before anyone could get over to the bridge and across it," Colin said.

"Today's appearance required her to be prepared in a different way," I said. "She had to do something to make the crowd want to keep their distance. Covering her neck in gore, which I imagine would not be difficult for someone acquainted with the use of stage makeup, would—and did—do the trick."

"I agree," Colin said. "You don't have any mysterious message in a pocket, do you?"

I checked my coat. "No. Nothing."

"What can she mean to achieve?" He took my arm. "Walk. I'm half frozen."

"It's no secret that I'm investigating Nemetseva's death," I said. "Perhaps the dancer is hoping to motivate me to work more quickly? Even if I didn't see her myself, I would hear about it. It's all anyone's talking about in the city."

"How could she possibly think her actions would have any impact on the length of time required to solve a murder? It makes no sense."

"Grieving people are ruled by emotion, not rationality."

"True, but I still think there is something else at play," he said. "What are we missing?"

We returned to the hotel for luncheon and had not yet finished our soup when the same German woman who, days earlier, had disturbed my breakfast marched over to our table, a look of triumph on her face.

"I have seen her myself, Lady Emily, and can assure you she is a ghost."

"The ballerina?" I asked. "You were skating, too?" This surprised me, as I had not expected someone of her girth would be drawn to athletic pursuits.

"Skating? No. Why do you ask? I was in the Hermitage, with my husband, looking at Flemish paintings. My Friedrich does not like Flemish paintings and had grown most annoyed at my insisting on taking so much time in the gallery. He wanted to see the Egyptian antiquities, you understand. I told him to entertain himself by looking at the ceiling in the adjacent room—have you been in the Tent-Roofed Room, Lady Emily? It is most impressive—but my Friedrich does not like to leave me unattended, you understand."

She paused here, to shoot an amphibian-like grin in the direction of a man I can only assume was her Friedrich.

"No, I have not," I said. "However, I am unable to see how any of this connects to the dancer you're claiming is a ghost."

"You rush me, I understand. I take too long. Forgive me. My Friedrich went to look out the window, to see the view of the Palace Square. He has great admiration for monumental architecture, my Friedrich, and the column of Alexander, built by—"

"Yes, quite," Colin interrupted. "It is magnificent. Pray, do continue, madam. Did he see the ballerina?"

"Oh, sir, you are, like your wife, in a great hurry, aren't you? No matter. He saw her and called out to me. Soon everyone in the room was jockeying to see out the windows. She flitted all the way across Palace Square on her toes. No one living could have done so. She did not sink in the snow." At this revelation, she paused again, smiling smugly. "You see? She is a ghost."

"I make it a practice never to argue with a beautiful woman," Colin said. I did my best to avoid any obvious reaction to this ridiculous statement, because I saw how much she enjoyed the compliment. "If you say you saw a ghost, who am I to question you?"

"Your wife, I think, does not agree with you," she said.

"She often doesn't." He dabbed his lips with his napkin, folded it, and set it on the table. "My dear, will you despise me forever if I tear you away from our meal? I'm quite desperate to see where this ghost appeared."

Within moments, we had retrieved our coats, hats, gloves, overshoes, and my muff, bundled up, and headed to Palace Square. The dancer must have rushed there immediately after finishing her performance at the river. She was long gone now, as were, so far as we could gather, all the people who had seen her. That did not stop those we questioned from giving us detailed accounts of what had happened. Most of them claimed their stories came from someone who had witnessed the performance, but I suspected they were working more in fiction than fact.

As our German friend reported, the square was covered in snow. It was packed tightly enough that one did not sink into it far when walking, but the surface would not have allowed for the graceful crossing of the space en pointe that everyone claimed the dancer had made.

"Emily!" Colin called to me. "Look, here someone has created a narrow path of ice the length of the square. Stand on it, will you, and see if it supports your weight." He took me by the hand to steady me, lest I slip on the slick surface. It did hold my weight.

"She could have prepared by sprinkling water and letting it freeze overnight," I said. "If fresh snow had fallen, she would only need to discreetly brush it away before starting her performance."

"And she could have done that while wearing a coat that disguised her costume," Colin said. "But as it was, not that much snow fell. I don't think the trace amount would have interfered with her."

"It must have been extremely difficult, regardless," I said. "Dancing en pointe is no small feat, but to manage it on ice . . ."

"She must be a professional," Colin said. "Until now, she had done nothing that an amateur might have been able to accomplish—"

"I don't agree," I said. "Her movements were so graceful. I have never doubted she is a trained professional."

We walked back to the hotel along Nevsky Prospekt, taking our time and listening to the conversation on the street. No one was speaking of anything but the mysterious dancer. We heard references to each of the incidents we knew had occurred, but the story, or rather the apparition, had started to take on a life of her own. A young lady was telling a young man that the dancer had stood at the end of her bed the previous night, waking her from a deep sleep. An elderly woman spoke of having seen her in the market, early in the morning. And two gentlemen were entertaining the ladies on their arms with a tale of having seen the ghost hovering above the imperial box at the Mariinsky during a performance of *Swan Lake*.

"There has not been a performance of *Swan Lake* since Nemetseva's death," I said.

"The truth, my dear, often falls aside when one is in search of a good story. Whatever her goal, the dancer has certainly managed to capture the attention of the entire city. I only wish we knew what she means to achieve in the process."

Ekaterina Petrovna
June 1898

Katenka had spent ages trying to convince herself that she cared nothing for Mitya, but she could no longer deny the truth. Emotions she hardly recognized rushed through her as she saw his prostrate form on the floor. She could hardly breathe. Feeling as if she were choking, she rushed to him and knelt at his side. Concern turned to anger when she realized he was drunk. She slapped him soundly across the face, knocking his spectacles onto the floor.

"What do you mean by coming here in this condition?" she asked.

He reacted slowly at first, but then shook himself awake and smiled at her before picking up his eyeglasses. "I apologize. Perhaps I should have stayed away, but I needed to speak to you most urgently."

"You have ignored me for months," she said. "What can be so important now?"

"I think we should go inside," Sofya said. "Your neighbors are not likely to appreciate being disturbed by an argument."

Katenka unlocked the door. Mitya stumbled through and dropped onto the settee.

"I shall make us coffee," Sofya said. "Very strong coffee." She disappeared into the tiny kitchen, leaving Katenka alone with her friend.

"I have treated you badly, Ekaterina Petrovna," Mitya said, looking down. He leaned forward, his hands clenched together, his forearms on his legs. "I tarred you with a brush tainted by my opinion of Irusya. She betrayed my best friend, and I thought you would do the same to me."

"I never—"

He raised a hand. "Please. I know. I am entirely in the wrong and have come here, in this pathetic state, to beg your forgiveness. Lev has returned to Petersburg."

"Where is he?" Katenka asked. "Why has he not come to me?"

"He is living with me at the moment but said he will leave again if I do not make things right with you."

"So you came not because of any feelings you have for me, but because my brother wanted you to?" She shook her head. "I wish you had stayed away."

"No, no, he pressed me to come because he knows how I feel. He is plagued with terrible guilt because he believes he catalyzed the break between us."

"Was there something to break?" Katenka asked. "You kissed me a few times and gave me some books. We had no understanding." She wanted to be cruel, but when she looked at him in his worn and rumpled suit, his glasses badly smudged, her resolve abandoned her.

"I deserve no kindness. I know that," he said. "And I shall not press you to take me back, not now."

"How can I take you back when I never really had you?"

"Did you want me?" He was looking at her now, holding her gaze, his steel-gray eyes burning with intensity.

"I did." Her voice was barely a whisper.

"*Love passed, the Muse appeared, the weather / of mind got clarity new-found; / now free, I once more weave together / emotion, thought, and magic sound.*"

"You return to Pushkin?" she asked.

"Do I dare?" His voice broke.

"Love passed, you say, and you are now free."

"Emotion, thought, and magic sound I weave for you, only you, my dear Katyushenka." He leaned so close she thought he would kiss her but pulled back when Sofya returned with coffee.

"I see you two have reconciled. Good." She picked up her coat and pulled it on. "I shall leave you now. Promise you won't do anything that would horrify me."

Katenka flushed and asked her to stay, but Sofya refused, leaving her alone with Mitya. They talked for hours, about everything and nothing. When he left, not long before dawn, Katenka walked him to the door of her flat and called goodbye as he started down the stairs. He ran back, caught Katenka in his arms, and kissed her.

"I will never be without you again."

18

After Sebastian's revelation about the pamphlets in Nemetseva's dressing room, I had arranged to return to the Mariinsky to conduct more interviews but would have to wait until the following afternoon and, hence, decided to spend the morning at the Hermitage with Cécile. When I called to collect her at Masha's, Vasilii was there breakfasting with them. His spirits seemed marginally improved from when I had seen him last, but the pain he felt at Nemetseva's death remained evident, not that I could mention it in front of our friends, as neither Cécile nor Masha knew about his affair with the ill-fated ballerina.

Masha was regaling them with tales of the ghostly dancer when I arrived, and I could see how difficult the topic was for the prince. Wanting to spare him from the conversation, I pulled him aside on the pretense of Colin's having given me a private message for him and told him what we had learned about the dagger.

"You think Katenka has something to do with this?" His face turned a sickly shade of gray. "I did not think it possible for this horror to be made worse, but if her dearest friend . . ."

"Emily, don't upset the poor man," Masha called from the table at which she and Cécile were finishing their pastries. "Let us discuss something pleasant, like a lovely young lady whose acquaintance I made last week. She would be the perfect bride for you, Vasik."

Cécile rose from her seat. "Comé, Kallista, let's remove ourselves before this conversation goes any further." She patted the prince's arm sympathetically as we took our leave and called for the carriage, which was ready for us by the time we had finished swathing ourselves in coats and scarves and hats and muffs. "Whatever were you speaking about so secretly with our prince?"

I debated how to respond. Knowing that I could trust Cécile absolutely—she was as steadfast as Colin—I decided to come clean to her and detailed everything I knew about the prince and Nemetseva.

"I am not often shocked," she said. "But this . . . *mon dieu*! I should not have thought Vasilii had it in him. He's so very serious and focused. How I could miss a passionate nature hidden beneath the surface? Perhaps I am losing my touch, Kallista."

"Unlikely," I said. "I have never met someone more discreet than he. He was protecting his reputation as well as hers but has expressed much regret over not having married her."

"Married her?" Cécile looked to the heavens and shook her head. "Nemetseva would never have agreed to marry him."

"How can you possibly know that?" I asked.

"Think of your own experience, *chérie*," she said. "What state naturally follows marriage? Motherhood. Why would a dancer in the prime of her career enter into a situation likely to interfere with everything she has worked for?"

"Well . . ." I hesitated. "Obviously she, er . . . I mean . . . if she and the prince . . ."

"*Mais oui*, perhaps this is a subject better abandoned without further discussion. Yet I remain aghast at learning that Vasilii is a heartbroken lover. The poor man."

"Don't even think about consoling him," I said.

Cécile gave me a look of utter disdain. "Really, Kallista, you should know better. When have I ever expressed interest in a military man? That dancer, Yuri, is infinitely more appealing."

We had arrived at the museum and entered its vestibule through the portico on Millionnaya ulitsa. After depositing our coats and accoutrements in the cloakroom, we climbed a staircase between walls finished to look like marble and emerged in the gallery above it, which was lined with twenty granite Corinthian columns. I knew from reading that the designer had modeled this path into the museum's collections on the approach to the Acropolis in Athens. The lacunar ceiling above contributed to the feeling of having stepped into something ancient, a sensation that only increased when one crossed from the stairs and into a brightly colored gallery, on whose walls Georg Hiltensperger had painted nearly a hundred scenes inspired by descriptions of classical images.

Very few paintings from ancient Greek and Rome have survived, but the German architect Leo von Klenze wanted visitors to the museum to pass through a hall dedicated to these works as well as to the sculpture of the period before entering rooms containing more familiar European pieces. This, he felt, would serve as a reminder that western art as we know it could not have existed without the contribution of our ancient counterparts. Hiltensperger used the encaustic technique, the same employed centuries ago in Greece, covering the walls with neoclassical decoration and mythological scenes. The room also held a collection of eighteenth-century sculpture, much of it classically inspired, as well as a fine bust of Voltaire and one of Catherine the Great.

The European picture galleries followed from here, but I did not enter them, instead leading Cécile back down the stairs and into a series of galleries displaying a stunning collection of ancient Greek vases.

"Oh, no, Kallista," Cécile said. "I have not come here to spend the entire day looking at pots. I know your passion for them—"

"Fear not," I said. "I shall return to study them on my own, but I want us to see the Scythian gold and Peter the Great's Siberian collection." I led her through room after room filled with the most marvelous Greek antiquities but resisted stopping until I had reached my stated destination. We were marveling at a stunning piece from the seventh century BC, a recumbent stag, more than a foot long, fashioned from solid gold, its spectacular antlers a masterpiece of its Scythian creator, when I caught sight of a familiar figure.

I grabbed Cécile's arm and pulled her alongside me. "That man over there—do you see him?"—I pointed to a tall figure in a drab suit coat—"It's Lev. Let's follow him. I want to see what he's doing."

"Most likely he is looking at art," Cécile said, squinting. "This is, after all, a museum."

"He's walking with obvious purpose and doesn't seem interested by anything on exhibit. I want to see where he goes. Perhaps he's planned to meet someone here."

Cécile and I stepped toward him, moving (figuratively) as one man. He passed through three more rooms filled with classical antiquities and then turned into one that housed medieval arms and armor. From there, he entered a large hall lined with dark granite columns. I found the contents of the room—the discoveries from excavations near Kertch, in the Crimea—so distracting I nearly lost sight of our quarry. I must be forgiven, however, as there are few finer examples of Greek artifacts from the fourth and fifth centuries BC to be found in the world. Needless to say, I soldiered on, and we pursued him (discreetly, I need hardly say) into the medieval and Renaissance galleries.

After traversing an exhibit devoted to more arms and armor, he mounted a narrow marble staircase that took us to the first floor. He strode past magnificent paintings by Rembrandt and Rubens without so much as pausing and all but sprinted through at least two galleries filled with Dutch and Flemish masterpieces to a corridor that connected the building of the New Hermitage to that of the Small Hermitage, the first gallery space built for Catherine the Great.

This area of the museum was considerably less crowded than those through which we had just passed. As a result, we had to take more care to avoid his seeing us. Cécile accomplished this by walking more slowly and allowing herself to fall far behind me, confident she could easily enough keep me in her sights. I, however, had to employ a different strategy. How I wished depositing one's outwear at the museum's extremely convenient cloakrooms was not compulsory! My fur hat would have gone a long way in helping me disguise myself.

Having no ready method of changing my appearance, I had to rely only on my wits. I pulled a slim Baedeker guide, *Russland*—no English edition was yet available—from my handbag and held it so that it partially blocked my face. We were in a long, narrow gallery full of paintings featuring views of St. Petersburg. I did my best to look rapt with attention, so that if Lev spotted me, it would appear that I was nothing more than an ordinary tourist.

When he reached the end of the room, he paused before continuing into the next. His manner was casual and indifferent as he looked up and down the space. There were only two other parties in the gallery: a mother and daughter and a group of German students. I did not count Cécile, who was hovering on the far side of the entranceway. I gave every appearance of studying a large canvas, moving my eyes back and forth between the painting and my raised guidebook.

Lev gave no sign of having recognized me and continued to move toward a door on the western wall. Then—I peeked over my book to watch—he nimbly opened it—it looked as if he used a key to unlock it—and passed through, closing it behind him. I waited a few beats and then motioned for Cécile to come to me. We tried to follow, but, as I suspected, the door through which he had exited was locked.

Knowing that pulling out my lock-picking tools would most likely be frowned upon by the museum staff, I left them in my bag and crossed to one of the room's windows.

"He has gone into the Winter Palace," I said, frustrated. The buildings of the palace and the museum were connected.

"You are looking for the Winter Palace?" One of the German students had wandered near enough to hear us talking. "You may enter through there." He pointed to the adjacent room, a gallery lined with portraits of the members of the house of Romanov. "It is accessible when the imperial family is not in residence."

I thanked him, and Cécile and I followed his directions. Near the passageway that led to the palace, we saw Catherine the Great's instructions for all those viewing her galleries, admonishing that everyone "*has on entering to leave his title, hat, and sword outside.*"

"Would it not have made better sense to post that at the museum entrance rather than here?" Cécile asked.

"In Catherine's day, the Hermitage was not open to the public," I said. "Those she admitted would have entered through here, having come from the palace."

We emerged from a beautifully decorated little room into the spectacular and vast Hall of St. George, the emperor's throne room. This would impress even the most cynical foreign ambassador. Its Carrara marble Corinthian columns supported a long gallery, and the sun flooded in through two tiers of windows, scattering light over an exquisitely detailed parquet floor fashioned from sixteen different kinds of wood. At the far end stood the imperial throne on a dais, above which St. George, in marble bas-relief, victorious and mounted on his horse, looked ready to defend the tsar.

The doors on either side of the throne opened into the Military Gallery, where hung portraits of all the generals who fought Napoleon in 1812. We turned left, heading in the direction of Palace Square, as that would put us nearer to where Lev had exited the Hermitage, and soon we found ourselves in the midst of a series of rooms that looked like living quarters.

"Excuse me, *mesdames*," a liveried servant said, seeming to have appeared out of nowhere. "I am afraid this is a private area. You ought to have turned into the Armorial Hall. I shall show you." He bowed and motioned for us to follow him.

"We're quite lost," I said. "We hadn't intended to leave the Hermitage." I, of course, was not lost, but saw no sense in winding through the imperial state rooms, as I doubted very much that we would find Lev in them. "Could you tell us the way back?"

His directions were difficult to follow, partly because the building was so immense. Rumor had it that earlier in the century, a peasant had moved his entire family into the top floor of the palace without anyone noticing until the smell of his cow, which he had also brought, gave them away. My feet felt like lead by the time we had made our way back through the Hermitage. Having both lost Lev and run out of time to explore the museum, we returned to the coat check to collect our belongings and found Colin there, sitting for us on a bench. When he saw us, he closed the slim volume of Pushkin's poetry he had been reading.

"I found myself nearby and thought you would want to know without delay what I've learned about Lev, particularly as you are planning to interview some of the dancers this afternoon. I knew I should never find you in the vast expanse of the galleries, so thought I would wait for you here."

"It is the most delightful surprise to see you, Monsieur Hargreaves, reading verse and looking very much like a poet yourself," Cécile said. "Byron was not nearly so attractive as you."

"Don't distract him with flattery," I said. "Let him tell us what he knows."

Colin smiled and his eyes danced. "We can discuss Byron another time, Cécile. I shall look forward to it. For now, though, we will restrict ourselves to a more mundane subject. Katenka's brother is affiliated with the League of Struggle for the Emancipation of the Working Class—as is the man who confessed to killing the Yusupovs' maid. Several of their members, including their leader, were arrested and exiled five years ago. They were publishing an illegal newspaper and organized a strike that resulted in the working day being limited to eleven and a half hours."

"That doesn't sound particularly alarming," I said. Cécile murmured agreement.

"In and of itself, it isn't," Colin said. "But the league believe that workers will never be treated fairly so long as the tsar is ruling Russia."

"And that, obviously, could lead to far more radical action," I said.

"Precisely," Colin replied. "As I have mentioned before, it appears one faction within the group is first seeking change without resorting to violence. Should that fail, however, I do not doubt they will become more extreme."

"And this, no doubt, is why Katenka hesitates to tell us anything about her brother?" I asked.

"I believe so," Colin said. "It would be dangerous for him, and for her as well. Her position in the theatre could be threatened by her association with someone like him."

"What legitimate business, Monsieur Hargreaves, can a man with such views have in the Winter Palace?"

"None, Cécile. None."

Perhaps Katenka was right to worry about her brother. Perhaps she was right to try to protect him, even if it meant lying to me. Regardless, I could no longer entertain the notion that what was best for her, and by extension for him, would help solve Nemetseva's murder.

Ekaterina Petrovna
June 1898

How quickly things changed in those next weeks! It was as if Mitya's return had heralded a new era, one ruled by confidence and hope rather than insecurity and despair. Katenka's dancing now reliably reflected her talent, and she could feel a shift in the way her colleagues looked at her. She would not be trapped in the corps de ballet much longer. At least that was what Sofya said; Katenka could not bring herself to voice the thought aloud, fearing the possibility might vanish the moment she spoke it. But in her heart she knew her friend was correct, especially after Petipa cast her as the fairy Candide in *Sleeping Beauty*, which would be performed during the summer season at Krasnoye Selo.

Her good fortune was in part due to the fact that Mathilde Kschessinska was engaged to perform in Warsaw and would not be dancing at Krasnoye Selo that summer. With her gone, Irusya, who had established herself in the prior season when Pierina Legnani was ill, had a second chance to distinguish herself in leading roles. At last, she would play Aurora.

While warming up at the barre before class one morning, Sofya was complaining to Katenka and Irusya about a count who had been trying, unsuccessfully, to flirt with her for weeks. "As if I could be interested in anyone so stuffy," she said. "I'd prefer someone more like Katenka's Mitya. Or her brother."

"You know Lev?" Irusya stopped mid-plié.

Sofya placed her hands on the barre, turned her feet out in first position, and started to bend backward. "He's Mitya's best friend, so of course I do. It's impossible to miss him."

"He's back in Petersburg?" Irusya asked and then lowered her voice, staring at the ground. "I know I have no right to inquire."

"He is for now," Katenka said. "He's abandoned bookselling for politics."

Irusya smiled and returned to her pliés. "He always was an idealist. I suppose that will never change."

"I wouldn't dismiss him as an idealist," Sofya said. "His beliefs are quite profound." Finished with her backbend, she lifted one leg in front of her and rested it on the barre before stretching over it.

"I never suggested they weren't," Irusya said. "But no doubt you are better acquainted with him and his ideas now than I."

"Forgive me," Sofya said. "I forgot that you—"

"It is of no consequence," Irusya said. "He has every reason to despise me now."

"Lev could never despise you," Katenka said, lowering herself into the splits.

"Can you mean that, Katenka?" Irusya asked.

"Of course," Katenka said. "I know it for a fact. You may have broken his heart, Irusya, but he is incapable of thinking ill of you."

19

I took my leave from Colin and Cécile in front of the museum. He would escort her back to Masha's while I walked to the Mariinsky, burying my hands in my thick fur muff and delighting in the crunch of snow beneath my boots. Mr. Chernov, the theatre manager, greeted me warmly. Without directly mentioning the pamphlets Sebastian had seen in Nemetseva's dressing room, I asked him about the company and politics. He emphatically, if nervously, denied any knowledge of the dancers dabbling in politics, insisting that they wouldn't have time for such things. I thought it unlikely anyone would willingly admit to holding radical positions, but that would not necessarily prevent me from detecting undertones of political leanings. Mr. Chernov, I was confident, held no views to which the government would object. I also asked him who shared Nemetseva's dressing room. He looked relieved at the question, as if happy to have something that could be answered with ease, and told me that Nemetseva had invited Katenka and Sofya Guryevna Pashkova into her private space.

Finally, I asked him if he had any inkling as to the identity of the ghostly dancer who had captured the city's attention. He frowned, and told me in no uncertain terms that he could not imagine any member of the company stooping to such a thing. I thanked him, and he offered his office so that I might conduct the rest of my interviews in private. Once again, I met with each of the dancers in turn. None of them gave away even the slightest hint as to their political beliefs.

Yuri Melnikov, Nemetseva's partner, was the last person I saw in Mr. Chernov's office. He had proved not to have any useful information when I spoke to him before, but now I had specific questions for him. He admitted that one's relationship with one's partner was quite intimate. Not romantically, but emotionally. He and Nemetseva had been close since their school days. I asked him about Lev, and he smirked.

"I'm the only one in the company who ever noticed him," he said. "Apart from Katenka, of course. He came around a lot in our early days. I remember him from our first summer season. I kept an eye on him because I worried that if the relationship ended badly, it could impact Nemetseva's dancing, but it didn't. She threw him over and then fell in love with someone else and someone else again after him. No one broke her heart until that last one."

"The prince?" I asked. "Nikolai Danilovich Ukhov?"

"She always called him Kolya. He nearly destroyed her, but I needn't have worried about her dancing. Heartbreak only improved her artistry."

"Was there anyone after him?"

"She never mentioned anyone else, but I always suspected her of being in love. She was too happy. There was no other explanation for it."

"She never told you who it was?" I asked.

"No, and no one else either. I badgered Katenka about it more than once. Irusya became a master of discretion. No one in the company, Katenka and me excepted, even suspected she was in love."

I had waited to speak with Katenka until I'd finished with the others and went to her dressing room rather than summoning her to me. She smiled wanly when she saw me, barely looking up from the ribbons she was sewing onto a pair of pointe shoes.

"More questions?" she asked.

I had debated again and again the merits of asking her about the pamphlets, but in the end resolved not to. I couldn't believe anything she told me about them and was more likely to see her inadvertently reveal something in her reaction to something else: the knife.

"Just a single one, about an item that belonged to your father. A dagger—a naval dirk, to be precise. Have you any idea what happened to it after his death?"

"Not at all. I was very young when he died."

"I imagine your brother took possession of it. If not immediately, then perhaps after your mother died."

She flushed, slightly. "I can't recall ever seeing such a thing," she said. "Why do you ask?"

"Someone left a blood-covered knife of just this sort at my hotel, and subsequent investigation suggests it is the murder weapon. I recall you telling me that you and your brother were forced to sell most of your family's possessions after your grandfather's death, but surely you would not have parted with a memento of your father? Particularly as you were able to keep a significant amount of furniture."

She sat very still, the needle and thread frozen in her hand, and all the color drained from her face. "As I said, I don't remember seeing any knife."

"That's not altogether surprising," I said. "It's the sort of thing more likely to be given to a son than a daughter. As I suggested before, your brother probably has it."

"Lev has no connection to any of this," she said. "What do you mean to imply with these questions?"

"Nothing at all. Of course, should he still have the dagger, it would prove once and for all that it wasn't the one used to kill Nemetseva.

You might want to ask him about it." I was exaggerating. Him being in possession of the dagger did not preclude it from being the murder weapon. The one I had received could, theoretically, be a fraud, but Katenka did not know that, and I was hoping to goad her into giving something away. I took my leave from her without giving her any reassurance, hoping that any unease she now felt would, eventually, lead her to be more open with me, at least so far as her brother was concerned.

Colin and I had ordered dinner to be sent up to our suite that evening, not wanting to risk another interruption by our eager and verbose German friend. When we finished eating, we moved from the dining table to a sofa in the sitting room, where Colin poured port, my preferred after-dinner drink, for us both.

"Your day was productive," he said. "Do we have any other matters of business to which we must attend?"

"I think we have covered everything," I said.

"With our usual efficiency. Whatever shall we do to occupy ourselves for the rest of the evening? It's too late to go to the opera."

"Chess?" I asked, raising an eyebrow as I recognized both the tone that had crept into his voice and the heat in his eyes. "I know how you love the game."

"An excellent suggestion," he said removing from my hand the glass of port I had been holding and putting it on a table. "But I don't recall seeing a board here."

"We could call down to the desk. I'm sure they could locate one for us."

"If you'd like," he said, kissing the side of my neck. "If, on the other hand—"

Once again we were interrupted by a knock.

"If that is Capet, I swear I will—"

"Don't say something you'll regret," I said, and went to answer the door before he did, just in case. I found not Sebastian but, instead, a very tall, very grand-looking man in an officer's uniform.

"Hargreaves," he said, walking past without so much as acknowledging my existence. "I apologize for disturbing you but felt I should come at once."

"Think nothing of it. I understand urgency all too well," Colin said. "May I present my wife, Lady Emily Hargreaves? Emily, this is an old colleague of mine, Ilya Tabokov."

I smiled politely at our guest and offered him a drink, which he refused.

"Might we speak privately, Hargreaves?"

I excused myself, but I did not like it. Something about Mr. Tabokov irritated me; most likely the way he dismissed me as if I were a child. I went into the bedroom but did not close the door all the way, leaving it cracked open enough that I could hear the gentlemen's conversation. Colin's colleague may have wanted privacy, but not enough to bother keeping his voice low. He had come to discuss Lev Petrovich Sokolov, Katenka's brother.

"I had hesitated to say anything before now, but the time has come that I must confide in you. Sokolov is in my employ," he said. "I understand your wife saw him in the Winter Palace and expressed some sort of concern?"

"She did," Colin replied.

"Ladies so often like to make a meal of things, don't they?" I could not see Mr. Tabokov, but I could hear from his tone that he was probably rolling his eyes. "Sokolov has operated secretly as an agent of mine for the better part of a decade. I'm afraid I must request that you cease making any inquiries about him, as his work is most sensitive. There are many even within the government whom I cannot trust with this information."

"I see," said Colin. "You are aware of his political ties?"

"I made them for him," Tabokov said.

"You can depend upon me to take the matter no further," Colin said. "I would, however, like to speak to Sokolov, if you could manufacture an opportunity."

"Of course, of course. I shall organize it with expedience. Good to see you, as always," he said. "Apologies to that lovely wife of yours for stealing you away from her. You've done well there, old boy."

Ekaterina Petrovna
September 1898

Irusya had spent much of the summer in a state of despondency. Kolya had gone to Europe and would not return until the autumn. Katenka had noticed increasing tension between her friend and the prince and wondered if time apart might benefit them both—or, if it didn't, might provide the perfect opportunity for Lev to return to Irusya's life.

Although he was living in Petersburg again, Katenka did not see him often. She pleaded with him to return to his old habit of going to the Naval Cathedral with her on Sundays. He agreed to walk with her, but he wouldn't accompany her inside for the service. Still, she relished the time with him. He apologized time and again for having subjected Mitya to so much ranting on the subject of ballerinas being unable to resist the temptations of princes that he convinced his friend none of them was immune.

"I caused you so much unhappiness." Lev turned to face her and took her by the hands. "I should not have cut you out of my life, nor tried to separate you from Mitya. Can you forgive me?"

"It is all in the past now," Katenka said. "Irusya was asking about you not long ago, worrying that you despise her."

"I could never despise her."

"That's what's I told her." She stared at her brother. There was something in his eyes she could not quite recognize.

"What did she say?" he asked.

"She asked if I were certain," she said, "and when I told her I was, she looked very pleased to hear it."

Lev almost smiled. "I understand things are going well between you and Mitya. I am glad. I love him like a brother."

Katenka knew well enough to recognize the hesitation in his voice. "Are you sure you approve?"

"Yes, I do, of course, but I have my concerns," he said. "I know he used to tell you that Irusya and I would grow apart because we lived in different worlds. He was right about that, and now I must offer you the same caution. Mitya does not live in your world. The two of you may not be so far apart as Irusya and I, but I worry that—" He stopped.

"What do you worry?" she asked.

They had crossed the Fontanka River on the Egyptian Bridge. The route was not the most direct they could have taken to the cathedral, but they had fallen into the habit of prolonging their walks. Lev tried to make his sister too late to go to church, and Katenka did her best to keep her brother with her as long as possible afterward.

"I do not wish to see you hurt, Katyurushka. I know how strong you are, and I know the pain a ballerina faces every day, but the pain of heartbreak?" He paused. "That pain, Katyurushka, I do not want to see you turn into a beautiful dance."

January 1900

20

As soon as I had learned from Masha about Prince Nikolai Danilovich Ukhov's relationship with Nemetseva, I had tried to contact him, but he was away, in Vienna. He replied to me upon his return and asked me to call on him a nine o'clock the next morning. This was extraordinarily early for a meeting in Petersburg. As an early riser, this did not trouble me, even though the sun was not yet up and it felt more like night than day. The snow had stopped, and the cold infused the air with more ferocity than it had before. My lungs ached with every breath. I had asked Colin to accompany me, and despite the fact that the Ukhov Palace was only a few blocks from the hotel, we half regretted our decision to walk.

"I can't say I much like your colleague Mr. Tabokov who called on you last night," I said, my breath freezing against the soft muffler wrapped around my neck. "You did an excellent job of keeping me too distracted to mention it after he left, but he's exceedingly rude."

"You shouldn't have listened to our conversation." Colin had buried his gloved hands in the pockets of his fur-lined overcoat.

"He shouldn't have spoken so loudly if he didn't wish to be overheard."

"It is unlikely he has ever considered the possibility that a man's wife would be eavesdropping."

"Do I detect a slight note of criticism in your tone?" I asked.

"You do indeed, my dear," he said. "But it is Tabokov at whom I direct it. He shows an appalling lack of imagination for someone in his position."

"I wouldn't trust him if I were you. He's shifty."

"Is that so?"

"My famous intuition knew it at once," I said. "So be careful with him, will you?"

We crossed the last bridge before the palace and saw the pistachio-green dwelling sprawled before us, running an astonishing distance along the river. "A home fit more for a king—an emperor, I should say—than for an ordinary nobleman," I said. "Princes here aren't even royal, yet look how they live."

"The only significant difference between this and the homes of Britain's aristocrats is the color it is painted," Colin said.

"Yes," I said, and sighed. "So much wealth."

"Need I remind you, before you start adopting revolutionary tendencies of your own, that you personally are in possession of a very great deal of it."

"I am well aware of that," I said. "We must make sure we do something good with it. I don't know why it strikes me so now, here. Perhaps it is the way the Russian palaces shine against the snow. Devonshire House is probably no smaller, but it does not command one's attention in the same sort of way."

"Devonshire House was designed to be hidden from the public," Colin said. "One could argue it is less honest about its grandeur. Come, now, I'm beginning to freeze."

We went around to the front entrance of the palace, where we were admitted to a large drawing room decorated in gold silk. The prince, a tall man with finely formed delicate features and warm eyes, rose to greet us.

"I apologize most heartily for not being able to speak to you until now. As you know, I've been away," he said, after the requisite introductions had been made. "I imagine you've caused a bit of a stir in the city by looking into Irusya's death, Lady Emily. The official investigators, of course, haven't approached me on the subject, not that I thought they would. I assume you're here to make sure I didn't take care of her myself in a fit of jealous rage." His smile was charming, revealing rows of even, white teeth.

"No, of course not. That is not it at all—"

"I'm teasing you, Lady Emily. Forgive me. And you must call me Kolya." His voice grew more serious. "Irusya and I spent many pleasant hours together, and I loved her quite dearly. She returned my affection, most passionately. Our connection lasted nearly two years, ending when I got married. Irusya and I both knew it was inevitable, but it did hurt her, and for that I am deeply sorry. She was so young, so idealistic. I'm afraid she might have imagined that somehow we could have . . . well. She must have known that was impossible."

"She seemed a rather sophisticated lady," Colin said.

"She became one, certainly, but there was an innocence about her when we first met," Kolya said. "She was always very open and unguarded about her feelings for me, and that made it more difficult for her when the affair ended. We hadn't felt much need to hide our relationship— neither of us was married—which meant that when it ended, everyone was talking about it. I'm afraid she felt rather harassed. It is no surprise she became more discreet after the experience."

"Did you know her friends well?" I asked.

"Irusya had many, many acquaintances, but few friends. She often brought Ekaterina Petrovna—Katenka—to parties with her. I understand they had been close since their first days at school, but I could not claim to know her well. Katenka was not like Irusya, at least not when I knew her. She always seemed reserved and uncomfortable. Truth be told, I never quite comprehended how their friendship survived."

"Why is that?" I asked.

"Katenka always seemed to me jealous of Irusya's success," he said. "Not that she felt Irusya undeserving of it, but more that she believed they could not both achieve it. I do not know how to best explain my meaning. She thought one could not rise in the company without the other declining. After earning the rank of *coryphée*, Katenka confessed to me that the news had taken her by surprise, as she had never expected that she could receive a promotion because Irusya was the successful one.

"That hardly means she believed Nemetseva would have to have been demoted or in some sort of decline," Colin said.

"No, not literally, I suppose," Kolya said. "It was something in the way she said it, her tone, and that, combined with the way I had seen her interact with Irusya, made me come to believe what I do. I do not claim to be an expert on their friendship, and I may have interpreted things incorrectly. I am only telling you what I felt after observing them both."

"How did Nemetseva react to her friend's promotion?" I asked.

"With joy and delight," he said. "She believed Katenka to be the superior dancer and hated that she did not get better roles. What she wanted more than anything was that they would both be principal dancers. I often thought Irusya needed the friendship more than Katenka did. She certainly was the one who worked to keep them close. So far as I could tell, Katenka preferred other friends, a girl called Sofya in particular. She was a dancer, too, but I cannot claim much of an acquaintance with her. When they came to parties together, they kept to themselves and glowered at the rest of us. I believe they scorned the bourgeoisie."

"Were they vocal about their politics?" Colin asked.

"No, no, I draw the conclusion only from the feeling they gave me. Katenka never seemed comfortable in my presence, and I do not know if this was because she disapproved of me or if it had something to do with Irusya."

"Was she jealous of her friend?" I asked.

"Jealous enough to want Irusya dead?" the prince asked, smiling. He shook his head. "No, that is unthinkable. But then I cannot imagine anyone committing so vile an act. The poor girl. She did not deserve so terrible an end."

We thanked him, took our leave, and walked back through the palace's snowy garden to the pavement outside its large iron gate.

"What a devoted lover," Colin said. "Not a word against her."

"I quite liked him," I said. "I hadn't expected to."

"My dear, you always try to like people. I don't. The gracious Kolya is probably no worse than most other rich aristocrats, but I wouldn't take everything he said at face value," Colin said.

"Probing observations about Katenka, though, especially her friendship with Sofya, who I'm due to call on next. Care to accompany me?"

"I'm afraid I must return to the palace," he said. "Take care, my dear. You never know how dangerous a ballerina might be."

He was teasing, of course, but had he come with me to see Sofya he might have changed his tone, not because of her so much as her neighborhood. She lived not terribly far from Katenka, but in a section of the city even more wretched. Her flat occupied a corner on the second floor, which meant she did not have to climb the mountain of stairs Katenka did, but her rooms—she had only two—were small and dark, despite the tall windows. The glass, streaked with smut, let in very little light.

Sofya was expecting me. I had arranged to meet for further discussion when I had last been at the theatre. She welcomed me inside but offered no refreshment. No samovar stood in her sitting room, if I may so call the desolate little space whose sparse furnishings included a battered and lumpy sofa.

"I will not apologize for my home," she said. "I don't earn much in the corps de ballet, and, even if I did, I have never been tempted by material comforts."

"You have nothing to apologize for." My words were honest; an apology certainly was not required. One could not help but be a bit taken aback by the shabbiness of the dancer's apartment, particularly as it contrasted so completely with the elegance of the Mariinsky Theatre. However, it was spotlessly clean—everywhere but the windows—and Sofya showed not the slightest embarrassment at her humble surroundings. "I asked to see you here not to judge your home, but because I thought you might be more comfortable speaking openly than you were at the theatre." I did not want to approach the subject of the pamphlets directly, preferring instead to first win her trust. "As you know, I'm trying to determine who might have wished Irusya ill."

She sat next to me on the sofa. "I already told you I did not know Irusya very well, but I cannot think of anyone who despised her."

"You did share a dressing room with her, though?"

"Yes, but only because Katenka and I are so close. She's the best friend I have ever had. I adore her."

"Do you ever find her difficult? Some have told me she can be awkward."

"Who said that? Some of Irusya's grand friends?" Sofya snorted. "They never cared for her—nor me—because neither of us was interested in them. They weren't used to that and didn't like it."

"It must have been difficult for Katenka, though," I said. "She and Irusya had been close for so long, only to be pulled apart by differing social expectations."

"That's a convoluted, if delicate, way to put it," Sofya said. "I am not the only dancer who has spoken against those among us who choose to ally themselves with noble patrons. Some of us feel to do so would be beneath us, as if we were admitting that we weren't good enough on our own."

"Does Katęnka share that belief?"

"Katenka resides uncomfortably between two worlds. She does not object to the bourgeoisie, nor does she cultivate a relationship with them. Yet she does not give entirely into occupying the world she can afford to live in. She grew up in a wealthy household and found herself in reduced circumstances when her grandfather died. I would not expect her to be delighted at the change. She is a good friend, and I admire her greatly, as a dancer and as a human being. She has never made me—or, for that matter, Irusya—feel bad for choosing a path different from her own."

"Do her brother's politics put her in a difficult situation?"

"Lev's politics? I didn't realize he had any." She knew his name, and the speed with which her words tumbled out told me she knew more than she was inclined to share.

"We are both aware of the dangers than can arise from . . . unconventional ideas. It is unfortunate that one must take things like that into consideration. We are not accustomed to doing so in Britain. I'm sure Lev agrees that the people there are in a much happier situation than those here in Russia."

"Your working class is not better off than ours, and I don't believe for a minute that Lev would agree with you." Her cheeks darkened. "I am in a far better position to understand his views than you are."

"I apologize for my mistake. I took you at your word when you said you didn't realize he had any politics."

"It has nothing to do with this anyway. Lev would never put his sister in harm's way," she said. "If anything, he would defend her to the death. He adores her. There's nothing he wouldn't do for her."

This was precisely what I suspected. "Nothing?" I paused for a moment, wanting her to feel the silence. "What about your political views? Are you content with society?"

"Of course I am. Why wouldn't I be? I have everything I could possibly want," she said. "I've never been overly ambitious. I love the ballet but don't have to be consumed by it. I'm happy where I am and delighted to see Katenka getting the adoration she deserves."

"Was Irusya standing in the way of her friend's success?"

"No, not precisely," Sofya said. "Katenka was the one holding herself back." She looked me in the eyes, as if challenging me. "What do you make of this mysterious dancer who has been seen all over the city, en pointe in the snow? She's causing quite a stir, isn't she? Of course, no one can dance en pointe in the snow. Not well, at any rate."

It was an odd way to change the subject. "I can't imagine what she means to accomplish by it," I said. "Have you any ideas?"

Sofya shrugged. "Perhaps she means to draw attention to herself. She could want an audition with the company." She laughed. "I am jesting, of course. I have no idea what her intention could be. The only thing I know for certain is that she is not Irusya's ghost. Her pointe work isn't nearly delicate enough."

"You've seen her?"

"Only once, when she was across the Neva and caused a commotion among the people ice-skating. I was on the bridge."

"Did you recognize her?"

"No," she said. "I was too far away. I would have preferred to see her later that day in Palace Square, where she's said to have danced in the snow, but then I've already told you no one could do that well."

"Not even Nemetseva?" I asked.

"She would never have wasted a pair of shoes trying."

Ekaterina Petrovna
December 1898

Kolya had not been especially attentive to Irusya when he returned from his foreign travels. There was no official break between them, but they were not so close as they had been. Irusya showed no outward signs of this causing her grief, but Katenka knew her friend was unhappy. So when, one Sunday morning, Katenka's landlady brought her a message from Lev, saying he would not be able to make their weekly "pilgrimage"—his choice of word made Katenka smile—she decided she would forgo services and visit her friend instead.

She knew that Irusya, who despised mornings, tried to force herself to wake up early on Sundays, as it was the only day she had entirely to herself. Katenka, stopping first at a bakery to buy sweet, cheese-filled *vatrushkas*, which Irusya adored, arrived at her friend's door before nine o'clock. Not wanting to risk waking her in case she had decided to stay in bed, Katenka used the key Irusya had given to her when she first took the apartment. Katenka had protested, saying she didn't need it, but Irusya had insisted. It was closer to the theatre than Katenka's, and she might on occasion find it convenient to come there instead of going all the way home. Katenka had taken it but had never used it until now.

She opened the door and closed it quietly behind her, hearing no sounds as she stepped into the flat. Irusya was still asleep. Katenka lit the coals in the samovar and started to prepare tea, arranging the *vatrushkas* on a plate while she waited for the water to heat. Once the tea was ready, she filled two cups and put them, along with a bowl of sugar cubes and the pastry, on a tray, which she carried to the bedroom. Realizing she could not open the door while holding it, she placed it on the soft carpet in the corridor and then hesitated. Should she knock?

Of course not. So far as she knew, Kolya had never spent the night, and, regardless, they hadn't been together for weeks. She cracked the door and retrieved the tray, pushing gently against the door with her shoulder as she made her way into the dark bedroom. She paused, waiting for her eyes to adjust, and when they did she walked toward the bed, stopping almost as soon as she had started.

Irusya was not alone, but it was not the prince sleeping beside her; it was Lev.

Swallowing a whoop of mingled horror and delight, Katenka retraced her steps and exited the room. Quietly, so quietly, she retreated. She closed the draft of the samovar and dumped the tea she had made into the kitchen sink. She washed out the cups and the plate on which she had put the *vatrushkas* and returned the pastries to the bakery box. Confident that she had left no trace of her presence, she tiptoed out of the apartment, locking the door behind her.

The sun had not yet started to rise, but rosy hints of dawn colored the sky. Filled with an all-consuming happiness, Katenka ran back to her own flat, completely unaware of the bitterly cold air. The snow squeaked beneath her boots as she raced along the streets, her heart ready to burst. Now, at last, they could all be happy again.

January 1900

21

—❖◈❖—

By the end of our conversation, I was certain the pamphlets in the dressing room belonged to Sofya. After leaving her, I spoke to the two other dancers I had arranged to meet in their homes. Larisa, whose scorn at Irusya's aristocratic lovers had concerned me, lived in a modest apartment. Her salary in the corps de ballet would not allow her to afford more, but she was unquestionably living better than Sofya. (Sofya, I decided, had selected her domicile as much to make a point as to provide shelter.) I spent half an hour with Larisa before determining that her ire was motivated by petty jealousy, not the sort that leads to murder.

My final appointment was with Nina, a soloist. All ballerinas are slim, but Nina was so lithe she seemed more like a spirit than a person. She wore her dark hair pulled back in a bun and was dressed in a simple gown devoid of ornamentation. She did not need it, or jewelry, for that matter, as she possessed a pair of impossibly large eyes, a bewitching shade of emerald with which the most brilliant gems could not compete. She greeted me warmly, led me into her modest but elegantly furnished sitting room, and reminded me that she had entered the Imperial Theatre School at the same time as Katenka and Nemetseva. She had been on extremely friendly terms with the latter.

"Our parents were close," she said, passing me a slab of ginger-bread cake filled with jam. "We used to play when we were little and went together the day we auditioned. I thought we would be best friends, but Irusya and I never really confided in each other; we were too young to have anything to confide."

"And as you got older?" I asked.

"She took Katenka under her wing from almost the first week of school," she said. "Katenka was so shy and had difficulty getting to know the other students. Irusya liked playing mother."

"Did she always look after Katenka?"

"In her way, yes," Nina said. "Not that Katenka required it much once we had graduated. She was disappointed by her graduation performance, as I'm sure you have already heard, and was brought into the company in the corps de ballet. Everyone had expected she would be at least a *coryphée*, but she remained in the corps for more than a year. I can't remember how long exactly."

"Was that why Nemetseva felt she had to continue looking after her friend?" I asked.

"Katenka was despondent for quite a while. There was nothing anyone, including Irusya, could do to improve her mood. To be honest, most of the rest of us found it rather irritating. Lots of us start in the corps. It isn't a death sentence. But it was not all bad, for Irusya, anyway. She was distracted by falling in love."

"With whom? Nikolai Danilovich?"

"The prince? Kolya? No, not he," Nina said. "This was her first love, before she took grand lovers. He was a very sweet boy, older than us. I remember we used to watch him out the windows at school every Sunday."

"He is a dancer?"

"No, no, he's Katenka's brother," she said. "Her grandfather had got permission for her to go to church with her family instead of suffering through services—we had a very long-winded priest in the chapel at school. Lev Petrovich used to collect her every week and walk her to . . . I don't remember which church. He was a very handsome boy with the most marvelously unruly honey-colored curls. The older girls were all madly in love with him, but then we didn't have many options. We weren't allowed even to socialize with the boys at school. They kept them on a separate floor."

This was an unexpected development. The romance would have changed the dynamic between Nemetseva and Katenka and could have had a profound effect on their friendship, especially after the relationship ended. "So they were childhood sweethearts?" I asked.

"No, no, I was not clear," Nina said. "Irusya did not meet Lev Petrovich until perhaps the summer before our final year as students. I cannot be exactly sure, but Katenka could tell you. Irusya's parents invited them both to join the family at their dacha. I don't know when they became more than friends, but I can assure you that by the time we had graduated and were dancing our first summer season at Krasnoye Selo, Irusya was madly in love."

"Do you know how the affair ended?"

"I wasn't close to Irusya when it happened. After a certain point, Lev no longer came backstage. Irusya never spoke of it, to me at least, and then she fell in love with Kolya."

I thanked her for her assistance and set off on my way as quickly as possible without seeming rude, ordering the driver of my hired troika to take me directly to Katenka's apartment. She was not home. I gave myself a minute to catch my breath after having climbed the five flights of steps and, with only the slightest hesitation, used my lock-picking tools to let myself into the dancer's flat.

I felt very little guilt as I searched through her belongings; she had told me too many lies. The armoire in her bedroom contained a modest wardrobe, and the chest of drawers on the opposite wall was crammed full of dance wear: cotton chemises and batiste bodices, short knickers, long pink stockings, and carefully folded practice dresses. Two boxes, one stacked on the other, stood against the wall. The bottom contained several pairs of thick cotton ballet slippers; the top, six pairs of pristine satin pointe shoes. Six more pairs of the latter hung from a row of hooks on the back of the door. They were all well used, and when I inspected them I found each contained a slip of paper with the name and date of a performance. Souvenirs. One solitary pair had not been hung, but its ribbons were wrapped around the shanks, holding the dainty shoes together. I wondered if that was the pair Katenka had worn in *Swan Lake.*

I found nothing of note in the rest of the apartment, save a framed photo of her, Nemetseva, Mitya, and Lev, standing in front of a lake. She had a few books, a stack of newspapers—unread, by the look of them—and no letters at all. I was about to leave the apartment when I heard someone at the door. I waited for the sound of a key, but it did not come. After a firm rattling of the knob, knocking started.

"Katenka, let me in," came the voice. "It's Lev! You told me you would be home." He knocked harder.

My heart pounding, I went to the door and opened it. "Mr. Sokolov, how convenient to find you here," I said. "I've been hoping to have a word with you so that you might enlighten me as to your relationship with Nemetseva. Your sister neglected to mention your romantic involvement with her, and I suspect the omission was deliberate. What is she trying to hide?"

"What are you doing here when Katenka is not home?" he asked. "Leave at once. My sister would never have failed to lock her door, so unless you can show me a key, you have broken in, and I shall summon the police."

He had me on shaky ground there, and although I did not doubt I could avert any problems that might arise, I preferred to avoid them altogether, particularly as the man standing in front of me shared his line of work with my husband.

"I am investigating Nemetseva's murder and came to inquire about your relationship with her."

"My relationship with her is irrelevant," he said. "It ended long before her death."

His piercing eyes, icy and intense, unnerved me, but I was not dissuaded from my pursuit of the truth. "Did it end badly? Badly enough that you are not mourning her death?"

"That is a despicable accusation," he said.

"I mean no offense," I said, "although I do find it awfully strange that Katenka never mentioned your connection to her friend. Why was she hiding it?"

"Only she can enlighten you on that point. As for me, I have always held Irusya dear in my heart. We were young when we were in love—too young, and too different. Our lives never meshed. Did she break my heart? Is that your question?" He took a step toward me, forcing me to back up against the wall. "She did, but I have never despised her for it, and I certainly did not kill her as a result."

"She was your sister's professional rival."

"Neither of them ever viewed it that way and I will thank you for not looking for trouble where there isn't any. This has all been difficult enough for my sister. Can't you understand that? Her heart is broken because she has lost her dearest friend."

"She is trying to protect you," I said. "That is the only reason I can conjure to explain her behavior. Why does she feel that is necessary? Could it be, perhaps, that she knows you kept your father's naval dirk—a knife identical to the murder weapon? Or is it, in fact, the murder weapon?"

He recoiled. "You ought not make accusations you cannot prove."

"Did you receive the knife after your father's death?"

"Of course I did. Who else would inherit it? But I haven't seen or thought about it in years. We sold nearly everything after my grandfather died. His debts were not inconsiderable." He drew his eyebrows together. "I assume that you searched the flat after breaking in. Have you found anything that suggests where my sister may be? She was expecting me and it is not like her to miss an appointment. Perhaps your presence scared her off. It's clear what you think of me, but I wonder what, exactly, have you been accusing her of?"

He did not wait for my reply, instead turning sharply on his heel and slamming the door behind him as he left. I could hear his boots on the stairs. I leaned against the wall, considering his words. Katenka may never have chosen this outcome, but could her brother have orchestrated it on her behalf without her knowledge? Or had she asked him to eliminate her rival without realizing how profoundly the crime would affect her emotionally. In such a case, one could say that she had not chosen this outcome in particular. I gave little credence to his claim that he bore no ill will to his former love. What else would he say when being confronted? Still, I doubted that he would have acted alone so many years after the relationship ended. Something else would have had to catalyze his action—if he took any—and what better impetus than to invigorate his sister's languishing career? If he avenged an old hurt in the process, so much the better.

I went down to my waiting troika, bracing myself against the cold wind that nearly ripped my hat off my head, and instructed the driver to return me to the hotel. Nothing I'd discovered about Nemetseva's personal life provided in and of itself an adequate motive for murder. And as for the professional, I kept recalling Agrippina Aleksandrovna's words: *Irusya did everything she could to forward her friend's career. Even die.* I was still musing them when I arrived at the hotel and hardly heard the concierge call out to me when I entered the hotel lobby.

"Lady Emily! There is a gentleman waiting to see you. He is in the lounge across from the restaurant. Would you like to meet him there, or should I send him up to your suite? Of course, if you would prefer I send him away, I will do that without delay."

Sebastian! He was the last person I wanted to see right now, although a small—very small—part of me was tempted to ask him what he would have done had he encountered Katenka's brother at her apartment. No doubt he would tell me he would never have got caught.

"Forgive me, madame, I did not tell you the gentleman's name," the concierge continued. "It is Prince Vasilii Ruslanovich Guryanov."

"Oh! Is it?" This was a surprise. "I'll go to him in the lounge. Could you send my coat up to my room?" He helped me out of it and then took my hat, gloves, and muff. I thanked him and went to the lounge, where Vasilii was sitting alone at a table, drinking a cup of coffee, an open newspaper in front of him. He leapt to his feet when he saw me and stepped forward as if he meant to embrace me. I moved out of the line of fire, so to speak, and took the seat across from the one he had occupied.

"You know why I am here, of course. I came the instant I heard the news. You cannot imagine what joy it brings me to have this matter settled so well and so quickly." He frowned, but his expression did not dim the shine in his eyes. I had never seen them look so alive. "Well, perhaps settled well is not quite correct. It is not the outcome for which any of us would have hoped, Irusya in particular."

I had not the slightest idea what he could possibly mean. "I'm afraid I'm quite at sea. You'll have to explain."

"Yes, I see your point. I suppose Irusya wouldn't have known, and I am grateful that in her final moments she was not faced with the knowledge of her friend's heinous betrayal."

"Vasilii, I had no point," I said. "What are you trying to tell me?"

"Can it be that you've not heard? Katenka presented herself at the office of the judicial investigator and confessed to Irusya's murder."

"She did?" I reeled with confusion, although it did explain why she had not kept her appointment with her brother. "But she couldn't have killed—"

"She did not strike the fatal blows herself," he said. "She hired someone else to do that, a ruffian who was passing through her neighborhood."

"I had considered that possibility but did not think . . . . this is quite a shock." She had so little money; there was only one person whom she could have turned to for assistance in the crime.

"None of us would have suspected her," he said. He seized both my hands across the table. "I cannot tell you how grateful I am for your assistance. She may not have confessed to you, but there can be no doubt that your work is what drove her to turn herself in. You did what I asked with more expertise than I could ever have hoped for. Thank you, Lady Emily. I cannot get my Irusya back, but at least now I shall see justice served."

"I'm afraid I cannot take the credit, Vasilii, I—"

"You must call me Vasik, and there is no need for such modesty, not among friends. And I do hope you consider me your friend now."

"You're very kind," I said, still unconvinced that it was all over so suddenly. "But I assure you I am not being modest. I am glad, though, that you will have your justice. I can see in your eyes the peace it brings you." Truly, I could. He looked much improved: his eyes brighter, his complexion less sallow.

"If there is ever any service, small or otherwise, I can provide for you, promise me you will not hesitate to ask. I owe you everything and shall never forget that. May I order you some tea? Or perhaps the occasion calls for champagne?"

"No, thank you, I—"

"But I am being an absolute beast," he said. "I all but accosted you on your way to your rooms. You're probably in the midst of something. I shan't trouble you any longer, but please do accept my deepest thanks. I hope you will save a dance for me at the imperial ball." He bowed neatly and smiled after me as I left the lounge.

Our suite was empty. Colin had left a note saying he was embroiled in something complicated and would be back late. Still confounded by Vasilii's news, I rang Cécile at Masha's and asked her to come to me. They had already heard about Katenka's confession and arrest and wanted me to go to them so that I might regale them with further details, but I declined. Cécile, knowing me as she did, recognized something not quite right in my voice. She was at my side within half an hour.

"You should be delighted with this development, *non*?" she asked. "This is hardly the first time you have exposed a murderer whom you had grown to like." She was quite right on this point. In one case, I discovered that a woman I had considered a close friend was guilty of the crime, and the knowledge had struck a terrible blow. "Although I never felt that you *liked* Katenka."

"I don't know her well enough to form an opinion," I said. "I certainly don't trust her, but something about this feels all wrong."

"If you are going to start talking like that, it is a good thing Monsieur Hargreaves is not here," she said. "The crime is solved. There is no further need for instinct."

"Consider the last conversation I had with Katenka. My focus was on her brother, and she might have concluded that Lev was in danger of being arrested for murder. I'm convinced she didn't tell us about his relationship with Nemetseva to protect him."

"He is not Nemetseva's only former lover," Cécile said. "Their romance ended years ago. Why would he have waited so long to exact his revenge?"

"I have not figured out the details," I said, "but I have no doubt she knows more than she's told us and that she is willing to do anything for her brother."

"Confessing to murder is going a bit far, don't you think?"

"Perhaps not when you consider their history. They've always been extremely close, and since her mother and grandfather died, he's her only family. And the murder weapon, Cécile—do not forget that. A naval dirk just like the one her father had. It is hardly a reach to think his son would have received it upon his death."

"C'est vrai." Cécile stood and got her coat.

"You're leaving me?" I asked.

"No, I'm going to the prison with you to speak with Katenka. That was your plan, *non*?"

Ekaterina Petrovna
December 1898

The morning after she had seen Lev in Irusya's apartment, Katenka was desperate to talk to her friend, but by the time Irusya arrived for company class, the pianist had already started to play; she would have to wait. Irusya was perfect in class: her pliés, her tendus, her ronds de jambe, but most of all her work in the center, culminating with one of the most gorgeous adagios Katenka had ever seen. Irusya was glowing.

"You had an excellent class," Katenka said when Petipa had dismissed them.

"On some days, everything works, doesn't it?" Irusya said. "This is a good day and will be a better night. Are you ready for *Esmeralda*?"

Rife with love, jealousy, betrayal, honor, and loyalty, the ballet told the story of Esmeralda, the gypsy girl who enters into a marriage of convenience to save a man from execution. She finds true love in the end, but only after first experiencing profound feelings of heartbreak. "It is so full of emotion," Katenka said. "There is nothing I would rather dance. But what about you? I haven't seen you so happy in ages. Has something happened?"

"I'm just excited that you are performing in a role that could very well lead to a promotion," Irusya said. She was right. Petipa had cast her as one of Esmeralda's friends in the pas de six in the third act.

"Surely that alone does not account for your improved mood?"

"I've heard rumors Petipa plans to revise the choreography next season for Mathilde. She told me she plans to train Esmeralda's goat herself." The company always used a real goat to play Esmeralda's pet, something that never failed to delight the younger students in the Imperial Theatre School.

Katenka could not understand why Irusya wasn't telling her about Lev. Perhaps the reunited couple wanted to share the news together. Satisfied by this explanation, Katenka asked no more questions.

Katenka's performance that night was a spectacular success. All of her additional practice and the hours of lessons with Cecchetti had paid off; she outdid herself in the pas de six. Petipa announced her promotion to *coryphée* after the performance. Their Esmeralda, the sublime Olga Preobrajenska, was flawless. Irusya missed the landing on one of her jumps but recovered seamlessly and did a credible job as Fleur de Lys, the young maiden unlucky in love.

As soon as the final curtain fell, Mitya rushed backstage, clutching a book to his chest and grinning when he found Katenka. He picked her up and spun her around with such vigor he nearly sent his spectacles flying.

"I am so proud of you," he said, kissing her on both cheeks and handing her the book. "*Notre Dame de Paris* by Victor Hugo, the inspiration for this ballet."

"Thank you, Mityusha," Katenka said, beaming. She looked around for Lev but did not see him. "Where is my brother?"

"He could not come but sends his congratulations with me. He knew you would shine," Mitya said. "Now, we must celebrate. You go change and I will wait for you by the stage door, with the rest of your admirers."

"You're my only admirer."

"Not after tonight, Katyushenka."

Flushed with excitement and exertion, Katenka headed for the dressing room she shared with the rest of the corps, passing Irusya's on the way. She stopped to speak to her friend but then realized Petipa was there, giving Irusya a lengthy set of corrections. Her performance had disappointed him. Katenka's elation faded a bit, and she waited in the corridor until the ballet master had finished. He congratulated Katenka again as he walked out of the room.

"You have impressed me so much tonight, Ekaterina Petrovna," he said. "Now, at last, you are becoming the dancer we all knew you could be."

Katenka thanked him and went to Irusya.

"He ought not to have been so severe with you," she said.

"He said nothing that wasn't true," Irusya said. Her demeanor, so perfectly calm and measured, would have led someone who knew her less well to believe that his criticism had taken no emotional toll on her. "It is of no consequence. Not every performance can be perfect, and I will do better tomorrow. Let's talk about you instead. I am so happy for you! No one deserves promotion more." She kissed Katenka on both cheeks and embraced her.

"Mitya is waiting for me outside. Will you come celebrate with us?"

"I want to more than anything, but I'm afraid I have a previous commitment that cannot be broken." Irusya blushed as she spoke, and looked at the floor.

"Ah," Katenka said, smiling. "I believe I understand."

Irusya squeezed her hand. "I knew you would. I have been waiting for this for so long. Tomorrow, after *Sleeping Beauty*, we will celebrate together. Promise?"

"Promise."

22

Before we left the suite, I rang the judicial investigator, who told me where Katenka had been confined. Cécile had Masha's carriage outside waiting to take us across the Neva to the St. Petersburg Prison for Solitary Confinement. Although not so infamous as the jail in the Peter and Paul Fortress, the conditions inside the large red brick building appalled me. This was a place where tuberculosis thrived and suicide seemed preferable to life.

The warden agreed to let us see Katenka and had two guards bring her to a small room not far from his office. Wretched did not begin to describe the ballerina. Her eyes were red and swollen, a dark bruise blooming beneath one of them. Her golden hair had escaped its pins and hung around her face like straw. She was no longer wearing her own clothes, and the woolen dress and felt boots of her prison uniform were coarse and ill-fitting.

She sat across a roughly hewn table from us and stared at the floor.

"Why have you done this?" I asked.

"The truth always finds its way out," she said. "I should have thought you'd be glad. I could tell you suspected me from the beginning."

I chose not to correct her. "Describe for me exactly what happened."

"I came here and asked to see the warden—"

"No, not in the prison," I said. "With Nemetseva."

Katenka drew a deep breath. "I had been jealous of her for years and could stand it no longer. I arranged to have her killed. I am ashamed of myself, but I acted out of a desperate passion to succeed in my chosen profession, something not possible so long as I had to compete with Irusya." She spoke as if reciting lines written for someone else. They did not fit her.

"Whom did you hire?"

"A wretched man who skulks about my neighborhood. Don't bother to look for him. He's long gone by now, and I don't even know his real name. We agreed on a price and I told him where he could find Irusya. I knew she always waved to Agrippina Alexandrovna during the interval. I chose the date I did because I was the understudy for *Swan Lake*," she said. "I knew I would triumph when I took on the role for the remainder of the ballet at the last minute in difficult circumstances. As you see, it all went just as I planned."

"And what about your brother?" I asked.

"My brother has nothing to do with this." She spat the words. "Why do you mention him?"

"Partly because you've consistently tried to mislead me about him and partly because of how you reacted when I told you about the knife wielded by the murderer. If the crime were committed as you claim, you would not have permitted your neighborhood brute to use a weapon that could be tied to your family."

"I did not tell him what knife to use. He probably stole it from someone. You've got what you want now, so can't you just leave me be? Your case is solved. There's no need for you to torment me any longer, and you certainly have no right to try to bring my brother into any of this. I'm no fool—I realized that you had begun to suspect him.

It's what spurred me to confess. I had made an uneasy peace with my conscience over my crime, but it had never occurred to me that I might be putting Lev in danger. Once I realized that you were rushing to the wrong conclusion, I had to come forward. He would never have received a fair trial."

I cocked my head and raised an eyebrow, but Cécile spoke before I could. *"Porquoi pas?"*

"His politics would preclude it." Her voice was barely audible. "Can you be so ignorant about my country? We are not allowed to think what we want. The fact that he had nothing to do with the murder would be irrelevant. They'd send him to Siberia regardless to punish him for his ideas."

"They could do that without accusing him of murder," I said. "What is he involved in, exactly? You must tell me. I can help you, but only if—"

The warden threw open the door and told us our time was up. The guards pulled Katenka roughly from her chair, knocking it over and nearly sending her flying with it. Cécile admonished them to be more gentle, but they ignored her. My stomach churned as I watched them take their prisoner away.

Neither of us said another word until we were back in the carriage and out of sight of the prison.

"What a horrible place." Cécile looked as disturbed as I have ever seen her. "It is as bad as the Bastille. Something must be done."

"Do you believe she is telling the truth?" I asked.

"She is lying, *bien sûr*, but whether to protect her brother or because she is innocent, I cannot say."

"I have been suspicious of her, but her confession does not ring true. If anything, it argues for her innocence. What if she's wrong about Lev needing protection? At least wrong about who is threatening him." I thought about Mr. Tabokov, Colin's colleague. If Lev were his agent, he wouldn't be worried about the government objecting to his politics, and surely he would have found some way to reassure his sister. Unless . . . but I could not worry about that right now. "If that's the case, the murderer may still be wandering free. I know where we need to go next."

This was not precisely accurate. I knew, in theory, where I wanted to go, but had no idea as to the actual location. I ordered the carriage to Katenka's building, but rather than going to her rooms, I knocked on the doors of the other apartments in the building, inquiring in Russia if the occupants were acquainted with Katenka and her friend Mitya. Most of her neighbors knew and liked her, and a few recognized my description of Mitya, but it took nearly an hour to find anyone who could claim an acquaintance with him.

"Yes, of course, Dmitri Dmitriyevich Ivchenko," said the young man who lived on the second floor. "I was in school with him, and we often speak when he comes to see Ekaterina Petrovna. He has a room not far from here in the building above a butcher's shop. I will write down the address and directions."

We thanked him and set off. Finding the building was simple enough, but reaching the apartment was another matter. Mitya lived on the top floor, up a seemingly endless succession of stairs. When at last we reached his door, I knocked repeatedly while Cécile caught her breath. No one answered. A woman poked her head out from across the narrow corridor.

"He's not there," she said. Her dress was filthy and torn and she was missing most of her teeth. "So you can stop making such a racket."

"Do you know when he will return?" I asked. She replied, but I could not understand her well enough to grasp her meaning. I tried to clarify, but she only laughed at my failure to speak Russian fluently.

"I don't like her, Kallista," Cécile said. "Did you see the way she looked at us? Sizing us up? It is not safe for us to stay here."

"We need to get inside," I said, once again turning to my lock picks. I worked quickly, not wanting to be seen by anyone, and soon we were inside. Mitya had only a single room, with a narrow couch and a small table with three mismatched chairs. There was no electricity, and only one window. I pushed aside the curtains to let in some light, and we began to systematically comb through his belongings.

"I think we may be getting ourselves into more trouble than we realize," I said, holding up a stack of leaflets.

"What do they say?"

"My Russian is only so good, but as far as I can tell they first document the plight of the workers and then urge them to rise up against their employers. Along the bottom, here"—I pointed—"it says League of Struggle for the Emancipation of the Working Class."

"This name is familiar to me," Cécile said.

"Remember the maid murdered at the Yusupov Palace? The man who confessed to killing her is a member of this very organization. If Lev is not loyal to the cause, as Mr. Tabokov tells us, and his friends have realized he's a fraud, they would want to punish him."

"Wouldn't they simply kill him? Is that not how thugs deal with each other in these situations?"

"Not if they were concerned that eliminating him might alarm their enemies, who, in this case, are the government. Better to have him lawfully arrested for a crime, don't you think? That would remove him from their organization without the police or anyone knowing that his cover was blown. It's a much subtler approach, and a more useful one."

"Except that he has not been arrested."

"Only because his sister has intervened," I said. "Think about it. How did we get the murder weapon? It was left at my hotel. They knew we would identify its origins, and they knew that we would see the connection to Katenka's family. Her confession will have thrown off their plans. We must be very careful as to how we proceed."

"I cannot imagine Monsieur Hargreaves or anyone else is going to want us—or rather, you—to proceed. You won't be able to prove your theories, and he will want proof. Evidence, hard evidence, as he always says."

"Colin knows the league is planning something. He will listen to me."

We continued our search of Mitya's pitiful lodgings, hardly expecting to find something more explosive than what we already had. But there, inside a narrow cupboard next to the window, hung a white tulle ballet costume, perfect for *Swan Lake*; below it, a pile of neatly folded crimson scarves.

When we left, closing the door behind us, the neighbor woman was waiting in the corridor. She did not speak, but followed us to the stairs and watched as we descended. I have never been better pleased to leave a building, nor more grateful to have a carriage waiting outside. We returned directly to the hotel, where I nearly yelped with joy when I saw Colin was already in our rooms.

"I hardly dared hoped I would find you here," I said, embracing him before even removing my coat. "What a brilliant surprise!"

He returned my embrace and kissed me quickly, but looked over my shoulder to Cécile and then whispered to me. "Much though I am enjoying your enthusiasm, I fear it is not a precursor to any sort of pleasant activity. What have you two learned? I can't remember when I've seen you so agitated."

He pulled away, greeted Cécile, and took our coats. Cécile lowered herself next to him on the couch, but I found myself too on edge to sit and stood in front of them to recount the events of the day. He already knew about Katenka's confession and assured us that she was being well treated in prison, a statement I could not reconcile with the bruise I had seen on her face.

"There is more, however," I said, and handed him one of the pamphlets I had taken from Mitya's room.

"Where did you get this?"

I explained, and as I spoke his countenance grew dark. He rose to his feet and started to pace.

"I am relieved you got out unharmed, Emily," he said. "I do not admonish you, because you had no way of knowing. This group is radical and may be dangerous—you remember Anna?"

"I do," I said. "It is the league's connection to her murder and information I overheard from your colleague Mr. Tabokov that prompted me to come up with a new theory. Katenka did not hire someone to kill Nemetseva. The league eliminated her themselves." Still pacing, Colin listened as I explained how I had reached my conclusion.

"I agree that your idea has merits. If Lev's colleagues realized he is a spy, they would want to deal with him, but framing him for murder seems a clumsy and unreliable way to do it. Nonetheless, it is worth considering the possibility. I agree that Katenka's confession leaves something to be desired, but if she stands by her words, there is not much we can do." I told him about the ballet costume. "So the revolutionaries are behind our ghostly ballerina."

"Her first appearance coincided with Anna's murder," I said. "Perhaps it was meant as a distraction."

"Possibly, but there have been many subsequent appearances that did not occur simultaneously with other crimes," he said.

"Yes, but she has been appearing more and more frequently, and the city is consumed by stories of her. If they manage to whip the public into a frenzy, only imagine what they could do if they arrange her to materialize at just the right moment? No one would be able to pull their eyes away from her."

Colin frowned. "It is as reasonable an explanation as I've heard, and I shall share what you've learned with my colleagues. If nothing else, they may be able to keep the police on high alert and warn them not to be distracted by ghostly dances."

"And what about Katenka?" I asked. "We cannot let her languish in prison."

"Unless you can prove that someone else committed the crime, I don't see that we have any choice. She has brought this on herself. And I would remind you, Emily, that until now you had no other viable suspects."

"But now I do; I just don't know precisely whom. I'm convinced there is more to this, and I shall do whatever is necessary to find the truth."

Ekaterina Petrovna
December 1898

Irusya kept her promise to celebrate Katenka's promotion after *Sleeping Beauty* the following night. Katenka had not danced in the production, so her friend came to her flat and gave her a bottle of champagne and an enormous bouquet of flowers.

"Tell the truth," Katenka said. "These flowers were meant for you, weren't they?"

"They were, but I want you to have them." She popped open the champagne and poured it into two tea cups. Katenka had no wineglasses. "Soon enough you'll have more flowers than you can stand. I am so very, very happy for you. You'll be glad to know that I have redeemed myself after yesterday's fall." She had danced the Lilac Fairy, and Katenka got her to admit she had acquitted herself beautifully. "I know we planned to celebrate, and I have every intention of doing just that, but I've arranged for something more special than the two of us sitting around alone. Kolya is throwing a party for you."

"Kolya?" Katenka balked. What about Lev?

"Yes." Irusya's smile was radiant. "We've reconciled. It happened last night. His carriage is waiting outside, and I'll tell you everything on the way. Get your coat."

Katenka felt as if she were being held underwater. She could not breathe and her limbs felt heavy. She did as Irusya said, but only because she was too stunned to do anything else. Kolya offered his congratulations the moment Irusya led her into the room, but that was the last he spoke to her. He had eyes for no one but Irusya. Katenka had seen them in love before, but that paled to the way they looked at each other now. Something had changed, and she could hardly reconcile it with what she had seen in Irusya's apartment only two days earlier. Horrified by what her brother must be going through—did he know, she wondered?—she retreated into a corner and asked a waiter to bring her tea.

Sofya proved her salvation. She had arrived late and came immediately to Katenka's side. Recognizing at once that something was wrong, Sofya collected their coats, waved down a droshky, and bundled her friend into it without asking another question. Katenka did not speak during the drive, or back inside, after Sofya helped her up the long flights of stairs.

The weeks that followed Katenka's promotion should have passed in a blur. She would be given new parts to learn, and would hardly have time even to see Mitya anymore. When she was not in class, she would either be rehearsing, taking her private lessons with Cecchetti, or performing. She would get no break until New Year's, at which point the company would rest until two days after Christmas.

But she could focus on none of this. The next morning, when she woke up, she did not go to class. Sofya had stayed with her overnight, and Katenka told her she was ill. Sofya promised to explain her absence. Katenka lent her practice clothes and watched from her window after Sofya left for the theatre. When she had disappeared from view, Katenka dressed and set off on an errand of her own.

She needed to talk to Lev.

23

The next day, as I considered the evidence, I became convinced that the revolutionaries were behind Nemetseva's murder. Even if their goal weren't to frame Lev, they might have killed her for another reason altogether. Their ghostly ballerina wouldn't cause such a stir and, hence, prime the citizens of Petersburg for their ultimate distraction if it weren't for Nemetseva's death. Could the prima's final role have been that of sacrificial lamb, murdered to forward the league's revolutionary cause?

Even I had to admit it was something of a stretch. Unless . . . What if Lev had suggested the nefarious scheme himself as a way of proving his loyalty to the league? I sighed. Colin, who'd been called to the palace and said he would not see me until the imperial ball that evening, would rebuke me for letting my imagination run away on this flight of fancy. Best that I be left alone with my thoughts.

Except. An idea struck me. I needed Sebastian. If only there were some simple way to contact him. Pondering the matter, it occurred to me that each time he had come to the hotel, despite behaving as if he had come from elsewhere, he never looked cold, not in the slightest. No hint of red on his cheeks, no sign of snow on his boots. I rang the front desk and asked if they knew whether Fedor Dolokhov was in his room; after a brief pause to check the keys, the clerk confirmed that, so far as he knew, yes.

"Could you please give him a message for me?" I asked and then hesitated, only briefly. "I need to see him in my rooms at once."

He was knocking on the door fewer than five minutes later, his sapphire eyes dancing. I must have caught him unaware, as he was not in his Cossack uniform, but rather an ordinary suit that, though excessively well tailored, was not nearly so striking as the long woolen *cherkeska*. Truth be told, I almost regretted the absence of his hat, even if I still hold it to be ridiculously tall.

"It warms my heart that you summoned me here, Kallista," he said, stepping into the room and holding his arms out to me. "Where is your husband? Dare I hope I find you alone?"

"You do find me alone," I said. My reason for hesitation when deciding whether to bring him to my room or to have him meet me in the lounge or restaurant should be obvious to anyone of even moderate intelligence. Although I knew it would subject me to impertinent comments, I decided braving them was an adequate price for being in a position to better persuade him to confide in me. "I shan't waste my time reminding you that this is not a romantic assignation. Despite your criminal activities, I do believe you are, in other ways, a gentleman, and that you shall not threaten my virtue."

"Kallista, you wound me," he said, emphasizing his words with a ridiculous demonstration of pounding on his chest. "You know I hold you more dear than anyone. I would call out any man who attempted to smear your reputation."

I didn't bother to point out that he had not, in fact, addressed my concern. "Sit." I motioned to a chair and stood in front of him. "We do not need to mince words, you and I. We have been acquainted with each other for far too long."

"I should hope you consider me more than a mere acquaintance."

He crossed his legs. "Does your beastly husband have any whisky left? I'm rather parched." I poured him a glass, which he accepted with a gracious nod. "I can't stand much about the man, but I do admire his habit of bringing his own single malt when he travels. But we are not here to discuss Hargreaves, are we? Why have you summoned me, Kallista?"

"You said you saw pamphlets in Nemetseva's dressing room when you left the imperial egg for her. Can you remember if they were similar to this?" I passed him the one I had taken from Mitya's room.

"Similar? Quite," he said. "Identical, more like it."

"You're certain?"

"I do read Russian, Kallista. What kind of a savage do you take me for? I recognize it. Whoever wrote it has an appalling style. No elegance whatsoever."

"I doubt elegance is what revolutionaries strive for." If I could connect—through firm evidence—this pamphlet with the ones in Nemetseva's dressing room, I might be able to begin to build a case. Someone had brought the pamphlets in her dance bag. Sofya was my prime suspect for this, and, furthermore, she was eminently qualified to have performed the role of the ghostly ballerina. She could have lured Nemetseva outside. It still required a leap of logic, but at least I felt I was moving in the right direction. Suddenly I realized what Sebastian had said. "Identical? You're sure?"

"You can look at the lousy thing yourself if you'd like. I kept one as a souvenir."

"Why didn't you mention this before?"

"I had no reason to think it pertinent. Would you like to see it now? It's in my room. I can be back in the flashiest of flashes."

On this point, at least, he was telling the truth. He returned with the paper in a matter of moments. It was identical to Mitya's. I could now prove Sofya's connection to the league. Unless it could be Katenka? Sofya, so proud of her shabby apartment, seemed more likely to harbor revolutionary tendencies. One other thought struck me.

"What did you write on the note that you left with the egg?" I asked.

"The girl was Russian, so I quoted Pushkin, of course," he drawled. "*The wondrous moment of our meeting . . . / Still I remember you appear / Before me like a vision fleeting, / A beauty's angel pure and clear.*"

"Not particularly enlightening," I said, frowning.

"It's a lovely selection, perfect for its intended purpose, and I will brook no criticism on the point." He paused. "You didn't mean the poetry, did you?"

"No. I thought there might be a chance the message could have been misinterpreted, but it is quite straightforward. Forget I mentioned it."

"Forget? That I shall never do, especially a conversation with you."

"You are abominable, Mr. Capet, but as this is one of the only conversations we have had in our lengthy acquaintance that involved any significant amount of truth, I shan't fault you. Perhaps there is hope for you yet."

He pulled himself to his feet and kissed my hand, lingering far longer than necessary. "You make me do terrible things, Kallista, but I will not stand for you reforming me."

"I have not the slightest interest in embarking on such a futile endeavor," I said. He started to kiss my hand again. I wrenched it away. "I assume I will see you at the imperial ball tonight. Please try not to steal anything while you are there."

Ekaterina Petrovna
June 1899

Months had passed since Katenka rushed off once again to warn her brother about Irusya's perfidy. Lev had shaken his head and smiled when she told him the awful things she knew. "I am already aware of it all, Katyurushka. She told me herself, before I agreed to stay with her. First loves are not always meant to last, you know, but we gave each other a wonderful farewell."

"She went immediately to that awful man—"

"Who broke her heart soon thereafter," Lev said. "That is censure enough. I take no pleasure in her suffering."

Irusya had grown more serious after her second and final parting from Kolya. She vowed to never again get caught up in so public an affair and dedicated herself to discretion. Both girls danced brilliantly for the rest of the season: Irusya fueled by a new maturity; Katenka, by a fiery passion she could at last control.

As usual, Katenka summered at Irusya's dacha, but this time Sofya came as well. Three was not so easy a number as two, however, and Sofya took to having long conversations with Mitya, who was visiting his parents nearby. This did not trouble Katenka; she was glad for Mitya to have someone with whom to discuss politics.

Irusya still loved to row, and they spent a great deal of time on the lake, but she made a point of always returning to the house in time for the mail delivery. Every day, she would flip through the stack of envelopes, smile at the sight of one, and disappear, glowing, to her room to read them in private.

"Who writes you these missives?" Katenka asked on a sun-dappled afternoon as she and Irusya were walking in the woods adjacent to the house.

"A man I love like no one else," Irusya said. "I became very close to him over the final weeks of the spring season and have no intention of making the same mistakes with him that I made with Kolya. I have learned."

"Will you marry him?"

"No," she said. "He could never marry me, which makes him all the more perfect. I hurt Lev so very much, and that would have never happened if we hadn't had such different hopes for our relationship. He desired marriage; I didn't. All I want is to dance and to love someone who will ask very little of me. I have that now and couldn't be happier."

"I am glad for you, then," Katenka said. "When will I meet him?"

"Never. I'm keeping him to myself and avoiding all hints of rude gossip."

"But what about later, Irusya, when you retire from the stage? Won't you be lonely?"

"Maybe, but I can't think about that now. Perhaps I'll be fortunate, collapse in a blaze of glory, and never have to retire."

"That's a terrible thought," Katenka said.

"Not to me. The only terrible thought is never dancing again." Irusya looped her arm through Katenka's. "Now what about you and your darling Mitya? When will he propose?"

"I don't know that he ever will," Katenka said. "We've never discussed it."

"Perhaps he's too obsessed with revolutionary politics to take such a bourgeois step," Irusya said, laughing. "Or perhaps he won't propose until you vow to learn how to use those wretched hectographs he and Lev use for their pamphlets." They walked a little farther and then stopped short when they saw a figure ahead of them, standing very close to someone else, engaged in a heated discussion.

"Isn't that Sofya?" Irusya asked.

"It is." Katenka squinted, trying to see better.

"But that can't be Mitya. He would not—" Irusya pulled Katenka around. "Come, let's go back to the house. We ought not be spying."

January 1900

24

---※◎※---

Still taken with the theory that Nemetseva's murder was somehow tied to the revolutionaries, I debated trying to find Sofya before the imperial ball, but there was no time. The sun had set long ago, and I had to tend to my toilette. I had asked a hotel maid to press the gown I ordered from the House of Worth and found it hanging in the dressing room by the time I had finished bathing. Much though I still missed their father, I could not deny that the brothers Worth were continuing his work admirably.

The dress they had made for me was princess cut, dark sapphire velvet. A slightly lighter shade of blue satin, its skirt was embroidered with long silver floral garlands. Delicate handmade French lace hung in frothy layers from the sleeves, trimmed the bodice, and formed a delicate fall from just below the waist to the bottom of the modest train in the back.

It fit perfectly, skimming my hips and clinging to my waist. The hotel maid assisted me in getting into it, as I had no hope of fastening the numerous hooks and eyes and tiny buttons myself. She also managed to tame my hair, never an easy task, twisting it into a Gibson girl pompadour. I completed my ensemble with a parure of sapphires and diamonds, consisting of a necklace, two bracelets, drop earrings, and a small tiara. Over this I draped a long shawl, to protect the gown from any fur that might come off my coat. Satisfied that my appearance would suffice for the occasion, I went to the lobby. Masha and Cécile were outside in the carriage, waiting to collect me.

Palace Square dazzled. A golden spill of electric lights blazing from the chandeliers inside the imperial state rooms cast a soft glow on the snow, complementing the dancing lanterns on the line of carriages waiting to deposit their occupants at the gate and the bonfires that roared from braziers to keep the coachmen warm. The gilt details on their uniforms shimmered, and it all looked like something out of a painting done by an artist who had perfected the art of capturing light and all its magic.

We passed through the courtyard and went inside, where imperial footmen relieved us of our coats, hats, muffs, and overshoes. Music came from the rooms above, and the excited chatter of the guests, resplendent in their finery, had the effect of birds chirping to each other on a bright spring day. These birds, however, were deliberately and blissfully forgetting the snow falling outside and the chill of the air blowing off the Neva.

Sweet incense filled our nostrils, competing with the scents of the thousands of flowers placed in the palace halls, along with potted lemon and orange trees. We passed through a room where Gypsies were playing traditional music with an urgency that all but commanded one to stand up and shout with approval and into another room where a string quartet was playing a melody from Mozart. Masha prodded us to continue until we had reached the Nicholas Hall, called after the first tsar to bear that name. The enormous space—the largest room in the palace—was illuminated by eleven sparkling chandeliers and boasted a wide balcony that overlooked the Neva. All gold and white, it was as elegant as the guests pouring into it.

"The imperial family will process from the Malachite Room to here, and then the real fun will begin," she said. "I hope you are both ready to dance."

I was looking around, hoping to find Colin, but did not see him in the crush of people surrounding us. The room was growing unbearably warm, and I accepted with sincere thanks a cool glass of wine from a servant in blue-and-gold livery. As I drank, I felt someone pushing against my elbow and turned to see a tall, slim man with black hair and a narrow moustache.

"Sir!" I exclaimed.

He adjusted the monocle in his right eye. "My apologies, madame." He bowed. "Masha, introduce me to your friend."

"This is Prince Kalenischeff," Masha said. "Don't pay him the slightest attention, Emily."

"Kalenischeff," I said. "The name is familiar. Were you embroiled in some sort of trouble in Cairo not long ago?"

"Not at all, madame," he said. "You have confused me with an extremely unfortunate cousin of mine who met an untimely end in that city." With that, he disappeared. The orchestra began to play Glinka's *A Life for the Tsar*, signaling the approach of the imperial family. A uniformed man banged on the floor with a tall ebony staff bearing the double-headed eagle and shouted, "Their Imperial Majesties!"

The tsar, dressed in the uniform of a hussar guard, and his wife, resplendent in a dress of heavy silver brocade, led the procession, which included all the grand dukes and grand duchesses, other than, of course, the emperor's two small daughters, and the rest of court. When it finished, the orchestra began to play a polonaise, and Nicholas led Alexandra to front of the dance floor.

"She dances badly," Cécile said. "It is a disgrace."

"She takes no pleasure in it," Masha said.

"It shows." Cécile frowned. "Very bad manners."

Seeing the empress brought the imperial egg to mind, and as I thought about it, a sickening feeling crept into my stomach. Could I have missed something critical to my case? Something that might prove Katenka's innocence? I stood on my tiptoes, searching for Vasilii. He was standing with four other army officers on the opposite side of the room. The crowd made it impossible for me to reach him, so I waited until the imperial couple and the line of dancers behind them had moved on to the next room. The tsar was expected to dance his way through all the halls being used for the ball. The instant they had snaked through the arched doorway, I crossed the dance floor and chatted nonsensically with Vasilii and his friends. When the orchestra started to play another tune, he asked me to dance. I had counted on him doing exactly that.

"I'm afraid I don't know the mazurka," I said, but I gave him my hand and did my best to follow his instructions. Although I made rather a mess of it, he laughed good-naturedly and assured me that I would get the hang of it before the night was over.

"I much prefer a waltz," I said.

"Yes, but now you are in Russia, Lady Emily, and you must learn to dance like a Russian."

The intensity of the steps did not allow for much conversation, but by our third turn around the room, I had started to warm to the mazurka, and was even reveling in its accents, clicking my heels with abandon. I was out breath, and the room had grown even warmer once the dancing began. I begged my partner for a breath of air. We stepped out onto the balcony, the biting cold a welcome relief from the hot ballroom.

"You have converted me to a devotee of the mazurka," I said. "I'm so pleased we have the opportunity to talk. I've been thinking about Nemetseva and Katenka, and there is one thing that doesn't make sense: the imperial egg. How on earth did Nemetseva come to be holding it?" I all but fluttered my eyelashes. "I can't imagine why we've never discussed it before." I, of course, knew exactly why we hadn't. I had avoided the topic because I knew it had nothing to do with the murder. Vasilii, on the other hand . . .

"I assumed you must have learned what I did, that it was nothing more than a copy," he said. "The genuine egg never left the empress's rooms. I myself collected the fraudulent article from the police and discovered the truth when I went to return it to its proper place."

"I did not know." I studied his face. There were still beads of sweat at his temples, but that was from dancing, and I detected no change in his countenance. "Not that it matters now." I met his eyes with mine and smiled so sweetly my teeth began to hurt. "I did find the sentiment on the accompanying note lovely."

"Only because you are not Russian. It was the most obvious choice to anyone even vaguely familiar with Pushkin. But, then, I've never considered 'The wondrous moment of our meeting' as his best work."

"Why do you think the murderer gave it to her?"

He sighed, his breath hanging like a veil between us in the frozen air. "I believe it was a message from Katenka, a farewell of sorts, evoking the time, so long ago, when they first met. I can hardly bear to think about it. If only they had never become friends . . ." He shook his head. "We will freeze if we stand out here much longer. Allow me to escort you back inside."

A fellow officer approached him almost as soon as we had crossed through the glass doors back into the ballroom and told him he was needed immediately to attend to something in one of the other rooms. Apparently an unruly guest was causing a commotion. Vasilii bowed neatly before excusing himself. I watched him disappear in the crowd of dancers until I was distracted by movement above me on the mezzanine level across from the orchestra gallery. I blinked to better focus my eyes and thought I saw a familiar face. Mitya? I recognized his spectacles and strained, trying to get a closer look. If it was him, he had no business being in the palace at all, let alone during an imperial ball. I went to the nearest footman I could find and asked how to access the orchestra gallery.

He directed me to a small staircase hidden behind a wall panel. I climbed it and stepped into the gallery. There was no sign of Mitya, only musicians. I went back toward the stairs and emerged into a passage that led to the rest of the galleries on the level. From there, I began to methodically make my way through the labyrinthine corridors that wound their way through this mezzanine level of the palace. Some members of the court had rooms here, but they were empty now, their occupants downstairs at the ball.

The sound of music grew louder whenever I approached one of the galleries above the state rooms, and peeking in through them helped me maintain a basic idea of where I was. I heard voices rather than music behind one such door, but found only musicians preparing for their performance, which would not start until midnight, when the guests would have a buffet supper. In the hall below, a veritable army of servants was making final adjustments to the long tables set with Sèvres china, silver polished to perfection, and sparkling crystal glasses.

From here, the corridor became quieter, quiet enough that I was able to discern voices. Voices I recognized. Mitya and Lev were standing fifty-odd feet away from me. I moved closer, stepping silently in my satin dancing shoes, and pressed myself against the wall next to a longcase clock to avoid being seen.

"This is the culmination of everything we have been working for," Lev was saying. "We must proceed with extreme caution. You are certain you have Tabokov in line?"

"Yes," Mitya said. "I implored him not to act on his own again."

"Can you trust that he will do as he's told?" Lev asked. "I will never forgive what he did to Anna."

I had never warmed to Tabokov, but he was more dangerous and more treacherous than I had ever imagined. He told Colin that Lev was his agent, but what I was hearing now told a different story. There was an agent in the league, but not the way Colin believed. Tabokov had lied to disguise his own loyalties, which were decidedly not to the tsar. Anna had worked with my husband; Tabokov had killed her, probably because she had threatened to expose him.

"He does not think we are going far enough but has agreed not to deviate from the plan," Mitya said. "He understands how important it is."

"We should have found someone else." Lev's voice was gravelly.

"Evgenii Orlov was the only one who could ever control him, and he is not here."

"There was no time to find another safe house for him, and he cannot risk being arrested again. If only—"

Mitya interrupted him. "You cannot dwell on that now. It will distract you. We have done everything possible in the circumstances to ensure our success. I am confident that when we stand before him, the emperor will listen to our petition."

I was half tempted to step forward, right then, and tell them that Tabokov could not be trusted. I could offer to bring their petition to the tsar myself—I would have no trouble gaining access to him. But, of course, I could not do that. I had no idea what the petition said and, furthermore, had no way of proving to them that Tabokov was crooked. If his murdering Anna didn't convince them, what would?

"We haven't been able to persuade him to do so yet."

"No, that's why we are taking more dramatic action."

"I don't want anyone hurt," Lev said.

"Nor do I," Mitya replied. "Violence at this point would destroy all chances of peacefully reforming our country. It is almost time now, Lyova. Be safe, my friend."

Ekaterina Petrovna
December 1899

Katenka was sewing ribbons onto pointe shoes when Irusya banged on the door of her flat and then stormed in demanding tea. Katenka poured her a cup, but Irusya did not stop pacing long enough to be able to drink it. She was wild with anxiety about Sofya after learning that she had agreed to help Lev and Mitya with some political scheme they were planning.

"She ought not involve herself in any of this," Irusya said. "It's dangerous."

"There's no need to whisper," Katenka said. "I can guarantee no one is listening in my flat."

"Can you? What if they know about Lev? If they do, you can count on them watching you. They know he's your brother."

"Lev—and Mitya, too—are extremely careful. They have never drawn the attention of the Guard Department."

"I think you are being naive," Irusya said. "The Okhranka have men in revolutionary organizations. What if—"

"How have you become so well versed on this topic? I shouldn't have thought you even knew what the Okhranka are," Katenka said, cringing at her friend's mention of the secret police. "You've never shown the slightest interest in politics before."

"And I don't have any now," she said. "But my . . . friend . . . he knows about these things. Lev believes he is careful, but he needs to realize that the palace isn't wholly unaware of what is going on."

Katenka did not reply. She knew Irusya would resist any effort to identify her *friend,* and Katenka had begun to find the whole situation more than a little tedious. She had never before wondered if it was possible to take discretion too far. But she could not deny being somewhat alarmed by Irusya's sudden concern about politics and revolutionary ideas. "I will speak to my brother and implore him to take more precautions than usual. Do remember that we have no idea at all what he is doing."

"We know he's drawing Sofya into it."

"Only to distribute pamphlets. That's what she told me." Katenka had finished stitching and tugged at the ribbon to make sure it was firmly in place. "If she—or they, for that matter—were involved in something truly dangerous, they would never breathe a word of it to us, as doing so could endanger us as well. Pamphlets advertising some sort of rally or whatever it is might be frowned upon, but they are not likely to cause Sofya any lasting harm."

"I don't know why it's bothering me so much." Irusya flung herself into a chair. "Something about it frightens me. I can't explain why. It may be that it's only on my mind because I came here directly after seeing—"

"Your friend."

"Yes," Irusya said. "My friend."

"It would be much more entertaining to tease you about him if I knew who he was." Katenka hoped Irusya would take her bait and change the subject.

"I shall never reveal that particular secret."

"Do you have others?"

"Of course I do, one of which I may eventually share with you. In the meantime, I will tell you my primary purpose for coming to you. It's the most spectacular news. Pierina Legnani has chosen me to dance Odette and Odile in *Swan Lake*."

"How marvelous!" Katenka threw down her pointe shoes and embraced her friend. "You'll be brilliant, absolutely brilliant. And what a triumph to be selected by her. No one thought she would ever let anyone else take her place, even if she is fast approaching retirement. I could not be happier for you. You deserve this, Irusya."

"Thank you," she said. "There is one more thing. You deserve it, too, Katenka. I am tired of you not being given the roles you deserve. That is why I spoke to Petipa this afternoon. He has agreed to let you be my understudy. We can learn the choreography together."

"He's allowing me—"

"Yes, you." Irusya leapt up and pulled Katenka by both hands, spinning her around and whooping with joy. "And I am certain that, in time, you will be cast yourself. This is the beginning of a whole new path for you. You may only be my understudy, but one can never predict what might happen. I could fall on my head in the second act and be unable to finish the performance. And then you, the little-known *coryphée*, would step on stage and complete the ballet flawlessly, winning the hearts of all of Petersburg. Petipa would promote you on the spot."

"Unlikely in the extreme," Katenka said.

"Oh, let me have my dreams, will you?"

"For you, Irusya, anything."

January 1900

25

Almost time! My heart was racing and my mind reeling. I desperately wanted to find Colin, but the daunting odds of doing so quickly, when I had not seen him even once all evening, deterred me. I wished I could rush at the men and overpower them, but although I am quite confident in my physical abilities, I did not think I could achieve such a thing, particularly in evening dress and with nothing more than a fan as a weapon. I could go to the Palace Guard, but their revelation about Tabokov's role in Anna's death reminded me that I might not be able to trust even the military.

I could follow them, but with what aim? Whatever they were planning was bound to be directed at the tsar, and while I did not know the specifics, I could warn him, at least, that something was about to happen. Mitya and Lev had parted with a quick embrace, each turning a different direction at the end of the corridor. Cautiously, I retraced my steps and entered every gallery, searching the crowded rooms below, trying to find the emperor.

Locating anyone in such a swarm might be an exercise in futility, but I remained undaunted and refused to give up. What else could I do? When I stood above the Field Marshals' Hall, I spotted the empress's tiara. The gallery had ample space for the musicians but also included a narrow walkway that skirted the perimeter of the room. I ran along this until I reached the nearest point I could above where Alexandra stood, her husband beside her. In his uniform, the tsar was much more difficult to pick out of the crowd.

I waved my arms and shouted, but I could not be heard over the music and conversation below. I considered throwing my fan in the unlikely hope that whoever it hit would look up and see me but rejected the idea. Why ruin a good fan for nothing? I shouted again and then started back to the staircase.

All of a sudden the music came to a crashing halt as shrieks emanated from the crowd and everyone in the room surged toward the windows facing Palace Square. Their cries of "ghost" and "Nemetseva" told me what they saw. The tsar, now surrounded by a small group of uniformed officers led by Tabokov, was being hurried out of the room. I knew what to do. Lev and Mitya might have faith that this odious man would do as ordered, but I did not.

I raced down the stairs in pursuit. They had led the emperor into an antechamber. Following, I burst through the door—surprised to find it unsecured—and flung myself through the guards and at the tsar.

"It's a plot!" I cried. "A trick! Do not let them take you anywhere!" Rough hands grabbed me and wrenched my arms back. "You are in grave danger!"

Summoning strength I did not know I possessed, I freed myself and again rushed toward the emperor. In a flash, I saw Tabokov draw a gun. Catapulting myself forward, I knocked the Autocrat of All the Russias onto the floor, shielding him with my body. A shot echoed through the chamber, but, so far as I could tell, the man below me was unharmed. Chaos erupted. More guards poured into the room, and the incident stopped as quickly as it had started.

Then, another commotion. I had not seen Lev in the room, but now he was wrestling with Tabokov. Mitya emerged from the crowd and into the fray. With his assistance, Lev managed to pry the gun from the would-be assassin's hand.

"This was never meant to be violent," he said. "We came here to talk, nothing more." Tabokov lunged toward the tsar, who was still beneath me on the floor. Lev raised the gun and fired. Tabokov crumpled to the ground, dark blood pooling under his head.

Now more rough hands grabbed me, pulling me to my feet. Someone helped the emperor up as well—not so roughly—and Nicholas immediately made a quick motion to his guards, who released me.

"Emily?" Colin came running across the room. "What are you doing?"

"Exhibiting more bravery than all of my guards," the tsar said. "This lady saved my life."

"As did these men," I said, pointing to Lev and Mitya. "They stopped the assassin. You must not—"

"Take her somewhere safe," the tsar said. "This is no place for a lady."

"Colin, Mitya and Lev did not—"

"I know, I know," he said. "I shall take the matter into hand."

My husband started barking orders to two uniformed officers who had wrenched Mitya's and Lev's arms behind their backs. He was motioning for them to be released, but I could not see what happened next. Three more soldiers had all but dragged me into the empress's private drawing room in the family apartments, where, despite repeated requests, I refused the attentions of the imperial physician.

"I am quite unharmed, as you see," I said. "The tsar?"

"He is in perfect health," the doctor said. "The empress sends a message of deep thanks and asks that I tell you she will forever be indebted to you."

He left me, and for nearly three-quarters of an hour I sat alone in the room, save for two tall Cossack guards, one who never took his focus off of me, and the other who stared at the door. I pleaded for them to let me go, but they never spoke a word.

I was left with nothing to do but study my surroundings. I have never made secret my disdain of our era's passion for clutter. Rooms whose every surface brimmed with trinkets, mounted birds, picture frames, vases, candlesticks, and heaven knows what else held no charm for me. Fashionable households—my mother's included—were crammed with the stuff. But never before had I seen the style applied so vigorously as in this space.

The room itself, in the northwest corner of the palace, was of comfortable proportions and from its large, arched windows afforded stunning views of the Admiralty and the Neva. Otherwise, however, it was a hideous exercise in eclectic excess. A motley assortment of paintings—some of fine quality, some questionable at best—offered a bit of relief from the dizzying effect of the fussy print on the wallpaper. An ornate screen stood in front of an even more ornate iron fire guard, and above the highly decorated marble fireplace hung an enormous gilded mirror that would have been more appropriate in one of the grand formal reception rooms in the palace. The furniture looked as if it had come from a London department store catalog of middling quality, and every square inch of every surface was covered with objects Alexandra had chosen herself.

There were snuff boxes, cigarette cases, tiny stone statues of a variety of animals, enameled and jewel-encrusted frames that housed pictures of her husband and daughters, and a shocking number of icons. And there were, of course, Fabergé eggs, among them the one Sebastian had given to Nemetseva. I picked it up and looked at it closely. It was a gorgeous piece. I had just figured out how to release the tiny pictures of the tsar and his daughters when Cécile, Colin, and Vasilii burst into the room.

"*Mon dieu,* Kallista, is it true? You have saved the tsar?"

"Not alone," I said. "Mitya and Lev—"

"Yes, alone," Prince Vasilii said. "These reprobates have no scruples and are quick to abandon their principles when their own well being is threatened. They saw the game was up and did what they thought necessary to save themselves."

"That is not true," I said. "Their aim was not violence. Tabokov acted against orders. I overheard their plans."

"She speaks the truth," Colin said, waving a crumpled stack of papers stained with blood. "They were armed with nothing more than this petition, asking the tsar to consider social reforms."

"Tabokov had a gun," the prince said.

"Neither of the others did," I said. "And their quick actions saved the emperor's life."

"How did you become embroiled in this, Kallista?" Cécile asked. "I thought your investigation was over. What made you start skulking around again when you should have been dancing?"

"I thought it was, too," I said. "I only began skulking, as you say, when I caught sight of Mitya in one of the galleries above the ball. I followed him."

"So it had nothing to do with Nemetseva?" Cécile asked, knowing my theory about the revolutionaries, which I now knew to be incorrect.

"In some ways the two crimes are unrelated," I said.

"The two crimes are entirely unrelated," Prince Vasilii said, his tone measured. "Has the doctor been in to see you, Lady Emily? You look quite unwell."

"Your concern is touching," I said, "but I make a practice of never taking a murderer's words at face value."

"Whatever can you be suggesting?" he said, his face darkening.

"You very nearly got away with it," I said. "But after we danced tonight, you admitted that you had read the note to Nemetseva that accompanied the imperial egg. When did you see it?"

"When I read the police file, of course. I couldn't risk examining the evidence myself, for reasons of which you are well aware."

"The trouble, Vasilii, is that the note wasn't part of the police evidence. They never saw it."

"You must be wrong, because otherwise I wouldn't have—"

"I'm not wrong, although, looking back, I realize it was foolish of me to so completely dismiss the presence of the egg. I did so because I am aware of the thief's identity and have always been confident that it had nothing to do with the murder. Further, I had no way of proving whether Nemetseva had even found the egg before she was killed—it was left in the pocket of her cloak. I concluded that it must have fallen out during the attack, but that is not how it happened, is it?"

The prince's face had taken on a ghastly pallor, and the tortured look in his eyes as he winced at my words almost made me wish I could comfort him. Almost.

"I know *what* you did," I said. "What I cannot understand is *why*."

"It is appalling that you would consider me capable of such a thing." Vasilii's voice, brittle and dry, cracked.

"She must have found the egg almost as soon as the thief left it for her. Maybe she brushed against her cloak and felt something hard, or maybe she felt chilled and put it around her shoulders and noticed the weight of it. The specifics don't matter. When she saw it, she must have panicked, realizing at once that it belonged to the empress. Not wanting to be accused of having stolen from the imperial family, she would have wanted to rectify the situation without delay. Fortunately, her lover was an adjutant to the major general in charge of palace security. Who better to return the egg to its rightful owner, possibly even before anyone noticed it had gone missing? Which is exactly what you told me you did."

Vasilii frowned, but I saw confusion on his face. "No, I never said that. I told you I intended to but then realized the egg Irusya had was nothing more than a copy."

"I am impressed that you managed to construct your lie without so much as hesitating. A falsehood, however, does not change the facts." I moved to stand directly in front of him and looked him in the eyes. "Nemetseva trusted you completely, which is not surprising. You shared an intimate relationship for two years. Was it that trust that destroyed her and her dearest friend, who is now imprisoned for a crime she did not commit? Thank heavens Nemetseva at least was spared the knowledge that you would stand by and let Katenka ruin her life, too."

He staggered back, covering his face with his hand. "Stop, please, I cannot stand anymore. You are right, right about everything, but you must believe me when I say I never intended for any of this to happen. I loved her so, more than should have been possible. She was like a dream to me, a dream of perfection."

"She asked you to come to the stage door, didn't she?" I reached for his hand and pulled it away from his face. "Did she send you a message?"

He answered in a whisper. "Yes. As you know, I never made a habit of seeing her backstage as neither of us wanted our relationship to play out in public, but that does not mean I was anything but desperate to see her. I was so thrilled that night, knowing she would triumph. No one could dance like her. The stage will never see her equal. Much though I love *Swan Lake*, I could hardly pay attention to the first act of the ballet, as she did not appear in it. I was probably more excited than she was. But that is not what you want to hear." He sighed. "I always order champagne to be delivered to my box, preferring that to balancing a glass in the foyer during the interval, and that night, when my tray arrived—just before the second act began—I found a note in Irusya's handwriting. It said *Stage door, interval.*"

"Were you alarmed by this?" I asked.

"I had no reason to be," he said, his deep voice louder and stronger now. "I knew she waved to Agrippina Alexandrovna during intervals, and I assumed she wanted to see me, too, if only briefly, before she went back on stage. It was an historic occasion to make her debut in such a role and no shock that she would want to share it with me."

"Let's sit down, shall we?" I led him to a long couch and sat next to him, taking his hand in mine. "I know this is difficult, but you must tell me exactly what happened when you saw her."

"She rushed straight toward me without even waving at her mentor," he said, "and I could see from her face that something was terribly wrong. She could hardly get out a coherent sentence—she was so agitated—but she forced herself to calm down. As you so aptly deduced, she was worried about being implicated in the theft, but that was the least of her problems."

His forehead was beaded with sweat. "She kept saying 'the wondrous moment of our meeting' over and over, as if hearing the phrase repeatedly would make me understand. Finally, she took me by the shoulders and shook me, as if that would clarify her fears for me. And then, at last, she explained. She told me that she had a lover long before I met her and that he had copied out that same poem of Pushkin's for her the day after he first kissed her, on a swing at her parents' dacha." His voice changed, becoming almost wistful. "I don't know why she felt that detail was important, but it endeared her to me, and an overwhelming feeling of love swelled in me like none I had felt before. I tried to embrace her, but she pushed me away, imploring me to listen.

"This lover had recently reached out to her, she explained, not looking for romance, but assistance. She told me he was involved in a political movement that had met with a certain amount of trouble with the police. Their leader had been arrested and exiled some years back, but he was planning to return to Petersburg, to participate in some sort of demonstration. She swore she did not know the details. I have considered her words many times since then, and I am convinced she was telling the truth. She knew nothing more. I believe her. I do."

"You may now, but did you believe her then?" I asked.

"It all happened so quickly I had no opportunity to consider the veracity of her statement. All that mattered was what she said next. This man had been a dear friend of hers, before and after they were lovers. She confessed to me that she had treated him badly and felt that she owed him. So when he asked if his colleague, the exiled leader, could hide in her apartment, just for two nights, she did not refuse him. She believed him when he said there would be no danger, because a ballerina of her reputation and stature would never be suspected of harboring a fugitive."

"When was she hiding this man?" Colin asked.

"She never did." Vasilii closed his eyes. "I had interrupted to beg her to reconsider, insisting that such things are always dangerous, but she would not let me finish. She pulled the egg out from her cloak and thrust it at me, along with the note she had received with it, the note that referenced that same poem her former lover had given her. She was convinced it was a warning, meant to tell her that their plan had been compromised and that the authorities knew what she planned to do. She said her friend had connections in the palace who could easily have stolen the egg, and it was then that my emotions started to churn. Only a few moments ago, I had felt so consumed by love, but now she was telling me this? Admitting to aiding would-be revolutionaries?

"I have spent my entire career working toward the position I hold in palace security and now am responsible not only for helping to keep the imperial family safe, but I am also tasked with rooting out members of the staff who have revolutionary leanings. Discovery of her treason would lead to my destruction as well as hers. I did not try to explain this to Irusya then, though. She was too agitated and so wholly unable to contain herself, I knew that the instant the police began to question her, she would be incapable of resisting their barbaric methods of interrogation. They would ferret out every detail of her life, including the identity of her lover, and they would never believe that I was not a party to all of this."

He pulled his hand from mine and rose to his feet. "I was furious, enraged, utterly unable to reconcile myself to what she had done. She had ruined everything for both of us. For a flash, I pictured the wives of the Decembrists, following their traitorous husbands to Siberia, but I knew Irusya was not made for such a fate. I looked at her again, at her beautiful face, her refined features, her dark eyes. I remember holding my breath, wanting more than anything to be able to stop time, to go back, to keep her from making such a dreadful mistake. I felt dizzy and could hardly remain upright. I started to gasp, desperate for air, and then I saw her face again. I could no longer read her emotions. It was as if she were a stranger. And after seeing her as a stranger, something deep inside me, something of which I will always be ashamed, made her my enemy. Some primal evil lurking in my soul led me to protect myself—my worthless life and my career—instead of helping her."

He covered his face again, this time with both of his hands. "I do not recall pulling the knife from its sheath, or the feeling of the blade sinking into her flesh. I ought to remember it. I deserve to be haunted by it, to be capable of thinking of nothing else but the hideous details, but all I know is that there was blood, so much blood. She hadn't fastened her cloak and it must have dropped when I—" He swallowed hard. "It was there, on the ground next to her, when I realized she was dead. There was no blood on it, not a drop. I don't know how that is even possible. I picked it up and stood over her, unable to comprehend what I had done. Never had I thought myself capable of such grotesque and hateful violence."

Colin had moved closer to him and laid his hand on the prince's shoulder. "You are right to speak the truth now. Your crime cannot be undone, but you can stop an innocent woman from being branded a murderer."

This was small consolation, but more than the prince deserved. "What did you do with the cloak?" I asked.

"A terrible calm came over me after I left her there, on the ground. I put the cloak around me to hide the blood on my clothes and then took it home and burned it. I suppose the note must still have been in the pocket. I changed into a clean uniform and then went to the palace."

"Where you said you had been called away from the ballet for a meeting," I said.

"Yes. I remained there until long after the performance would have finished and then went to Masha's, where I met you, and what a fortuitous event it seemed to me! After you left, Masha told me of your talent for detection, and I decided to enlist your assistance, hoping I would either be able to manipulate you in your conclusions or, at least, know if you discovered anything that might implicate me. The latter, of course, is precisely what you have done." He lowered his head. "And now there is only one honorable thing to do." His eyes darted to one of the Cossack guards standing at the door, and he lunged forward, reaching for the man's gun. In a single swift movement, Colin pinned him to the floor.

"There's already been quite enough killing," he said. "If you're lucky, you'll get nothing worse than a decade or so of hard labor, given your rank and the fact that your crime wasn't directed at the imperial family. You deserve far worse." The guards approached, and my husband handed over control of Vasilii to them. As they led him away, I saw tears in his eyes.

"*Mon dieu*," Cécile said, snapping open her fan and waving it in front of her face. "I never suspected him. Masha will be mortified. She was in the process of trying to marry him off, you know. But what about the rest? These revolutionaries and Nemetseva's ghost?

"You know perfectly well there never was a ghost," I said. "Given the scant evidence—the pamphlets in Nemetseva's dressing room,

Sofya's pride at refusing to live a bourgeois life, the costume in Mitya's room—I am forced to rely on my intuition, which tells me that Sofya is our culprit."

"In this case, your intuition is correct," Colin said. "She was arrested less than an hour ago. You were quite right, Emily, that her role was to provide an ever-increasing distraction, and she knew that her performance tonight would be her last. She would not be able to disappear into the crowd when Palace Square was filled with guards on high alert. She was aligned with Lev and Mitya, who split off from the League of Struggle for the Emancipation of the Working Class because they both wanted to pursue nonviolent methods of revolution. Their immediate goal was to make a direct appeal to the tsar, but it soon became clear that they were being spied on. A young woman, working as a maid for the Yusupov family, was passing their plans to the government."

"So they killed her?" Cécile asked.

"That was not the original plan," Colin said. "But one of their members took matters into his own hands."

"Tabokov," I said.

Colin nodded and continued. "Sofya had agreed to provide a distraction to the houseful of guests by dancing outside in a costume similar to the one Nemetseva was wearing when she died. The idea was that while everyone was looking at what they thought was a ghost, one of their men would slip inside and get Anna. He was to bring her to a designated spot, so that they could question her. They wanted to know the identity of her contact in the government. But, instead, the man they sent, Tabokov, killed her."

"Why?" Cécile asked.

"Because he was afraid she would reveal his identity to her contact," Colin said. "He was a well-respected naval officer, whom no one, myself included, suspected of maleficence."

"Did she reveal the name of her contact?" I asked, knowing full well my husband was the man in question.

"Fortunately, she did not," Colin said, looking grim. "Once she was dead, there was no more hope of learning his identity, but the distraction provided by Sofya was successful beyond all their expectations. They staged similar appearances multiple times throughout the city, until they had worked the population into such a frenzy that they could count on getting their desired reaction tonight."

"They certainly succeeded in distracting everyone at the ball," Cécile said. "No one was paying attention to anything but the dancer when they removed the tsar to the antechamber. If it were not for your intervention, Kallista, we might now be mourning the emperor's untimely demise."

Colin replied to her, but I hardly heard him. I walked across the room to a window and gazed upon the frozen expanse of the Neva below. The world had lost an incomparable artist when an ordinary man, in a moment of catastrophically reckless rage, had destroyed both her and his humanity. A Christian believes there exists no sin that cannot be forgiven, but Vasilii would never forgive himself. Whatever punishment he received, it could not cleanse from him the grief and guilt he would carry for the rest of his life. He had taken from the world the woman he loved, Katenka's dearest friend, and a mother's and father's daughter. His act could never be redeemed.

A carriage passed by on the road parallel to the river, its lantern's golden glow bouncing in time to the rhythm of the horses. A couple stood beneath a streetlight, embracing. And although I could not see it from my vantage point, I knew that the monumental bronze statue of Peter the Great on his horse looked over the river, daring any enemies to threaten his magnificent city. Vasilii's crime had caused a ripple of anguish, one given greater attention than usual because of his victim's fame, but for most of the citizens of Petersburg, life would continue unaltered. In the end, even public tragedies ebb to the private, their breadth of pain narrowing until they all but disappear. Everything has changed, but it all remains the same.

Ekaterina Petrovna
January 1900

Katenka couldn't stop crying. They had released her from prison after the Englishwoman came and explained to her what had happened. And now Mitya was here with her, by some miracle having escaped winding up in a cell of his own.

"What were you thinking, my darling girl?" Mitya asked. "You would have languished in a cell for so many years."

"I could not risk Lev being found guilty. They might have executed him."

"They could not have found him guilty of a crime he didn't commit."

"Neither of us is naive enough to believe that," Katenka said. "It is over now, and I am grateful for that. But how is it you have eluded arrest?"

"Hargreaves and his wife convinced the emperor that we had not intended any violence," he said. "Sofya has been released as well. The empress intervened on her behalf. She is grateful that Lev and I stopped Tabokov and, hence, is feeling most generous."

"What else?" Katenka asked.

"Sofya was fired from the company, which comes as no surprise, but she and Lev are getting married," Mitya said. "I was not supposed to tell you as he wanted to give you the news himself, so pretend to be surprised when he comes to you."

"I always suspected her of caring more about politics than ballet."

He took her hands in his, feeling a dart of pain as he saw how bettered and rough they had become during her prison stay. "What about you? Is there anything you care about more than ballet?"

"I want to dance." She didn't look at him, terrified of what she might see in his eyes. Could they have a future? She loved him, of that, there was no doubt, but she would not give up the opportunities now open to her. Irusya would rise from her grave and strike her down if she did not seize this moment.

"Then dance you shall," he said. "I can wait for you."

"I will not get my pension until nineteen seventeen," she said. "You can wait that long?"

"To have you as my wife, yes," Mitya said. "Although I worry it will harm your career if you are known to be involved with me." Neither of them was naive enough to believe that politics wouldn't eventually come into play. One could never escape it in Russia, but Katenka was not willing to give him up.

"The emperor himself has said you are a hero, regardless of your politics," she said. "If he can accept that, so can the rest of Petersburg."

January 1900

26

Vasilii made a complete confession, including admitting to having sent the Fabergé card case and all the notes I received. He had paid an old woman to slip one into my coat pocket at the funeral. He thought that his actions would spur me toward seeking a quick resolution to the case and that having sought my assistance would protect him from suspicion. The dagger came from a shop on Nevsky Prospekt; he had chosen one with naval origins thinking it would further shield him, an army man. It wasn't the one used in his crime. For that, he had used his own dagger, part of his uniform, hanging from his belt.

"He was afraid, momentarily, when Sofya began to make her appearances as the ghostly dancer," I said to my husband. I had ordered a large spread of *zakuski* and a bottle of vodka, all of which now lay before us on the table in our sitting room. I intended to be as Russian as possible while still in St. Petersburg, but I had given up on converting Colin to my ways. I poured his whisky for him myself. "He thought she might actually be a ghost."

"To be fair, I don't think anyone would have leapt to the conclusion that she was a revolutionary providing distraction. Unless, of course, one were as gifted with an imagination as fertile as yours,"

Colin said. "His main error—other than committing murder in the first place—was underestimating you, my dear. He thought a refined lady would never suspect a gentleman like him capable of so hideous a crime and assumed he could manipulate your investigation."

"We ladies are smarter than you gentlemen think."

"Not smarter than I think," he said.

"He was truly devastated by what he did," I said, "and ashamed that he was willing to go to such terrible lengths to hide the crime."

"Mitya, Lev, and Sofya owe you their lives," Colin said. "I don't think anyone else could have persuaded the tsar that they are not a threat to him. You made him believe their organization seeks only peaceful negotiation with his government."

"It is nothing but the truth."

"I am not quite so certain about that as you are. Eventually, their methods will change. In the meantime, however, Tabokov's trial will be short," Colin said. "He admitted that he lied about Lev being a government agent. He has no defense for any of his actions and will be convicted quickly, but I am afraid the government considers his murder of Anna a lesser crime than his attempted assassination."

"I am very sorry she is dead," I said, taking his hand.

"And I am immensely proud of you for figuring it all out."

We stayed in the city for four more weeks. While he returned to his work, Cécile and I went to the ballet, the opera, and countless parties and balls. I was left deliciously exhausted, but nonetheless hated the thought of returning to the quiet of our estate. Russia had grabbed a piece of my soul.

"If it weren't for my being so desperate to see the boys, I don't think I could bear going," I said after having overseen the last of our packing.

"I promise we shall return," Colin said. "In the meantime, I shall do my best to keep you distracted from any distressing thoughts that might prevent you from thoroughly enjoying our last evening in Peter's magnificent city." He bent over to kiss me just as we heard a sharp knock on the door. "If that is Capet—"

"No, it can't be," I said. "He sent a message saying he was leaving yesterday." Before he had come to Russia, he had surreptitiously removed from the studio of Edgar Degas in France a charming pastel of two dancers in traditional Russian costume and had carried it with him to St. Petersburg. He had hung it on the wall in Katenka's apartment before fleeing the country in what he considered a blaze of glory. His note explained that he had known he would find a dancer worthy of the piece in the city with the greatest ballet in the world. I had already agreed to return it to the artist.

I followed as Colin opened the door. No one stood on the other side. We looked up and down the corridor, but it was empty. Then I looked down. There, on the carpeted floor, was a box covered in gold velvet. Colin retrieved it and handed it to me.

I brought it inside the suite, unfastened the clasp, lifted the top, and gasped. "The lilies of the valley egg? No, he wouldn't. He couldn't." I removed it from the box and set it on a table. Below it was a note:

ἠοῦς ἄγγελε, χαῖρε, Φαεσφόρε, καὶ ταχὺς ἔλθοις
ἕσπερος, ἣν ἀπάγεις, λάθριος αὖθις ἄγων.
Farewell, Morning Star, herald of dawn, and quickly come again as the Evening Star, bringing secretly her whom thou takest away.

"He'll never forget how much you love *The Greek Anthology,* will he?" Colin asked, reading over my shoulder.

"No," I said. "But how could he steal this again? And why?"

"Just to show off." Colin picked up the egg and turned the pearl button on the side. Up from the top popped three miniature portraits, but they were not of the emperor and his daughters. Instead, the faces of my own three boys looked out at me.

"Please tell me it's a copy," I said. "Surely he didn't—"

Colin had already popped the glass off one of the tiny frames and removed Henry's picture to reveal that of the emperor.

"He really must stop this," I said, taking the egg from my husband and examining it. "Or at least learn to make copies. Perhaps if I were to speak to him—"

"Stop, Emily." Colin took the egg back and returned it to its box. "If you start believing you can reform him, I shall divorce you. This is our last night in Petersburg, and I intend to do everything in my not inconsiderable power to keep you from thinking about that man for even another instant."

I have always said that when Colin sets himself to a task, he refuses to fail, and, hence, I knew there was only one way forward. I pulled him to me, ready to submit to his extremely delicate attentions.

AUTHOR'S NOTE

While the principal characters in this book are fictional, there are a handful in supporting roles (beyond Nicholas II and his wife, Alexandra) who were real. Marius Petipa, the renown choreographer, made Russian ballet the greatest in the world. He hugely admired Pierina Legnani, who pioneered the now-famous thirty-two fouettées still performed by ballerinas in *Swan Lake* (she did, in fact, first perform the feat in *Cinderella*). Mathilde Kschessinska, another prima ballerina assoluta, was Nicholas II's mistress before he married his wife. In her memoirs, she records him as hesitant to consummate their relationship because of her inexperience. He did not want her to regret her actions. Somehow, she must have overcome his concerns. I based many of my dancers' experiences on incidents from her life. Olga Preobrajenska danced with the Imperial Ballet and later became a teacher, eventually settling in Paris after the Russian Revolution. Not so well known among her many famous pupils (including Margot Fonteyn and Tamara Toumanova) was Marie Buczkowski, who eventually moved to South Bend, Indiana, where she opened a ballet studio. I was fortunate enough to be one of her students.

The League of Struggle for the Emancipation of the Working Class was a real organization, formed when Vladimir Lenin organized disparate groups of workers in St. Petersburg. I have invented the schism within the group that allowed Mitya and Lev to pursue their own agenda.

I have tweaked by a few years the date of the installation of the spectacular stained glass window in the restaurant at the Hôtel de l'Europe so that Emily might see it. She always appreciates Apollo.

The story of the peasant who moved his family and his cow to the top floor of the Winter Palace is true. According to Greg King in his magnificent book *The Court of the Last Tsar,* only the smell of manure gave them away.

ACKNOWLEDGMENTS

Myriad thanks to . . .

Charlie Spicer, editor extraordinaire who makes every book better. My wonderful team at Minotaur: Andy Martin, Melissa Hastings, Paul Hochman, Sarah Melnyk, April Osborn, and David Rostein. Anne Hawkins, Tom Robinson, and Annie Kronenberg. You're my secret weapons.

My dear friends: Brett Battles, Rob Browne, Bill Cameron, Christina Chen, Kristy Claiborne, Jon Clinch, Charlie Cumming, Zarina Docken, Jamie Freveletti, Chris Gortner, Tracy Grant, Nick Hawkins, Robert Hicks, Elizabeth Letts, Carrie Medders, Deanna Raybourn, Missy Rightley, Renee Rosen, and Lauren Willig.

Xander, Katie, and Jess . . . I can't believe you're all adults now!

My parents, for their constant support.

Andrew, the best husband ever.

FOR FURTHER READING

Bowlt, John E. *Moscow and St. Petersburg 1900–1920: Art, Life and Culture of the Russian Silver Age.* New York: Vendome Press, 2008.

Brezzo, Steven L., Christopher Forbes, Johann Georg Hohenzollern, and Irina Aleksandrovna Rodimtseva. *Fabergé: The Imperial Eggs.* Munich: Prestel, 1989.

Figes, Orlando. *Natasha's Dance: A Cultural History of Russia.* New York: Picador, 2002.

Frame, Murray. *The St. Petersburg Imperial Theaters: Stage and State in Revolutionary Russia, 1900–1920.* Jefferson: McFarland, 2000.

Hall, Coryne. *Imperial Dancer: Mathilde Kschessinska and the Romanovs.* Thrupp: Sutton, 2005.

King, Greg. *The Court of the Last Tsar: Pomp, Power, and Pageantry in the Reign of Nicholas II.* Hoboken: Wiley, 2006.

Kschessinska, Matilda Feliksovna. *Dancing in Petersburg: The Memoirs of Kschessinska (H.S.H. the Princess Romanovsky-Krassinsky).* London: Gollancz, 1960.

Volkov, Solomon. *St. Petersburg: A Cultural History.* New York: Free Press, 1995.